We're All Mad Here

Vicious Wonders Book One

By Leann Belle

Book Design and Cover Art by Leann Belle

Content Warnings

While there are many moments of fun and spice in this story, this is a DARK work of fiction. Proceed with caution if you're not comfortable with the following concepts:

Content warnings include (**May include spoilers**): Dubious Consent, Gore, Violence, Kidnapping, Drugging (magical), Murder of minor characters, Fear and Blood used in sexual context, Knife Play, Blood Play, Drowning, Choking

6

Chapter 1

Alice

"You ever have those days where you just need to get fucked, and you need to get fucked *hard*?" I asked to a tone that bordered on philosophical as I scrolled listlessly through pictures of my ex rubbing up on his new girl like a needy puppy dog. I should have blocked him just so I'd stop seeing his face on my feed, but I was still bitter about how it all ended. So many years of my life wasted.

Maybe it would have been easier if I had been the one to dump him, but no. When I found out he'd been two-timing me with my best friend for five of our nine goddamn years together, he had the audacity to officially dump *me*, like *I* was the problem. I didn't even get the satisfaction of a screaming match and a "burn in hell," and I would not be getting over that any time soon.

And then my ex-best friend had the gall to ask me to be her bridesmaid, when he'd been telling me he wasn't interested in marriage for our whole relationship. Amazing how a wedding sounds great all of a sudden when it's not with me.

God, now I'm just getting myself riled up again. Fuck you, Daniel. Fuck you, Clara. And fuck your cursed, tainted wedding.

"I thought that was why we were here, Alice." Dinah, my dear sister, interrupted my self and non-self loathing with a roll of her eyes in my general direction. The purple rotating lights caught in her pretty blue irises as she shot me a look of pure disappointment and frustration. "You were so adamant on coming out tonight, and yet you've spent the whole evening on your phone, staring at that jackass and your ex-best-home wrecker. You didn't even notice when hot guy number one offered to buy you a drink." She motioned with her chin toward a total chad, dressed in a half open button up and jeans that were too tight for any man to reasonably wear in public. I could tell from here that he wasn't packing much. "Or when hot guy number two asked you to dance." Her next target was a dark haired douche with more hair gel than rhythm grinding against some little curly haired girl on the dance floor.

"Yeah, I'm so sad I missed out." I shook my head before returning to my tequila sunrise. I needed something bright and sunny in the darkness that was my life lately, and the orange juice and grenadine was the only thing that seemed to be picking up my spirits.

"Look, I'm not saying these guys are marriage material, but you're in your thirties now and completely antisocial. It's not the same as when you were last single and twenty-one. You might have to readjust your expectations a bit."

"I'm thirty. I'm not ancient." I mumbled into my straw.

"That's ancient when you're at a club trying to get laid." Dinah corrected. She was twenty-five, a full five years my junior, yet she acted about fifteen years younger than me half the time. Not that she was wrong though. But I'd been with Daniel so long, I barely even knew who I was outside of a relationship. I'd built my entire adult life around him and the eternity I thought we were going to spend together. My hobbies, my friendships, my routines. It had only been a few months since it all went south. Well, I guess technically it had been five *years* since it went south on his side, but it still felt fresh to me. I just wished he could have told me that when he got "caught up at work" and missed a couple of my birthdays, that it was because he was caught up in Clara's vagina. I could have started over when I was still younger and more desirable to guys like… I glanced at Chad and Hair Gel…

Maybe the issue was just that I was legitimately over club life, and not that I was undesirable at all. I met my ex at a club, and we'd been all over the night life for half our relationship, before we both felt like we'd grown out of it. At least *I* felt like that. Maybe he only pretended to. Maybe that's why this made me more bitter than excited for new possibilities. I didn't want to meet another Daniel, after all.

Feeling even more down, I excused myself to the bathroom, where the annoying, thudding techno-rap-auto-tuned-whatever was somewhat muted by the thick walls. I shoved open the door and made no eye contact with the woman getting railed on the sink as I located an open stall. She seemed to be having far too good a time to care if anyone saw them.

Although *I* cared. Not about these two strangers fucking in the bathroom, but that Daniel and I had never had that kind of dirty spontaneity even at our best. He was more of a rollover-and-get-it-over-with missionary kind of guy.

I wonder if he's any more exciting for Clara? I doubt it. He was always selfish. How guys like that end up with multiple partners vying for their affection, I'll never understand. How he ended up with *me*, I couldn't understand either. I guess we all were prone to settling for comfortable and convenient instead of real, honest passion sometimes. I'd gotten so used to being disappointed that I started registering it as normal.

God, stop thinking about him. I definitely needed to get laid. But I didn't want to be faking moans like that girl on the bathroom sink. I wanted someone who actually knew what the hell he was doing this time. I wouldn't be settling for nine years without finishing ever again.

I returned to my secluded corner of the crowded club, where Dinah had long since disappeared to go dance with some random with bleached tips. I sighed and sucked on the last traces of tequila in my overly sweet and fruity drink. A drink that was by no stretch strong enough. I should have just ordered a long island and gotten it over with.

I hate this. It would be so much easier if someone would just approach me—

"Curiouser and curiouser." A deep purr of a voice buzzed behind me. I turned toward the sound on instinct, only to see a striking man with platinum hair and an ethereal rose gold tint to his eyes. Beautiful and unusual. They seemed to almost shimmer in the light. To add to that angelic presence, he wore a starkly white three piece suit, and he carried himself with an unusual elegance. Especially for someone in a place like this.

"What's so curious?" I asked, not parroting his strange grammar.

"That a woman who is so beautiful could be so very sad." He placed a single finger on my table as he pivoted around me. "Would you fancy a drink, Poppet?"

Cute nickname. I fought the urge to roll my eyes.

"It's Alice." I said dryly, before I'd realized exactly what he'd just done. "But that was a clever way to get me to tell you my name."

"I already knew your name." He smiled widely, as if that wasn't the creepiest fucking thing I'd ever heard. If he wasn't hot and dressed like some sort of angel or fantasy prince, I'd probably throw whatever was left of my empty drink in his face. But he *was* hot, and I was looking to get off tonight, so I ignored my better judgment. "I'm Coello." He said as he offered me a hand. "But most call me the White Rabbit. I'm charmed to meet you, Alice."

"Charmed, indeed." Poppet was weird enough, but *The White Rabbit*? All I could think was maybe he sold cocaine or something. That would be a precious title for a drug dealer. Though, if he was some kind of king pin, at least that would mean he had enough money to spoil me for a few days. I deserved to be pampered at least once in my life. Getting mixed up with billionaires and mafia always worked out great in Romance novels, anyway.

I should have just rolled with it from there, but instead, I just had to ask. "Why exactly do they call you the White Rabbit?"

"Why don't you follow me, and I'll show you." His grin was mischievous but disarming. Still, I couldn't shake the feeling that a name like 'rabbit' probably wasn't referring to a vibrator. A guy this hot wouldn't be approaching someone as plain as I was unless he thought I was an easy customer. After all, I'd probably gained a solid twenty or thirty pounds after nine years with the same person. I'd gotten complacent and stopped trying so hard to be model perfect when I thought our love was deeper than just our surface level looks.

I won't say I was ugly per say. I cleaned up very nicely, and I'd still put enough effort into looking attractive, but did I look like I belonged in a magazine? Not particularly. If anything, I was healthier now than I was when I skipped meals to impress people, and I was stronger than I'd ever been. I should have been content with that knowledge, but being in a club still managed to bring out the internalized insecurities about my body that I had pushed aside when I thought I'd found love.

Which is probably why I knew guys with that perfect styled-to-look-messy hair, enchanting eyes, and flawless bodies didn't pick girls like me over a dance floor of practical super-models. If I wasn't even good enough for Daniel despite sacrificing nearly a decade of my life, there was no way I was good enough for him.

"I'm not looking for drugs." I said, returning my attention back to my drink. "You're targeting the wrong girl."

He pursed those pouty lips perched atop that smooth jawline. "I'm not offering drugs, and I'm not 'targeting the wrong girl' either, *Alice*." Something about the way he said my name made me terribly uncomfortable. "I simply want to treat you to a lovely evening. And I really don't think that this is either of our definitions of lovely." He motioned toward the club, using a sweeping motion to encompass the whole garish thing, and I had to admit that he was right on that.

"Then why are you here?" I locked in our gazes, figuring I'd have some chance of detecting lies if I held that eye contact. *Because I was so good at detecting my last boyfriend's lies…*

"The same reason you are, I imagine." His expression was soft. Genuine, even.

"Mourning a wasted life?" I spat back sarcastically.

He blinked several times, his eyes widening just a touch on each opening. "Yes, actually. That's… exactly why I'm here."

12

"Oh." Well, now I felt like a bitch. Here I had a beautiful man in mourning looking for a rebound, while I was also looking for a rebound, and I was being about as cuddly as a dried up cactus. "Well, in that case, maybe I'll let you buy me that drink… uh… Coello was it?"

"Indeed." He gave me a soft smile of confirmation, then he stepped away to the bar. He seemed nice enough. *I guess I can stop getting in my own way for just one night.*

Chapter 2

Alice

I pried open my eyes, needing the force of a hammer and chisel to break the thick crust that held them shut. I blinked rapidly to verify I was successful, yet open or closed, all I saw was darkness. Darkness that felt innately threatening and unfamiliar.

I was in… a room. Somewhere. Coarse, uncomfortable sheets scratched at my back, and sweat had my hair clinging to my forehead. My throat was parched, feeling dry and scratchy as I tried to swallow nothing, and my body was sluggish to move or react.

How did I get here? And *where* was here, for that matter?

My head was splitting and even the slightest movements made me dizzy. An unpleasant retching teased at my stomach, leaving me in that uncomfortable limbo of feeling like I needed to vomit to feel better, yet not quite so much that I could go through with it without shoving my fingers in my throat.

Was this what it felt like to be roofied? Is… is that what happened?

But… who would do that? Why me? Maybe it was a drink meant for Dinah. She was younger and prettier and more fit than I was. And the only person I interacted with was…

It couldn't have been Coello. He was too pretty, and… he seemed so nice.

Tears stung at the corner of my eyes at the realization.

How stupid.

I knew better than to trust a random drink from a random man, no matter how attractive he was. *I knew.* There was no reason a guy like that would be into me, after all. I was the sad and thorny wallflower in a club packed full of flawless, scantily dressed twenty-somethings. If he was looking for an easy lay, he could have picked someone much more eager and naïve.

I guess I *was* naïve. And I was probably the most eager target of all, considering I wasn't going to have droves of other desperate men clawing at me like Dinah did. I was the perfect target.

How pathetic was I?

I used my slowly returning strength to leverage myself upright. My body felt stiff and confined. A corset? And a frilly skirt. I slid my hands up my body, feeling the lace and ribbing of a powder pink dress that definitely wasn't mine, then back down to the fluffy tulle of the skirt that lightly scratched against my thighs. I didn't know who had changed my clothing, but this certainly wasn't a dress I'd put on myself.

But that was the least of my concern.

I swallowed, drawing my attention to the heavy weight of steel that was heated by my own body temperature and coiled around my neck.

Fuck.

Fuck fuck fuck.

I gripped at the thick metal ring around my neck, before I felt around myself in the darkness, blinking rapidly to try to adjust my eyes to the total absence of light. Not surprisingly, that ring was connected to a heavy chain. And the chain? It was connected to a twisted iron bed frame.

Is this how I die? I gave myself one, single desperate night to forget my shit bag of an ex, and while he continued to go free, happy and content with his new victim, I ended up chained to a bed and getting sold for my organs or some shit?

Well, I hope my gluten free, vegan-fed heart catches half as high a price as the grocery bill had been.

"Fuck me," I groaned aloud, tainted with a bitter scoff.

"No, not yet. That wouldn't be any fun at all." That voice caught in my ears with a low purr. I swallowed.

He's here.

It was really him. Coello '*The White Rabbit.*' His footsteps grew closer. "I'm glad to see you're awake. Welcome to Wonderland, Alice."

Gloved fingertips grazed my neck from behind, slipping loose hairs back behind my ear. I whipped my head around to catch him, but no one was there.

"How are you feeling, Poppet?" The touch drifted to my cheek like a whisper, and I shot my gaze to follow the sensation. Still no one. Where the hell was he? How was he moving so quickly?

"Are you scared? Oh, don't be scared… Not yet, anyways." That feather touch moved along my shoulders. This time I held still.

"The game hasn't even begun yet." His hands cupped my breasts, as he leaned in close to my ear. "And the game will be terrifying." Tingling pressure circled my nipples until they were perked.

I bit my lip and wrapped my arms around my chest, not wanting to acknowledge at all what his magic was doing to me. "Where am I? Why did you kidnap me?"

"Kidnap you? That's a rather rude accusation." In a flash, the 'White Rabbit' was now in front of me, his loose platinum locks falling wildly around his perfectly symmetrical face, and whimsical yet piercing rose eyes boring into my soul. He leaned forward, lifting my chin with his hand, and parting my lips with his thumb. "You're exactly where I said I would take you. You told me you wanted to come here, did you not, Alice?"

"I-I thought you meant… When you said to follow you and you'd show me a lovely evening…" Finishing that sentence with 'we'd go back to your house and bang' seemed ill advised right now. In a way, I was gathering that's exactly what was going to happen and why I was chained to his bed.

"Go on." The smile that graced his lips was both sinister and painfully attractive in a way I didn't want to admit internally or otherwise. "What did you think I was going to do to you, Poppet? I'd love to hear you describe it. Please, be as detailed as you can."

His low, deep voice had me fidgeting in an effort to hide the way it was sending chills through me. The wrong kind of chills.

"Th-that's—" still every word had to be shaken from my throat. Cold sweat chilled me, a tightness contrasted with the racing pump of my pulse, my throat felt constricted, and my breathing was so short and shallow, air barely reached my lungs. It was a real and visceral fear in my chest. But that fear seemed to be tangling with…

something else. I resented the fact that my mind, for even the briefest flash, drifted towards my own wants from last night. Thoughts that imagined how it would feel if this was all some kind of act. A kink of his. One where he kept pushing me. Pushed into me. Held me down and made me…

My cheeks flared, and I forced myself to meet his eyes. "I thought you were…" Still I couldn't say it. Not with those eyes looking at me. Not when I was in this position.

"Human?" Pure delight finished that sentence for me. "Or do you mean to say you thought I was a sweet little game you could play for just one night?" He inched his lips closer to mine, until he was warming my skin with his hot breaths. I didn't move. I *couldn't* as he held the chain attached to my collar firmly, allowing not the slightest retreat. "I'll happily be your game, Alice, but you'll be playing with me for as long as I say you will."

"Then let's play." There was an imperceptible boldness that came over me. I was helpless, and I knew it, but showing him the panic I was feeling wasn't going to get me out of this mess. If I'd learned anything about dealing with narcissists, which sadly was quite a bit, it was that they responded better to even the most contrived acting so long as you said the words they wanted to hear. "What's the game?"

"Let's call it tag." He chuckled, letting every warm beat of breath feather against my skin. "You see, we collect 'Alices' here. But they never last very long." He clenched the chain harder, tugging me forward so my ear was now by his lips. "All so often, they get caught and give in before I've even had a chance to get my blood flowing. It's been so long since I've gotten to enjoy the hunt." He released me and stepped back. Then with a snap of his fingers, he created a faint, flickering light. Each of his fingertips acted as a candle, as he swept that hand through the room.

"The last Alice I collected," he began, "didn't even make it out of bed." His illumination briefly flashed by a dingy cot not far from my own. The reflective surface of a steel chain caught in the light. My gaze followed the flicker up the metal links, until the reflection hit the white of an eye. The dim, orange candlelight tinted the greyed flesh of a woman, not unlike myself, who laid lifeless on the surface of her prison bed.

My breathing hitched. I swallowed down the scream that was bubbling through me, and I stashed away whatever terror I could hide. "So you're going to kill me?"

The White Rabbit scoffed at such a question. "Not if I don't have to. I don't kill for *fun*, Alice." The playful look in his near metallic pink eyes didn't reflect that sentiment. "I only kill when it's absolutely necessary. And if you're a worthwhile Alice, it won't be necessary."

A worthwhile Alice. Why did it matter so much that I was named Alice? What was the obsession there? "So then how do I prove my worth?"

Coello returned to my bedside, and he grinned down at me with that charming, charismatic smile. "Well that's simple, Poppet." He slammed his hands back down on the bed with a suddenness that made me jump. "You're going to try to escape these chains, and then you're going to run. You're going to run as fast as you can, as hard as you can, and as *desperately* as you can, and if you're lucky, maybe I won't catch you."

Those last words shot through me like a piercing arrow. I wasn't a runner by any stretch. Getting thrown into a game of life or death, where my sprinting ability was my only lifeline, was the stuff of nightmares for me. Still, I didn't want him to see me stumble. "And how do I win? Is there a finish line?" My voice even sounded obstinate in my own ears. I was proud of that.

"Of sorts." He said with a grin, making it clear he would explain no further.

"If you can't even tell me that much, then I don't want to play with you." The more I pushed back, the braver I felt. This whole scenario of his reminded me of when I was a kid, and my teacher used to tell me that the boys couldn't chase me around the playground if I simply didn't run, banking on the idea that the chase was the only reason they gave me their attention. I don't know that it worked in the face of a murderer, but it definitely worked on Petey and Jack.

"You'd rather end up like her?" Coello shook his head in taunting amusement. "Oh Alice, my dear, following me here was optional. But running from me? That's mandatory." That laugh again. Now close enough that his lips brushed mine. I tensed at a sensation that was utterly threatening in its softness. "But go ahead and test me. I *love it* when they test me."

In an instant, he vanished again, leaving my heart pounding in my chest so hard, fast, and loud, it flirted with explosion. I couldn't contain the tremors anymore.

But he was gone.

The room was dead silent now, giving my mind free reign to race through my predicament and figure out what the hell I was going to do to fix it.

Run. I have to run.

If I didn't, he'd catch me and… and he'd… what would he do? Would he kill me? Fuck me? Possess me? Would he lock me to this bed forever, having his way with me whenever he chose? Would I die like the others? How many others had there been?

How did that girl even end up like that? Does he starve them? Torture them? Does he kill them himself with his own bare hands?

My eyes strained in the direction of the other bed, but it was still too dark to really see. Did it even matter *how* she died? Or how many he'd killed?

Whatever the case, I didn't want that. I didn't want to be a slave or a prisoner. I still had so much I wanted to do in life. Nearly a third of my existence had been wasted doting on another person, and if I died now, he'd have really won. My story would end having never defined myself beyond Daniel.

I wouldn't let that happen. Whether it was out of spite, revenge, or some form of desperately self-serving care, I wouldn't let my story end because of a shitty club and my bad choice in men.

I gripped at the metal collar around my neck and I pulled as hard as I could. Pointless. It was locked so tight that it cut into my skin. It hurt. It was heavy. It was extremely well secured. How was I supposed to free myself of this thing? He hadn't left a key. He'd left nothing but threats and frustration.

In my desperate denial, I clawed at the metal for several moments as if I could free myself on brute strength alone, but I didn't have any such strength in me. Those tears now threatened to overflow. The first drip dampened my cheek all the way down to my jawline.

Fuck. How was I supposed to get out of here? I was willing to play his game if it meant my freedom, but he'd made it impossible from the start. *This is so fucking unfair.*

With a huff, I placed my hands back on the coarse sheets to support myself, and I stared listlessly at the darkness. Under my concentrated weight, the mattresses compressed just slightly. That was when I felt it. A small bottle rolled into the indentation, stopping only once it hit my thumb.

Confused, I lifted the bottle to eye level. It was barely bigger than a thimble, and the liquid inside was a garish shade of pink. The tiny glass vessel was plugged with a cork, and a gift tag was tied around its neck. I squinted in the darkness to better read it.

Drink me, it said.

This had to be some sort of a trap. There wasn't a single bone in my body that saw drinking a mysterious bottle of mysterious liquid, right after having been drugged and chained to a bed, no less, as a good idea. It could be poison, or battery acid, or hell, it could be spit for all I knew. I'd be hard pressed to decide what would be the worst of those options.

And yet, this is Wonderland, right? I thought to myself sarcastically. He wanted to play the game. He obviously expected me to find a way out of here, so he could chase me around like some kind of animal out for a hunt. What if this bottle was what was going to save me? What if the first part of this depraved story was a test of my trust? That I trusted he was going to set me free. That he didn't want to kill me. That this was all part of some elaborate scheme to test the 'Alices.' Maybe that Alice over there died because she *didn't* trust this bottle.

Or maybe she died because she did.

Still, what was I out, really? It's not like I had any other options. It was just me and this suspicious potion versus otherwise guaranteed death. And if I was going to die either way, I may as well do it on my own terms.

Feeling committed, yet still uncertain, I pulled the tiny cork from its neck. I sniffed the contents, but there was no discernable scent. Maybe that was a good thing, or maybe it was a terrible thing.

Don't be a bitch, Alice. I told myself as if that was in any way encouraging. Maybe it was, because I was able to will myself to close my eyes and press the bottle to my lips. I hovered there, counting down in my head as I tried to psyche myself up to actually tip it back and swallow. I had no sense of what it was going to feel like, taste like, or do to me, and I couldn't seem to block those warnings from my mind. It was absurd, but so was this entire situation. With any luck, I'd drink this and wake up, realizing the whole thing was simply a vivid and curious nightmare.

Bottoms up.

My hand lifted the bottle to the point that the drink was spilling into my mouth before my brain had time to reconsider logic and consequences. The flavor hit my tongue in a bizarre parade of different meals, one after the other. Cherry-tart, custard, pineapple… turkey? Toffee? Buttered toast? It was a wild mix that shouldn't have worked together at all, but somehow was strangely pleasant as the thick liquid slid down my throat.

Then I sat, and I waited. And waited.

"You really drank it. How innocent." Coello's voice drifted through the room with a haunting laugh. "And naïve. You're the first to do that since the original Alice. The others usually throw it against a wall or cry until I get so annoyed, I have to fuck them silent."

"You're doing it wrong if they're silent while you're fucking them." I taunted back. Though I was trying to come off as cocky and unmoved, the nauseous feeling that started bubbling up from my stomach was difficult to ignore.

"By the Devil, you are obnoxious." His tone was a mix of annoyance and amusement. Though it was a weak comeback in my opinion.

"What, not used to your precious 'Alice' collection talking back to you? Is this your first time kidnapping a girl who isn't empty and scared?" Honestly, I was just buying time as the nausea gave way to a cool, tingling feeling that reached into the top of my chest. I was yelling any nonsense he might find offensive, hoping to push the right button while I figured out what was happening to me.

"It is, actually. You're unusually feisty, and I think I might like that." His voice echoed. "I especially like the part where you keep pretending you're *not* scared, as if I can't sense your heart beat and short, stifled breathing from here."

He had me there, but I wouldn't bend. "I'm just scared that your dick might not be as big as your ego."

"Oh no no, I'm not falling for *that*. You won't get it until you've earned it." Coello's rejection actually mildly annoyed me. I didn't even want his dick, but if he could fuck that corpse over there—well, theoretically… uh… *hopefully* while she was still alive—I'm fairly certain I should at least be on his list of possibilities. "How do you feel?" He asked, interrupting an inner monologue I was happy to put an end to.

"How do I feel? How do you think I feel? I'm chained to the bed by a sociopath who calls himself the White Rabbit. I feel like—oh…" I cut myself off with a swallow as that new sensation started to hit. I felt… sensitive. Every inch of me. Something as small as the way my clothing moved over my skin with the slight rise and fall of my chest as I breathed was suddenly sending small shockwaves through me. My nipples were perked beneath the cups of my rigid corset, my whole body was warm, and I was subconsciously clenching my thighs together. I bit into my lip and closed my eyes tight, now trying to focus on anything other than the throbbing sensation growing between my legs.

What the fuck.

"I don't want to presume and speak for you, so I won't tell you how *I* think you feel." His soft chuckle only made this worse. "But one of us knows what was in that bottle. The other just took a taste."

"W-what was in that bottle?" That nausea had dissipated completely, and now all I felt was heat. Heat that crawled through my nerves, and heat that soaked my panties.

"The secret to finding the key." In a white flash he was in the room with me again, now standing behind me, with a hand on each shoulder. He looked down at me, as though he was examining the cold sweat that had started to develop on my brow.

His hands directly on my skin only made it worse. So much worse. If that bottle was some sort of potent aphrodisiac, I'd ended up completely in its clutches, and it took only the slightest connection of body heat to get my pulse racing even faster. I fidgeted in his hold, but the tingles in my body were building to a point of overwhelming.

So when he leaned down and whispered in my ear, tickling flesh with his soft, warm air, I was ready to do anything to relieve the pressure. "Trapped and bound in my bed, with no way to escape. If only, if only there was some way to be… released."

He disappeared again, and I had to catch myself on my forearms, not realizing how much I'd been leaning into the security of his hold.

Release?

I squirmed in the bed, rubbing my thighs together with some misguided hope of getting friction where I needed it without having to be so voyeuristic as to use my hands. But… I wasn't going to find my *release* that way. And the White Rabbit was well aware.

Was he watching me from whatever dark void he kept disappearing into? Was he filming?

No, they probably didn't have cameras in Wonderland. As he'd said, he wasn't human. This didn't strike me as a place of technology.

My eyes darted around the room, as if there was any way to determine if the coast was clear in that darkness. Like I had a choice in the matter, whether he was watching or not. I drew my lower lip into my mouth and moistened it with my tongue.

Th… this is for freedom. I told myself as I let my hand drift slowly downward. *For freedom.* I nudged under the waistband of my skirt, hoping that thin veil of material was enough to shield me from a monster's eyes.

I was already so painfully aroused, just giving in to the temptation was nearly enough to push me over the edge. But only nearly. I slid my finger gently up my center, staying over my panties, feeling how wet I was through the thin, lacey fabric: A cute set I'd worn with the hope of getting laid that night. Yet, as was always the case lately, I was doing this myself.

Though it was hard to be mad when even the lightest feathering of pressure was *euphoria* under the influence of this potion. I rubbed careful rotations at the top of my stroke before dipping down to my depths to spread more of that wetness.

"That's a good girl." A glint of Coello's pure platinum locks, illuminated only by the soft glow of a cigarette, caught my eye from the far wall.

"You have no idea how good a girl I can be." I managed through slow breaths. I'd figured he was watching, but the confirmation that he was right there, his eyes squarely on me, sent an unexpected thrill through me.

I traced my clit again, keeping everything over the clothing. The light friction of the lace was exquisite. I couldn't help that he was watching me, but if that was my only option, I'd give him a real show. It would probably be his first time ever seeing a woman actually satisfied, so maybe he'd learn something. *What a service I provide.*

"Why don't you take off your panties, Alice? It'll go faster that way." A puff of white smoke trailed his words.

"For me or for you?" I nearly didn't finish my mocking with the way that last touch hit me. I pressed in with added pressure at the top of my folds before dipping down again.

His chuckle was cruel. "I'm not making you do this for *my* excitement. This is purely about you, my little Poppet. Only *you* can release yourself from the chains that hold you."

"Don't lie—" My voice hitched on 'lie.' *Fuck, I'm so close.* "You wouldn't do this if you didn't get off on it."

"On the contrary." Coello pushed off the wall and walked over to me, not using any of his usual teleportation-like speed or parlor tricks. "I do this because Wonderland simply needs its Alice." His heeled leather shoes clacked on the cold stone floor. With a snap of his fingers, that cigarette disappeared. "And I simply need a game to play so I won't get bored." He placed a knee on the side of the bed, and the mattress dipped under his weight. Real weight. He was no longer the phantom presence appearing and disappearing as he saw fit.

I inched back, my hand ceasing its movements, but with that chain secured to the bedframe, I could only retreat from him so far. He easily caught me, grabbed me by the ankle, then dragged me beneath him.

I froze, eyes wide as they met his. He supported himself on a hand on each side of my head, and he nudged my legs apart with his knees. This new position had me teetering dangerously between wetting myself in terror and drenching myself in orgasm.

He placed a hand on my chest, and he pushed me down against the bed, assuring I was completely trapped beneath him. Then he grabbed my wrist and tugged it from its safe haven between my legs. His grip clamped down on my arm hard enough that he'd likely leave a mark, communicating exactly how pointless it would be to fight back. So I remained still as Coello replaced my hand with his own. Though I couldn't stay still when he pressed the heel of his palm down on my clit, while subsequently tracing small circles around the dampest part of my panties.

My hips twitched into his hold, and I bit my lip to muffle the shameful sound he'd worked through me.

"Let me show you exactly how we play in Wonderland." He whispered, low and husky in my ear. He shifted the pressure slightly, kneading me with his palm. Those skillful fingers slipped the lace of my panties to the side, and his first finger dipped into me. Just his fingertip.

He stayed in that sweet spot of nerves, just at my entrance, and he massaged my inner walls with controlled slips of the wrists.

"Oh!" I turned my head away when I heard myself gasp. ... *Oh fuck.* It… it must have been the potion that made everything feel this good. It wasn't him.

A second finger slipped inside. Then deeper. *Please go deeper.*

He went deeper. He used more pressure. He slid in and out over just the right spot. *God, that was a good spot.* I gripped the sheets, bunching material between my fingers in a desperate bid to not acknowledge the pure electricity of his touch. I pressed my head back into the mattress to try to still how much I was shaking.

He didn't let up. My toes curled in my shoes. Then he… he…

Lightning. My soul was now leaving my body, off to another plane. My vision, my mind, the pulses through my every nerve—all of it went blindingly white. He pressed down again, still rubbing that brilliant high through me, and my body took it, giving in so completely to the building pleasure. I bowed my back against the bed, inadvertently drawing closer to him, while his fingers played me through the entire ride.

I resented the high pitched gasp that escaped my lungs as that magic radiated ecstasy to every corner of my skin. But it *was* ecstasy. True. Fucking. Ecstasy.

In a pronounced display, he slowly removed his fingers. They were wet with my natural fluids, glistening in that magical candlelight. He slipped slick digits between his lips, and he sucked on them with the most devilish smile on his face. He assured I held eye contact as he finished the job with a slow stroke of his tongue.

"Not bad." He smirked with his eyes still on me. "You even *taste* better than the other prospects. Maybe there's more to you yet."

I wanted to retort, but I was breathless and still running on trembles. He had no problem speaking in my stead. "But I'll only help you this once, Alice." His sinister voice now seemed distant, even though I could feel his warmth still teasing at my cheek. "The next time I catch you, I won't be nearly so kind."

Another flash of light, and I was alone in the bed. The room was illuminated now, and the chain had vanished completely from my neck. I heaved heavily, trying to catch some semblance of control again.

The last thing I wanted to think about was the fact that no man had ever made me come like that before, or how the terror had vanished completely under his skillful command of my body. Yet, not wanting to think about something had in incredible ability to make me think about exactly that.

Wonderland, indeed.

That comfort and satisfaction, however, didn't last long when the now brightened room slowly came into view. I was surrounded now. Well, I always had been, but now I could see it ever so clearly.

There were no windows. The walls were black, though they shone with a feint texture of metal that felt especially cold and unfeeling in this dark box. They created a sense of being closed in, trapped, and losing hope.

Then there were the beds, both lining the walls and placed in careful rows, each one numbered in sequence. Bed number one was empty and clean and neatly made. Bed two and three had flowers and framed pictures, each of a different woman like some sort of memorial. It seemed to mark the end of a much gentler time in Wonderland.

And those were the superficial details I was doing my best to focus on, because the reality of what filled my vision out classed the darkest and most depraved horror movies I'd ever covered my eyes through. Amidst beds four through sixteen, *Alices* were still chained, bound, and helpless in their various stages of decay and decomposition. Thirteen women before me, who all died without making it out of the room. Or if they had, they'd been replaced here, like a monument to their failure. Some were nothing but skeletal remains that were haphazardly strung throughout the sheets. Others still had hints of flesh. Alice number sixteen may have still been warm. Though… there was no smell. It was unexplainably flowery in this room full of corpses. Another strange trick of Wonderland, I suppose.

It gave me pause, but not as much pause as it should. It was difficult to conjure up any sort of concise feelings. All of these women had died confused and scared under the captivity of the White Rabbit, playing a game that none of us understood. Only I remained, like the next challenger ready to fight an impossible evil.

A large 'Seventeen' adorned my bed. If I had any say in the matter, that would be where this depraved count ended.

I stared blankly around the room, looking for the door, letting intentionally blurred vision ignore what was so vivid before me.

I should have felt dirty, having just gotten off while surrounded by death. While all of these victims had been lost to a game, I was touching myself to please and entertain their captor and their killer. But instead, I couldn't seem to manifest my feelings as legitimate anger or terror. I couldn't even find disgust in my emotional database.

Maybe the shock of it all had shut down my entire nervous system. I didn't know. I just knew I stared listlessly and detached at the horror show that painted the room with violent colors, and I didn't have any emotion available to so much as shed a tear for these fallen few.

What good would it do to panic now? These Alices were dead. I wasn't. And I wouldn't be.

No. I've dealt with enough men who thought themselves gods in my lifetime, and I knew how to beat them.

I gathered my wits about me, and I stood from the bed, now towering over a sea of corpses. I rolled my neck, then I bent over gracefully to stretch my hamstrings. *He wants a chase? Well, I'll give him one.*

My tough talk in my head was almost enough to calm my nerves. Almost.

Only silently would I admit that a pang of tightness clamped down hard in my chest as I took my first step toward the door. An unwanted sweat formed on my brow as that familiar voice filled the void, one last time:

"You'd best get running now, Poppet. It only gets worse from here."

Chapter 3

Alice

As soon as I stepped out of the White Rabbit's prison, I found myself in a gaudy hallway adorned with gold trim and trellis that framed garish red wallpaper. It appeared to be short in distance, with a door that brought in sunlight just a few yards opposite my position. Freedom was just a quick sprint away.

"I'll give you a head start. Don't waste it." Coello said in a voice that echoed through my mind like his words were my own thoughts.

I shook my head, as if such a simple motion would banish him from speaking to me, then I started to run.

My feet propelled me forward, but no matter how far I ran, the distance to the exit never closed. I glanced down at the ground to verify I wasn't stuck on some sort of fantastical treadmill, but a quick glance behind me showed I'd made substantial distance.

"Fucking Wonderland." I muttered to myself before I continued my sprint.

Moments more and the previously blank walls began to populate themselves with portraits. First with images of a mighty queen, dressed in a gown of small blue hearts that were linked together like chainmail. Her perfect body was clearly visible beneath this loose linked dress, as she posed seductively with all fifty-one of her soldiers. Each man was marked clearly as a different suit and card within the deck, but only the queen herself stood out as different and special. The rest had blank faces like mindless drones, even as the woman posed with her barely covered breasts pressed to their faces or with her legs spread before them. It was a montage demonstrating both sex and total control.

At least there was someone having a good time here.

I passed the last picture of the queen, but the door remained just as far away as it had started. Now the hall was lined with the pictures of young women, most vibrantly happy, pretty, and blonde. The first couple portraits I recognized as the Alices who had been memorialized on the first couple beds. The remaining pictures showed each Alice I hadn't seen alive, before they'd been left to rot in an ice cold metal dungeon. Many were barely more than children, with the same youthful exuberance I had once had when I was fresh out of high school and thought I had the whole world in front of me. Naïve, pretty, hopeful faces, not yet broken by reality.

How sad.

I kept my pace. I wouldn't falter. I wouldn't end up like them.

But the door remained at a distance. I passed by the sixteenth portrait, and the walls shifted again. Now there was a blank picture frame before me. The edges were ornate with twisted gold vines. The corners were speckled with sapphires that were strategically placed to resemble flowers. The center appeared like a blank wall that would put a stop to my escape.

It was an illusion, I was sure of it. At the other side would be my door. Coello wanted a chase, after all. It wouldn't make sense to stop me so soon.

On pure, unearned trust, I bounded through it, tearing the center like it was of the thinnest tissue paper, and coming out the other side unscathed.

A chill ran up my spine as I'd passed through, as though it had stolen a fragment of my soul in the process. Likely it did, but at this point, my soul may as well have been dead weight. I didn't need it around guys like Coello. If anything, I needed less of it. Compassion and logic would get me killed in a place like this.

Once I was on the other side of the picture frame, finally I was able to catch the door before it could shift away any further. The hallway seemed to have a life of its own, but my frustration was stronger than its magic. I caught the knob with the tips of my fingers, and I yanked the door open as suddenly as I could.

And on the other side was a glass box, where every wall held back a dark blue veil of water.

The door slammed shut behind me, so suddenly I couldn't help but jump. I checked the door from whence I came, but it was locked tight, not even jiggling when I tried to turn the knob. On the other side of the box was another door that led out into the water, while the top of the box, some five feet overhead, boasted a series of small black rings that had no obvious purpose. I glanced through the ceiling glass, trying to discern how deep I was and how good my chances of making it to the surface would be. I wasn't the strongest swimmer. If I held my breath and kicked hard enough, I might make it, but it would be a nail biter.

Drowning was high on my list of ways I didn't want to die, right next to being buried alive and/or general suffocation, so the prospect of failure wasn't something I wanted to think about.

And if it was possible for things to get even worse, a pair of creatures, long nosed like serpentine anteaters, began swirling around my cage. They were unlike any animal I'd ever seen before. Maybe a sword fish combined with a badger? They looked furry through the glass, but every time they caught sight of me, they bore a row of sharp teeth that lined the entirety of that stretched jaw line.

I swallowed and let my gaze fall back on that door. The water was bad enough, but having to outswim carnivorous fish-rodent-monsters didn't exactly give me confidence in my survival chances. But then, neither did going back into the tomb with Coello.

I gripped that door knob with white knuckles, having to perform Olympic-worthy mental gymnastics to convince myself to open it. The moment I set this in motion, I would have to swim with everything I had. And if the White Rabbit was chasing me, I likely didn't have long to psyche myself up before committing. *It's now or never.*

I took a three count, a deep breath, and I gave it a fast and hard twist and tug.

But… it wouldn't budge. The knob turned and turned and turned like it was just a loose wheel. I banged on the glass with one hard hit of my closed fist. How was I supposed to get out of here?

A drop of water tapped my brow. Then another.

Oh. Fuck.

The rings above me began turning slowly, and every rotation dropped a few more splashes of water at my feet. My eyes widened as those drops turned to small streams, then those small streams turned to waterfalls. Water began pooling at the base of this accursed tank, and before I knew it I was up to my ankles with no signs of if stopping.

No no no—

Terror ripped through me, and I started banging on the glass door. I'd rather be in the water with those things then in here. At least I had a chance out there. But the knob still wouldn't release, and the room just kept filling.

I squeezed my eyes shut in an effort to dispel more tears, lest they add to the water in the chamber, but the panic shaking through me made it impossible not to cry. I was crying so much lately, it was amazing that I had any tears left. What had I done to deserve this?

I pushed back on the door in frustration, stumbling backwards several steps, barely keeping my footing in the process. The water kept filling the chamber, up to my knees now, and my movements were sluggish as I pushed through the deepening pool. I tried the door I'd come through again, but it was just as locked and just as pointless. This game wasn't fair at all.

"Is this how you get off, Coello? Drowning pretty girls?" I yelled through my hysterics. The words sounded far more scathing and tough than I felt. I'd been so bold and determined when I'd walked out of that room, and now I was back to being a simpering mess. The water reached my hips. It was cold enough to chill me through as it inched up my core.

There had to be some way out of here. There had to be.

I filled my lungs enough to assure I was floating atop the water when it reached chest height. My feet left the ground, and I swam from one wall to the next, feeling along them for something—anything—that might get me out of here. But still nothing but smooth glass met my touch.

When the water was too deep to touch the ground with my head still above the surface, and the amount of air above me was less than the liquid below me, the panic set in much more intensely than even before. It was by survival instincts alone that I didn't completely hyperventilate. No, I took as deep of breaths as I could manage, just so I could keep my lungs full as long and as buoyantly as possible. As the top of the tank got closer, it sunk in that these were the lasts breaths I might ever take, and I wanted them to be good ones.

Three more feet of water filled the tank, and the top was just two feet overhead now. Everything was closing in way too fast, and still I had no solution. I was dead before the game even started.

Wonderland is what he'd called this place. It was supposed to be magical, right? Maybe even spectacular and fun and charming. Not like this. This was hell.

My mind was muddled with the disbelief that this was the end, and that I wasn't about to simply wake up from a bad dream. I'd had dreams like this before. Dreams where I was drowning, trapped, and there was no way out.

They say you can't die in your dreams, but I'd died in mine plenty of times. I thought back to one of my early dates with Daniel, back when I was so newly falling for him. We were at a lake, fooling around in his car. It started with an innocent kiss. It turned to a full blown make out session. Then he was climbing over the center console to get closer to me, and without realizing it, he'd knocked the car into neutral. We started rolling towards the lake, while Daniel fumbled to unhook my bra. I immediately felt the car start to move, but he didn't seem to care. He didn't take anything seriously ever. I pushed back on his shoulders, and he took it as foreplay, only kissing me more roughly and shoving my shirt up to my neck more eagerly. It took me screaming into his mouth before the blood in his dick made it back to his equally worthless head, and he realized we were about to roll head first into the lake.

He managed to get the car stopped exactly as the nose dipped into the drink. We were close enough for lake water to start leaking in through the bottom of the doors.

I saw my life flash before my eyes, while all Daniel saw was my half removed bra, and he tried to continue without even backing the car out of the lake.

Fuck, those red flags were on fire even back then. I should have known better than to commit nine years to a guy who cared more about getting off than our literal lives. I still had nightmares about that day. Maybe that had been a prophecy, really. A warning that if I didn't choose better men, one day I would drown for it.

The last foot of air between myself and a full tank started to disappear.

I felt along the ceiling now that it was easily in reach. I tried blocking off the seeping rings with my hands, but that did little good. I needed some kind of magic to survive at this point. *Where is all the goddamn magic?*

With the little air I had left, I kept my nose above water for what fleeting seconds remained, I scraped my nails along that glass, while I kicked and kicked and kicked to keep from drowning. Then the last inch disappeared.

I took all the breath I could in that fleeting final moment, then I was submerged completely, holding my air for my last few moments. It wouldn't be long now before a need for a fresh inhale would have my lungs drawing in the water around me and filling my body with the weight of drowning.

Just moments and it would all be over. I closed my eyes and dropped to the floor, landing softly under the weightlessness the water granted me. The first bubbles of my lost air started to dispense from my nose. Tiny little bubbles of life, just floating away. I glanced up as those bubbles gathered on the ceiling. They were my life force, soon to burst and disappear, just like the rest of it.

But they didn't disappear. Instead, they started to clump together. They shaped themselves. They formed… a key?

A key!

I pushed off the floor, and sprang up to this strange bubble key. It felt hard and firm in my hands, despite existing as little more than a transparent absence of water. That was the magic I needed. Frantically, and while the end of my held breath threatened to give, I shoved the key into the door knob, and the entire glass case dissolved into bubbles.

That's it!

I caught enough of the bubbles to take a new fresh breath, and I used that lucky air to start kicking towards the sunlight above. I was free. *Free.* I wasn't going to drown in a glass cage.

I could see the sparkles of sunlight atop the frigid surface, and I swam harder still. Then a swirl of water brushed my skirt, spinning me in place. I shot around and caught glimpse of the creature. I followed it clockwise. Another swirl of current twisted me around faster. I watched, wide eyed, as those animals began to circle me with increasing speed.

The whirling motion created suction, and before I knew it, I was being drawn back down into the depths again like I'd been caught in a tractor beam.

I looked up, wanting to sob despite the wetness against my face. I was so close. *So close.*

I kicked and kicked and kicked, but it was no use. They wouldn't stop spinning, and the whirlpool they'd created was more powerful than my doggy paddle levels of swimming skills. My only hope was if I could somehow get them to stop.

Another bubble shot upward, despite the downward suction, and I caught it like it was a ball, then shoved it into my mouth. The air dissolved on my tongue like the finest cotton candy, and my held breath renewed. What would have surely been impossible in the real world was so easy here. None of the same laws of physics applied, and I had to remind myself of that.

Wait, if that's the case, maybe I could just…

The two badger fish smirked at me—smirked!—as their circles dragged me down. I squinted at them, reading their movements, trying to pull apart what exactly they were doing. Clockwise circles created a downward pull, so… what if counter-clockwise circles could bring me up? That would be nonsense, but isn't that the point?

Instead of kicking up, I started kicking in circles, countering their movements with violent whips of my legs. I spun counter clockwise, rotation after rotation, and lo and behold, I started to rise.

I smirked at the bastards now, and I kept up my frantic spinning. Up and up and up. They couldn't catch me, even as they tried to swim harder and faster. I twirled like a possessed ballerina until I burst through that layer of surface tension that brought me into open air.

I was but feet from a shoreline, and I wasted no time paddling over to it with desperation. I crawled from the water, tugging on the grass like it was a life rope, and I came to my hands and knees to try to choke precious air back into my chest.

Water dispelled from my lungs and precious oxygen took its place.

I made it. I was alive. For now, anyway.

As I slowly found a sense of homeostasis again, I at last lifted my vision to get my first image of Wonderland in earnest.

And what an image it was.

Behind me, Coello's dungeon was now a perfectly still, sparkling lake painted by the reflection of the land beneath the morning sun. Before me was an expansive green field, speckled generously in flowers. And on the other side was a dense forest veiled in darkness.

So beautiful. I wanted to bask in that image forever. It was a picture perfect vacation retreat in a place I'd always wanted to go but never been able to commit to. Daniel had always been working after all. Or on work trips, at the very least. I'd been too scared to travel alone, and he'd promised that my vacation was supposed to come *someday*, after things *slowed down*.

I tried to shake the thought and just enjoy the warm sunlight on my face and the gentle sound of bird songs that enchanted the air, even if I could only do so for a moment. I smiled softly, nearly forgetting where I was, until I rubbed my neck to sooth the phantom sensation of the metal collar I'd just been wearing. That inner peace slipped away. I couldn't keep dawdling like this. It was time to run.

Chapter 4

I put my feet up on the desk and leaned back in my chair, watching my display orb with only mild amusement as the Alice-of-the-Week started running through the field towards the forest. Predictable. Boring. How long would this one last if her best idea was just hiding in the trees? There were more demons there than there were over here, after all.

I laughed to myself before grabbing a cigarette and snapping my fingers to create a small flame. I took a slow drag as the tobacco ignited.

This Alice seemed different though. She'd figured out the water trap much faster than the last girls. And she'd outsmarted the Slivy Toves and their suction cone like she was an experienced Wonderland creature out for a swim. I'd not seen that kind of resourcefulness in ages. So many of our captives were so quick to give up the moment they let the terror take hold. She had a bit of bite, and she used her fear as a tool instead of a point of paralysis. A sarcastic and snippy tool, but a tool none the less. It would be a disservice if I wrote her off *completely*. If anything, her attitude and little provocations were a bit refreshing.

I'd been telling The Cheshire Cat for years that we should be picking women with some experience under their belt instead of a bunch of barely legal children. Whether she'd perform any better was less significant than the fact that women often became more secure and more powerful as they got older, thusly being much more satisfying to try and break. I'd accepted we might never win this rebellion a long time ago, and if I couldn't win, I could at least have fun with it.

As always, I was right and he was wrong.

She'd already gotten further than half our candidates, after all. At some point I'd have to find an Alice that was resourceful enough to take down that sadistic cunt we were forced to call the Queen of Hearts. Maybe this one would be her. A veritable warrior princess.

I drew another toke, then I slowly exhaled the smoke. I still had doubts though. She was running with too much energy conservation in mind. It was a marathon not a sprint, sure, but at this rate, I was definitely going to catch her much too quickly. And then I would have to be terribly awful to her.

I sighed, though the grin across my lips betrayed the sentiment. Being nice to the Alices never made them tough enough. Even the ones who made it out of bed always ended up so broken by the rest of Wonderland that they were worthless by the time they made it to the Queen's court. And if they couldn't be useful, they could at least entertain me before I was forced to return, yet again, to the devil-forsaken Commonland, where all the humans grew up oblivious to this world of magic just on the other side of their looking glasses. *Such simple creatures, these mortals.*

I stared blankly at my fingernails, ignoring the image in my periphery as she bounded into the first trace shadows of the forest. *That's a good girl. Keep going. Faster now, right into the clutches of the Bandersnatch.*

I rolled my eyes, then I started counting down in my head. *Ten, nine, eight, seven...*

Another drag of the cigarette. These things always burned up too quickly. I should probably hit up the Caterpillar for something stronger.

Six, five, four…

A flick of my wrist, and the spent dart vanished.

Three, two… One.

I think that's enough of a head start. Good luck, Poppet.

Chapter 5

My feet pounded through the grass, the slight breeze from my pace helping to dry some of the dampness in my hair. I thanked my good sense that had chosen comfortable and reasonable dancing shoes last night instead of my six inch "hooker heels" that Dinah suggested.

Though Coello had changed my clothing for me, apparently, so maybe he would have given me better shoes regardless.

Because he so clearly wants me to succeed. I scoffed, as I ran my hands over the material of my soft pink corset. The boning restricted my breathing a touch, but I managed to keep air in my lungs despite. I'd never been much of a runner outside dread filled jaunts on a treadmill, but it's surprising the things a person can manage once they realize the alternative is death.

My hands snaked down to the frilly skirt that finished off this absurd costume. It flared out even with the heavy weight of water drenching every inch. Maybe this was what the original Alice wore when she ended up here, and these unoriginal clowns were just trying to replicate past success. *Who knows. Nothing makes sense here.*

The field disappeared slowly behind me as I neared the forest. Strange insects buzzed through the air, and birds flew upside down amidst clouds that were shaped with much too much definition to be natural. There was no science to the nature here. The grass would bounce beneath me, like springs throwing me forward, and the bees sang instead of buzzed. The visual was already enough to show me exactly how off this place was even beyond the confines of the Rabbit's lair.

The first trees sprang up beside me, bouncing to full height like an accordion letting loose. They speckled the grass in increasing numbers as I neared the blackened shade of the woods.

Before I could quite reach the densest tree line, I came upon a gaggle of strange men. They stood in different spots on a small running track, and they were all positioned as if they were ready to launch into an Olympic sprint race.

I rolled my eyes and kept running. Whatever they were doing was very likely absurd, and I had no time for it. As I bounded past, without warning, suddenly their race was on, and everyone began running beside me. I glanced at the man in my periphery. He looked strikingly similar to *fucking Daniel.*

More annoyed than anything, I picked up the pace. I wanted to beat them at whatever game they thought we were playing. I slammed my feet to the ground in rapid succession, and I outpaced one stupid clown after the other.

But that man who looked like Daniel began to catch up to me. I glanced briefly to my side, recording his image in my periphery. The same cheek bones, the same haircut, that slightly upturned mouse-like nose. The only difference between them was his height and muscle tone. I increased my pace even more, but he was much harder to shake than the rest, especially considering the lack of an obvious finish line and no obvious set of rules. Because why would there be? That would be much too logical.

I fucking hate this place.

"Where are you running to, my lady?" The man asked casually, despite running in full bore lunges that should be winding a normal person completely.

"Away." I snapped back harshly, partially because I didn't much want to talk to him, and mostly because that was all I could manage in my own heavy breathing.

"Away? I like it there." He nodded matter-of-factly, still so calm and composed for someone pumping along so wildly. "Then it's a race. I can't wait for my prize." He took off now, so fast his legs were a blur.

I scrunched my brows. *When he says 'prize,' he'd better not be expecting something from ME.* Yet somehow, I knew he did.

Again: I fucking hate this place.

But not wanting to be beaten by some bullshit Wonderfairy who looked like my ex, I gave that race my all. I was in an anger fueled sprint, straining my muscles with wild abandon, throwing myself forward, closer and closer to the forest. White lines appeared on the floor on either side of me, as if forming a clearly marked track. There was no clearly marked end, but at least I knew the boundaries. As my pace increased, his seemed to slow, as if his ability to run was inversely proportional to the effort I put in.

What a *wonder*, I thought with my tongue in my cheek. I'd have to stop myself from making that joke every five minutes as this place constantly ruined my day.

I pumped my arms in time with my legs, now completely dry. I left all of the other participants behind and made the final push to pass that asshole. The moment my toes touched ground ahead of his, he shouted. "That's it! You've won!"

I took that as permission to slow down. I had no clue how he'd determined the race had ended, but as long as he did it when I was ahead, I wasn't about to argue. I let my legs find a jog, then a walk, then stillness. I bent over, placing my hands on my knees, and I breathed heavily trying to catch anything that might resemble air in my lungs. *Goddamn, I'm out of shape.*

"Great. So what's *my* prize." I asked as if I'd suddenly cared. Maybe I kind of did.

"As the winner of the Caucus Race, the winner's pendant is your prize, of course." He smiled widely with dimples indenting his cheeks. His short brown hair and his equally brown eyes were styled so exactly like my ex, that I was more likely to stab him then take the hand he'd offered me. "It's Mishka," He said, presenting his hand a second time, as if I might be more likely to take it when presented again. "But most call me 'The Mouse.'"

I was not about to tell him *my* name. "Great. Cool." I ignored the outstretched hand, placing my fists akimbo, and I tapped my foot impatiently for this pendant. I should be running. I *needed* to be running. But I'd just sprinted fast enough that I'd probably earned myself a few seconds to collect some Wonderland jewelry. I deserved *something* for putting up with this situation.

Mishka frowned when I didn't accept his greeting, but he got to digging through his pocket. After entirely too many foot taps, he came up with a jeweled necklace that was worth every ounce of the patience I'd displayed. It was characterized by a large gem of translucent turquois, centering a ring of jeweled flowers and small diamond inlays. A gorgeous pendant fit for a queen.

My eyes widened in honest surprise. He stepped forward, and I remained still as he neared enough to present the prize to me. Despite being called the Mouse, he was quite a bit taller than me. Most people were, but the men of Wonderland made my five foot five seem downright miniature thus far.

I looked up into his brown eyes as he lifted the pendant over my head. I didn't fight him as he placed the chain gently around my neck, nor as he lifted my hair from its binding. It was gentle. Kind. Entrancing.

For a moment, I was back home, before everything had been broken beyond repair. I was cuddled up against Daniel, as he ran his hands through my hair, sweeping it away lovingly so he could better place kisses on my neck. He tugged lightly at the necklace he'd bought me for our first anniversary that I'd worn every day since. And I was smiling, filled with warmth, as I savored this peaceful and affectionate bond we'd shared. That we would share forever, I thought.

My eyes started to water without my permission, and I pushed back suddenly against Mishka in an effort to shove away those unwanted and sudden emotions. Though the "Mouse" effortlessly held his position, and it was only myself who I sent stumbling backwards. Those unfairly familiar brown eyes flashed a hint of confusion, followed by a hint of… surprise? Fear?

Fear because of… me?

My back hit something hard and warm. Two strong hands gripped my shoulders.

Fear *for* me.

"That was easy." Coello's voice warmed my ear with a harshness that rippled terror through my senses. "I gave you a head start—plenty of time to make plenty of distance—and already I've caught you? All because you let some silly *rat* distract you?" His chest heated my back. His fingertips drove into my shoulders until he was pressing hard enough to bruise the skin. Though he didn't care. "How dull. Perhaps I need to show you how serious this game is, because you don't seem to be *listening*, Alice."

My heart just about stopped as his grip slid roughly down to my biceps. I froze in his hold. The lump in my throat silenced me, so I used every ounce of fear in my quivering lip to beg this Mouse to help. Misguided as it may be, I hoped he might recognize how badly I needed saving right now, and that he might be brave enough to stand up to someone like the White Rabbit.

"I'm sorry, Coello. I didn't realize she was one of yours." Instead, Mishka bowed like a servant, speaking in a tone of groveling and submission. He was also as pathetic and as quick to disappoint me as my ex, it turned out. His gaze met mine with the kind of "I'm sorry" expression that offered neither relief nor solutions—only excuses for failing to put in honest effort. The kind of look that said *"I'm selfish and won't change my ways, but please don't try to unwrap yourself from around my finger."*

"Is that right?" Coello's voice dropped to something far more severe than I'd yet heard. "You thought this lovely woman was just out frolicking about in Wonderland of her own volition? Just a regular human girl in the magical realm with no ties to anyone." His hands inched back up toward my shoulders, sliding along their tops until they reached the nape of my neck. "Is that really what you thought, Mouse?"

"I-I mean… I just thought I might… I wanted to help you t-to… to test the new Alice." Mishka stumbled over every word, then he stumbled over his own feet as he tried to back away.

"And how were you going to test her exactly, Mouse?" Coello's hands now traced the chain around my neck, dipping down to the pendant resting atop the valley of my cleavage. I'm sure he felt me swallow. "Were you going to simply see how fast she could run?" Those fingertips now traced the edge of the bust on my corset. "Were you going to see how strong she was in a fight?" I didn't move as those finger tips just barely dipped beneath the rigid edge of my top. My breathing picked up pace. The speeding rise and fall of my chest only made the position of his touch more vivid. "Or do you mean you were you going to see how tight she was when you fucked her?"

"No, I swear, Coello. I-I wasn't—" Mishka flushed at the accusation, while his rambling only got more incoherent. My eyes widened as I watched him come undone. He didn't need to admit the words. The implication and intention was already quite clear.

In an instant, Coello's hands were off my breasts, I was stumbling to keep my balance, and he was standing opposite me, now holding Mishka prisoner from behind. "You know better than to touch my Alice." He hissed into the Mouse's ear. I remained perfectly still as I watched fear freeze in the man's eyes.

And as I watched Coello's powerful fingers plunge through skin, muscle, and bone into the cavity of this man's chest.

Coello's forearm tensed as he squeezed his fist around Mishka's heart. Red seeped everywhere, drenching Coello's skin, Mishka's chest, and flowing freely down the Mouse's body as that vital organ was crushed between the White Rabbit's powerful fingers. That squelching sound of fluid being wrung from flesh would likely echo in my ears for a lifetime. And the image of the life force fading from his brown eyes—Daniel's eyes—might forever haunt me.

Then, as casually as one might pluck an apple from a tree, he yanked the crushed organ from Mishka's ribcage, and he took a step back so this now lifeless and hollow body could crumple freely to the floor.

Coello tossed the heart over his shoulder with casual disinterest, then he shook out his wrist, scattering drops of excess blood in the nearby grass. He took a moment to examine his hand, as if the blood that now coated his entire arm somehow offended him for being there.

Then his gaze once again met mine.

And I realized, in that moment, that the White Rabbit had caught me.

Chapter 6

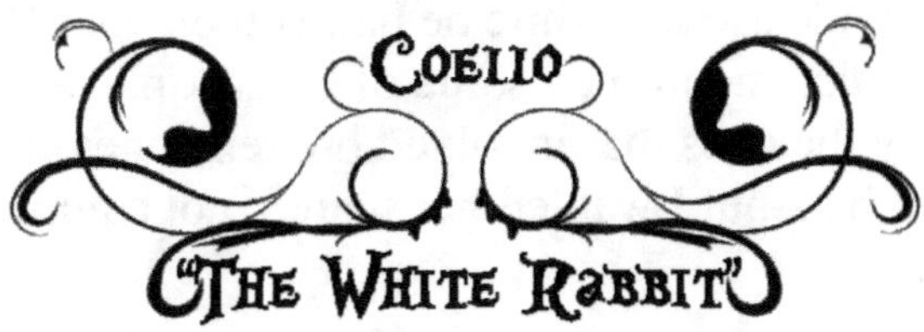

Coello

"The White Rabbit"

Alice took a shaky step back, nearly tripping over gravity itself as she struggled to keep her footing under those comically unsteady legs.

"You… You killed him." Her voice was barely more than a whimper. None of the snark and confidence she'd had while chained to my bed seemed to come through now.

The smirk on my lips was involuntary. She was much cuter when she was scared. I certainly wouldn't tell her that all Wonderland creatures were immortal, and that their lives reset with each new Alice. Though she might cry if I told her he won't come back until she disappears, and the cycle began anew.

"Would you have preferred I waited until he'd had his way with you?" I flexed my blood soaked hand, drawing a fist one finger at a time in a graceful motion.

"N-no but…" She wasn't crying like they usually did the first time they witness the end of a Wonderland pest, though she appeared to be in shock. She must not have ever watched a man die before. How nice it must have been to grow up so safe and sheltered. "I don't think he was going to—"

"You really are innocent." I interrupted her, not remotely interested in hearing anyone defend the fucking rat. "That pendant around your neck is a collar of total control. It taps into your nervous system and makes you a puppet for whoever controls it. And worst of all, it leaves its victim fully conscious while completely helpless. You'd have been wide awake, while he had you on your knees." I could have also mentioned some of his… kinks— Particularly the ones that involved broken bones and severed limbs—but I wanted her scared, not completely shut down.

"What?" Those wide eyes again. That's the look I wanted. *Fuck, I love that shock on her face.* She wrapped her fingers around the necklace and stared down at the gemstones in horror.

"It's powerless now that its master is dead. You can keep it if you fancy." I added nonchalantly. "The turquois matches your eyes. It looks quite nice on you."

"Oh." Was all she said in response. Though I couldn't tell if the red in her cheeks was out of distress or from blushing. "So you… you saved me." She blinked rapidly, as if processing the idea before she could look me in the eye again.

"Now, I wouldn't go that far." I took a step toward her. She stepped back. As she should. Amusement danced in my chest as nerves clearly danced in hers. "I was simply disappointed that you fell for his trap so easily, so I thought I'd remind you *whose* game you're supposed to be playing."

"I couldn't help it. He looked so much like…" She trailed off, frowning at the ground. "Like my ex-boyfriend." She managed to finish the sentence with the most disappointing answer. Human women were always so typical.

"I hadn't realized you had such poor taste in men." I taunted. *Who would date someone who was in any way like Mishka?*

"Wasn't that obvious when I gave someone as disgusting as you the time of day? Clearly I pick men based on how repulsive they are." *There* was that bite I'd been missing.

"You're such a liar, Poppet." I took another step to force her back another. Then I closed the distance with a speed she couldn't match, stopping her retreat with my bloody hand around her necklace, and my clean hand tightly around her waist. I held her tight to brace her body against mine. "If you find me so abhorrent, why are you so incredibly wet right now?"

"Tch—" She looked away, pure shame in all of her movements. "I'm not." She attempted.

"Are you hoping I'll call your bluff?" I released her necklace, and I moved that hand directly to her neck. I tightened my hold briefly, eliciting a small gasp from her throat, then I smeared blood over her soft, pale skin. Her heart rate and her breathing picked up pace as I drifted the trail of red down her chest, down to her right breast, then over the cup of her corset where I stained the pink lace crimson. I squeezed her gently, and she bit into her lip in perfect distress. She was so much more fetching than she'd been when she was clean. *Yes, I quite like this Alice.*

"What are you going to do to me?" That boldness was lost now that she felt so cornered. Though I had a feeling it would come right back the moment she'd figured out some sort of plan.

"What, indeed." Drifting my hand back up to her face, I drew a line of blood beneath her right eye, then another beneath her left. The war paint accented her face nicely, and the red really added a nice hue of violence to her. Moving lower to her lips, I used my thumb to color her mouth red, tracing each lip as though I was applying simple makeup. Her lip was still trembling under my touch, but I could tell she was trying her best to not flinch. She knew she couldn't win here. *Smart girl.*

With added pressure, I slipped my thumb inside her mouth. I press down on her teeth, granting myself more access until I was just touching the tip of her tongue.

"Suck, Alice." I whispered. "And I might give you another chance."

Her lips closed softly around my thumb, and her teeth tapped against the top of my finger nail before retreating a few millimeters. The instinctual desire to bite down must have been clawing at her mind, but she thought better of it. Alice met my eyes with those large blue orbs, looking much like a cornered doe.

Then her gaze narrowed in spite, and she bit down with everything she had.

Mmmmhmm, she thought she did something there.

"Harder." I held her eye contact like it was my captive. She bit harder. Hard enough to break my skin and draw my blood. *Heh. Good. She could enjoy that flavor, too.*

I kept my thumb in her mouth, and I used the leverage to forcefully redirect her chin upward. She kept on the pressure in a desperate last form of defiance. That fucking hate in her eyes made my cock twitch.

In one sudden motion, I yanked my hand from her mouth and shoved her away, sending her stumbling backwards into the grass. She fell on her hip, but was almost immediately scrambling back onto her feet.

"Consider that your first and only warning, Poppet. Next time I catch you, you'll be licking your own blood off my dick." I said as I placed my bloodied palm on my hip, making no effort to hide her dripping bite marks. I wanted her to see exactly how little she'd affected me. "What are you waiting for? Run."

Alice didn't say another word. She just turned her back on me and started running, as fast as she could, into the dense trees.

Ah, what fools these mortals be.

Chapter 7

Alice

"Run."

That single word went from being a curse to the command that dictated my entire life. I ran and I ran until my legs threatened to give. Until my lungs were desperate to hold onto a breath for longer than the fractions of a second my pace allowed. Until my feet bled and blistered, my body was drenched in sweat, and my throat was dry. I wanted to stop. *Dear God, let me stop.*

But after watching that display, stopping was hardly an option. I'd already deduced that the White Rabbit was a dangerous man, but not until I'd seen that level of brutality with my own eyes was the reality of that danger so apparent. He could kill with a smile on his face and no weapon but his bare fingers, and there was nothing I could do when he decided I was his.

But then…

He had also…

"Would you have preferred I waited until he'd had his way with you?"

Why did he save me? I would have thought it would have been to his amusement to watch me be hurt and demoralized and broken down by Wonderland. Maybe it was only fun for him if he did it himself? I couldn't imagine it being any reason more wholesome.

But that wasn't the worst of what I'd taken from that exchange. No, while I was focusing my hate on the White Rabbit, if anything, I was far more angry at myself for having even considered that affection from the Mouse just because he looked like Daniel. Why was I still so weak? He didn't deserve any of my mind or heart anymore, but I was more hung up on him than I'd realized.

I shook my head and squeezed my eyes shut, still cursing the way I'd craved, for just a few more moments, that fantasy that my ex hadn't been a complete waste of my life for the last nine years. I was supposed to be better than that. One of those tough, cool women who people said were "so strong" because I understood that I was better than I'd let him treat me. And yet, the first test reminded me that I was just an ordinary sucker who still clung to a lie.

Somehow, that concept upset me far more than having watched a man be savagely murdered before my very eyes. If anything, there was a bit of relief as I watched *Daniel* face consequences for once. As I watched the light fade from those familiar eyes, I'd be lying to myself if I didn't say there was a hint of satisfaction in it. Maybe something *was* wrong with me.

I was probably exactly as psycho as he told everyone I was to even be thinking such a thing. I shook my head in disdain as I continued my run into the darkening woods.

Every time a leaf rustled beside or behind me, I jumped. How much of a lead was Coello going to give me now? He'd caught me so easily, I couldn't help but think it barely mattered. I could have a mile on him, and he'd be at my heels in an instant if he liked. This wasn't the world I came from. These men weren't human. None of this was predictable or bound by the laws of earthly physics. I've already seen enough to know that.

What fun was a game of tag if there was no challenge? I couldn't understand what pleasure he got from this. But then again, it wouldn't be the first time a man picked something easy and unsatisfying for quick, short-sighted pleasure.

I exhaled sharply, and I kept up the pace into blacker and blacker canopies.

"You seem flustered, my dear." With the suddenness of a sniper's shot, a voice rang from the darkness from no obvious direction. My eyes darted from canopy to canopy, but it was pitch black beneath the branches now. The trees had come to gather so densely, it was pitch black *everywhere* now, so much so that I couldn't even see where the path itself had gone.

I ignored the taunting. I was learning my lesson not to engage with any of these Wonderland creatures if I could avoid it. Instead, I searched frantically for what direction I might go. I didn't have time to be indecisive. Not when I knew he was so near. Every second I wasted might be the one second too many.

Making an executive decision, I started to run to my right when the voice interrupted me again.

"Are you sure that's the way you want to go?" He said.

"I'm absolutely not sure at all." I lamented. "But if you're not going to help me, then please just leave me alone." Why I'd said 'please' could only be chocked up to distress so deep I'd reverted to my most basic ingrained politeness.

"Who said I'm not going to help you?" A wide grin, sparkling white, perfect, and punctuated with sharp fangs at each side of his smile, appeared in the trees like a beacon of light in a sea of black. "I would never let such a pretty girl end up a feast for the Jabberwock or the Bandersnatch,"

"Then tell me which way to go." I near pouted in my exasperation.

"How can I possibly tell you which way to go when I don't know where you're trying to get to?" That solitary smile was joined by full lips and high cheekbones. Striking violet eyes, and soft, dark hair that fell wildly around his handsome face. The ears of a cat, colored with purple stripes extended from his wide-rimmed hat, and his body appeared clothed in a fine suit of the darkest violet and burgundy.

I sighed, thinking silently to myself, *are all the men in Wonderland this gorgeous?* Though this one seemed particularly eye catching, with his whimsical dress, his devilish eyes, and that soothing voice.

"Anywhere that's not here." I attempted.

"Well any direction will take you there." He said as he hopped down from the high branches and landed effortlessly on his feet. "But I'm guessing just *anywhere* won't do."

"Well, how about anywhere where the White Rabbit won't find me." I tried again, this time more composed.

"Oh? You've crossed Coello, have you?" That perfect smile of his twisted with a hint of something slightly more sinister. I was starting to gather Coello had quite the reputation. "What's your name, my dove?"

"Don't pretend you don't already know." I scoffed at the question.

"A fair accusation. How rude of me, *Alice*." He said with a bow, removing his hat for effect. The cat ears came off with it, though if I'd learned anything about

Wonderland, I gathered they were only optionally attached to his head based on his mood. "It's just been so long since I've seen one of your kind out in the wild. He's gotten so sadistic, that silly bunny." He stood up straight and eyed me up and down. Something about his gaze made my skin crawl. "And judging by the blood, he's not improved much since the last girl came through."

I rubbed my cheek with the back of my hand, trying to clean the marks I knew were there. Having been so distraught trying to escape, I'd nearly forgotten that I was covered in Mishka's blood. I must have been quite a sight.

"I find it hard to believe you're any better." I mumbled inaudibly to myself. "It's rude to expect an introduction while offering none yourself." I didn't have time for this, and yet something told me I didn't have time to ignore him either.

"Right, of course." He offered me a hand gloved in white. "Mau is what I was called by my creator. The Cheshire Cat is what I'm called by the rest of Wonderland. You can use whichever name you fancy."

"By your creator, do you mean your mother?" While I asked the question, something about any of these men having mothers seemed purely ridiculous and highly unlikely, considering how uncouth they were.

But Mau chuckled. "The Devil would laugh if you called him that. I think I might try that next time I see him."

The Devil? That sounds about right.

"If you're a child of the Devil, then how can I trust any directions you might give me?" My eyes darted around the forest, still searching for some obvious out.

"You can't. And that's the fun of it." He tilted his head slightly to the side as he grinned. It was disarming. I might have even called it cute if not for the fangs in his smile. "If I were you, I certainly wouldn't trust me. But you would be a fool not to listen to me, despite, if you don't want Coello to catch you, Little Dove."

"I don't. I've already seen what he did to the other Alices."

Mau nodded. "That is a shame. Those poor girls." The way he said it told me he didn't care in the slightest. "But they weren't adequate Alices. Not adequate at all."

"Adequate for what, exactly?" I raised an eyebrow.

"You should probably get moving. Your adversary isn't far behind." The Cheshire Cat ignored my question completely. *Typical.*

"You still haven't told me which way."

He tapped his chin a few times with his finger, then he motioned to the left. "There, I'd say."

I shook my head, not willing to quiz him further on why this was the direction he chose. I just listened, like a naïve and obedient child, and ran into the trees to his left. At this point, if I ended up getting eaten by a Jabber-whatever, at least that would put me out of this misery. *How does anyone run for fun?*

"Please do be careful, Alice." He called after me with a tone that reflected possibly *genuine* concern. "Pick up the pace should you hear the outgrabe of Mome Raths, for the Jabberwock shan't be far behind."

None of those words even made sense, but whatever. I'd just sprint like my life depended on it if I heard anything other than the clatter of my own two feet.

Chapter 8"

I was staring listlessly at the darkness of the tree canopies, lost in thought, when the tapping of footsteps interrupted my peace and quiet, just a few brief moments behind Alice. I glanced down from my branch just in time to catch a flash of white.

"She went that way." I called down to Coello as he stood at the crossroads in my woods.

"You sent her towards the Jabberwock's nest? And you think *I'm* a sadist." Coello shouted up to the trees as he waited with obvious impatience for me to take physical form. I obliged him, and hopped down to face him.

"I do, because you are. But that doesn't mean I can't also enjoy a little bloodbath from time to time." I paced over to my companion, unable to miss the fact that he appeared a touch frantic. "You're not worried about her, are you? Here I thought you'd be pleased. That's not like you, Bunny."

The White Rabbit scoffed. He rolled his eyes. He did everything that someone pretending to not care might do.

I chuckled in response to his fidgety discomfort. "I have a feeling she's perfectly safe." I assured him. "This Alice strikes me a bit more tenacious than the rest."

"If she dies at the hand of the Jabberwock, then she wasn't good enough anyway." He huffed with forced indifference. How adorable.

"But you want her to be good enough." I stepped closer still, until I was enough in his personal space to draw his full attention.

"Don't we all hope she might be?" His expression was soft. A softness only I got to see. Though he was right. Of course we all hoped each Alice would be the last one we needed. The Queen of Hearts had been a terror on this land since her first day on the throne. The sooner she could be replaced, the better. In theory anyway.

And if I was being honest with myself, my first impression of this current iteration of Alice was somewhat intriguing. She was older than the last, but she seemed more determined. More jaded. And her beauty was more defined and comfortable, like she was settled into her body and personality. I wouldn't need to manipulate and reshape her mind to meet my expectations.

She amused me, quite frankly. I was willing to give her a chance. *If* she could outrun the Jabberwock. I had no need for women without resolve in the face of death.

But at the very least, she looked rather appealing painted red. That touch of death mixed with delicate lace and pouty lips was difficult to look away from, I'll admit. She might look even better if she was bathed in the Queen's blood.

I nodded in agreement, before addressing the dead elephant in the room. "I'm guessing you killed Mishka again."

"I never get tired of killing Mishka." Bunny smirked.

"I also never get tired of you killing Mishka." The uptick of my lips matched his. I reached over to grab his hand, and I lifted it level with our shared field of vision. He locked those pretty rose gold eyes in with mine as I touched my lips to the back of his hand. I sniffed along his knuckles, taking in that scent of dead mouse, then I licked along the length of his fingers. He held still, letting me clean the digits one by one. I wrapped my tongue around his skin to get the most out of every stroke. When I reached his thumb, I couldn't help but notice another flavor mixed in. *Coello's* flavor. Had Mishka injured him? Or was that from our new Alice?

"Divine." I purred, giving him one last once over with my tongue. "But why does it taste like you?"

"Alice has some bite, we'll say." Coello took back his hand, and he broke eye contact. Even in the darkness, I could see the flush in his cheeks. *Adorable. Did he have a crush?* In all his half-truths, he was still so easy to read.

I liked that about him though. I'd never tire of watching him try so very hard to be the most vicious of us all in front of the prospects, while for me, he was so often harmless and insecure. Messing with the little bunny rabbit was one of the few joys left in this Devil-enchanted place.

Coello glanced sidelong then addressed me again. "Anyway, have you heard any blood curdling screams yet?" He asked, breaking the tension with a return to the topic at hand. I'd allow it.

I shook my head. "No, I'm quite certain it hasn't caught her yet. Unless she's tough enough to keep her dignity even as she's being eaten alive."

"She might be." Coello said in seriousness. My eyes widened slightly at the unexpected compliment. That was high regard considering the last few women he brought here had been used as little more than chew toys.

"Curious." I said with a most genuine interest. "Well, if that's the case, I very much hope she survives. What gives you such confidence, Bunny?"

He didn't flinch at that nickname anymore. He'd accepted it some time ago. "A hunch." Is all he said in reply. "And if I'm wrong, then I at least suspect she'll be a particularly enjoyable toy."

"A toy you'll be sharing with the twins, if you don't get on your way soon." I reminded him with nonchalance. "Though I don't mind sharing with them sometimes. Or sharing *them* sometimes."

Coello rolled his eyes with clear amusement. "You've been in the Queen's Wonderland far too long, Mau."

"Perhaps. But so have you." We shared one more glance before Coello forced his eyes from mine.

"If she can't resist their charm...." That smirk of his took on its usual cruel bend. *My favorite expression.* "I plan to savor every minute of her punishment."

"I'd expect nothing less."

With that, he darted off toward the Jabberwock's nest. I watched him leave, waiting until he was out of sight to raise an eyebrow in curious disdain.

He seemed to like this Alice an unusual amount. He may even *genuinely* be a bit smitten. I wonder why that is?

Perhaps I should go take a closer look, myself.

First my body vanished, then my hat, my gloves, my ears, then my eyes, until all that was left were my lips. I couldn't help the grin as I let the last of my physical body disappear. I could move much faster than Coello could ever hope to run in this form. It would be easy to get ahead of both of them. Especially if they had some monsters to contend with along the way.

How fun. It's been a while since I had an excuse to leave the forest.

I'll have to give this Alice another visit.

Chapter 9

Alice

The forest didn't brighten up, no matter how far I ran. My only respite was that this made me more difficult to find. Though I'm sure someone like the White Rabbit could track me by scent or some other such primal, animalistic means. His magical swiftness certainly didn't beget the feeling of him being a man of ordinary senses and talents.

I hopped over a fallen log, and nearly slid out in a patch of moss on the other side. It was by the grace of nothing but luck that I managed to find balance instead of the ground. Still, I kept up the pace, collecting dew drops on the frills of my skirt, and light scratches on my bare arms and legs as I brushed small twigs and branches that protruded from the bushes.

In the distance, I heard the slight rustling of ferns. It was impossible to know *how* distant, though, with the way the forest amplified and carried sound. Trees seemed to absorb every frequency of noise, then they reflected it back in an untraceable echo. I swallowed, and I pumped my legs faster. My knees protested, and my muscles strained, but at no point did I even consider slowing. I wouldn't let him catch me again.

Another sound came from another indiscernible direction. A chirp? Maybe a growl.

Fuck, fuck, fuck!

Something told me that whatever made that sound was even worse than the rabbit. I squeezed my eyes shut, while still propelling myself forward, not wanting to look at my reality anymore. It was so dark in these woods, it made little difference whether they were open or closed anyway.

Just fucking get me out of here.

More rustling. I juked a quick right, in case it might throw whatever was out there off my trail. A howl that may have been wind or may have been a monster sounded from my new direction, so I juked back left again instead.

I could sense the creature's presence now. It was a suffocating darkness that overwhelmed my entire nervous system, more intense than Coello or Mishka or Mau, and it was *close*. My lungs were barely holding oxygen long enough to keep me alive, and my thighs were burning and begging for relief, but my heart beat told me not to stop. I could have relief when I was free.

The crunching of sticks came from behind me now. I began searching frantically for a place to hide. I could feel the first sting of tears in my eyes, but there was no time for crying. There was no time for anything. No time at all.

A heat now hit my neck. The heat of a monster's breathing. I didn't look back. I didn't want to see it. If it was right there, I was too late to get away. *Please just eat me quickly and make it painless.*

As hard as I was trying, there was no way I was going to outrun this thing. The forest could stretch on for miles more for all I knew, and I was going to run out of strength long before then. I needed something to throw it off my tail.

A chirp that sounded akin to an organ pipe announcing a funeral bellowed above me, and a screech of some scattering animal at my feet pierced the leaves below

me. Maybe one of these things were the mood rats...
Mom's wrath? Whatever the fuck the Cheshire Cat called
those things. He'd said they were typically followed by the
Jabberwock. Maybe they were its usual prey?

My slowly adjusting eyes caught just a glimpse of a
sparkling red set of eyeballs in the trees above. No, much
more than one. Thousands of them stared down at me from
the darkness now. I glanced up then resolved to keep my
eyes trained forward, not risking slowing my pace by
turning around to verify the monster I could already hear
and sense and feel. A gust hit me like a precursor to swipe,
and I stumbled as the adrenalin and survival instincts took
over my body. I ducked exactly as a massive paw covered
in razor blades swept overhead. Then I tripped exactly as
the reality hit me, sending me stumbling forward into a pile
of leaves.

Some clearly confused portion of my brain hoped
Coello might catch up now and save me again. But I had a
feeling I'd used up my only free pass on that Daniel-look-
alike. Now it was just me and all the hate in Wonderland
staring me down.

I needed something, *anything* to distract it.
Anything at fucking all. I felt through the leaf pile with a
desperate haste, until I located something hard and sharp
beneath the cover of foliage. My fingers grasped the rock-
like object, and I whipped around, using all of my strength
and momentum to huck that rock into the treetops.

The creepy sounding bird things screamed as the
stone invaded their safe haven, and the beast now standing
over me roared back. Its features were still veiled in
darkness. The frequency of the roar mixed with the
shrillness of the outgrabing... uh... whatever-they-weres,
and in an instant, stilled birds started raining from the
canopies.

Little bodies everywhere. I didn't know if they were dead or paralyzed, but the black feathers, sharp beaks, shining red eyes, and razor claws would be just as dangerous as the hulking demon in the woods if I were to get skewered by one.

That same waterfall of sharp beaks pierced the beast before me, and that seemed to be exactly the distraction I needed. I scooted out of the way of a falling bird, then I got back on my feet and back into a sprint. The bellow of the Jabberwock grew more and more distant. Then like a yoyo suddenly rolling back on its string, the growls and stomps and snapping twigs were right behind me again. It was a temporary distraction. Too temporary.

My legs pumped faster, listening to my survival instincts instead of my pathetic mess of emotions. The moisture of its breath, closer than even before, now dampened my skin like sweat. It had caught up again so quickly. And now it was impatient and angry.

Faster.

The vibration of a growl crawled up my spine. My lungs were on fire.

Faster!

A burst of blinding light suddenly hit my face, as the trees at long last gave way to a clear field on the other side of the forest. I kept running until I was completely clear of the tree shadows. Then I whipped around, suddenly, fiercely, and ready to face whatever had been following me out in the light. I knew I didn't stand a chance, but I clung to the notion that it had somehow lost its advantage the moment it could no longer hunt me within its own home.

But… nothing was there. All I saw was the shaking branches in the distance, as the creature retreated back into the hell of the forest.

Too close. Way too close. Whatever had been chasing me felt more evil than everyone I'd met thus far combined. I don't think I'd be returning to that forest any time soon if I could avoid it. Though, knowing I had this barrier between me and my other pursuer was a bit of a relief.

I hope Coello gets eaten trying to follow me.

With a deep sigh, I turned my back to the woods and scanned the horizon for some hint of where to head next. Up on a hill, surrounded by pops of pink and a backdrop of a waterfall, I spotted what looked like a small cottage. The perfect place that I was sure I absolutely should not be going, and yet the only clear destination at the same time.

But who knew—maybe whoever lived there would actually be half way sane. There had to be *someone* in Wonderland who wasn't a total nutcase.

Not a hope I should be gambling my life on, necessarily, but I didn't have a lot of other options that didn't involve returning to the forest. And not only that, but the longer I stood there, the closer the White Rabbit would get, so I really didn't have the luxury of time to think things through either.

So like the predictable idiot I was, I hiked up the hill toward the cottage.

Not running anymore, more because I was far too winded and my heart would likely explode if I tried, I was able to steal a glance at the flowers beside me. The light purple flowers resembled bubbles more than any sort of plant. They were small translucent spheres atop a stem.

Bumblebees that dared get close were swallowed whole by the lavender orbs, and it was by the flowers mercy that they were allowed to leave with pollen. Not all of them received that mercy.

The blue flowers were far more like what I was used to, with orderly pedals around a golden center. I considered picking one and putting it in my hair like a carefree child, until I saw a red and orange butterfly land on its center, only to be sucked into a mouth-like opening as though it was being ripped through a straw.

Fascinating and awful at the same time.

I set into a slow jog as I caught my bearings again to finish my run to the top. The cottage was much larger than I'd realized from a distance. The humble forefront had hidden a rather expansive mansion that extended backwards in deep and lengthy halls. It resembled more of a tunnel than a cabin when studying it up close.

Perhaps this tunnel would take me where I wanted to go.

Chapter 10

I moved swiftly through the forest, doing my best to assure I outpaced the Jabberwock. Mau commanded the creatures within these woods, so they shouldn't be an issue for me, yet I knew they weren't always ones to obey. And I also knew that sometimes the kitten got on a vicious kick, where he enjoyed toying with me entirely too much. I wouldn't be surprised if he loosed the monsters just to watch me sweat.

But I couldn't be thinking of the Cheshire Cat right now. I had a far more pressing task at hand.

I hopped a log, then sprinted ahead with swiftness. I didn't hear any creatures chasing me. A good sign or a bad one, it was hard to say. If Alice had caught its attention first, it was likely still up ahead. If *I'd* caught its attention, it could be anywhere.

But it was unusually quiet. I didn't see any of the glowing red eyes that typically followed me through the forest. Usually the Jubjub birds were almost worse than the Jabberwock itself if they took an interest in me. While they were small and easy prey on their own, they could rain down like a hail of knives, and the sheer numbers were usually enough to get a few kills that would feed their whole nest.

But the swarms weren't here.

Another downed log, and I vaulted myself towards a clearing I knew would soon be in sight. It was so dark in this forest. Dark enough for a cat or Mome Rath to see easily, but my eyes were straining. One more jump, and I landed on a pile of something small and plump. My boot slipped and sent me sprawling backwards into a patch of leaves. One that immediately gave in and dropped me deep into a hole.

"Dammit!" I shouted aloud as my back hit the damp muddy ground at the bottom of a solid fifteen foot drop. A small barrage of tiny blade like birds fell around me, likely from the pile I'd slipped on, nearly skewering me through the stomach in the process, then a light blanket of the upset leaves wafted down on top of me to add insult to injury.

This was definitely dug out by a Jabberwock. They didn't used to be smart enough to set their own traps, but the last few iterations of Wonderland had ushered in a constantly evolving set of monsters. This place just got worse and worse. I really hoped this Alice would be the last one.

A growl, loud enough to vibrate the entire forest, resonated through the walls of the trap. The outgrabe of Mome Raths wafted through the leaves like an eerie melody of death soon to come.

I sighed, still laying on my back, still staring upward at the dark opening in the ground.

Goddamn it, Mau. I couldn't afford to be one of the casualties in this cycle of Wonderland. Setting aside the annoying and obvious issue of the way dying warps a person, and how much more unhinged we all got on every reincarnation, my real issue was that I somewhat believed in this Alice. If I were to die this round, and she were to go on to survive, thrive, and defeat the Queen of Hearts, that would be it for me.

What would Wonderland be without its White Rabbit? I'd endured entirely too much misery to let myself die right before the revolution was successful.

I kept my gaze fixed on the entrance, waiting, watching, and readying myself for when the Jabberwock might reach in its claws and haul me straight into its hungry jaws. The dread sunk deep in my chest as the footsteps pounded closer.

To think I used to like this place. The woods, Wonderland, all of it. I once looked forward to skipping through the forest and running about with the Queen. To playing with animals, bickering with Mau, and enjoying an aromatic tea with the Hatter and the Hare.

Though I knew I had little time to spare before *it* came for me, still I closed my eyes only for the briefest moment, recalling what once was. It was a fleeting comfort, but if I died here, I wanted to cling to something pleasant for once, in the hopes that the reset might spare my mind an even more chaotic revival.

The memory had become so distant, I struggled to believe there was once a time when this monster we all feared was little more than a squirrel. It was downright inconceivable at this point that the woods were once a beautiful, enchanting, and magical place of lush greenery, deep swimming holes, billowing ferns, and colorful flowers. I could barely recall the sound of these leaves being filled with the music of laughter instead of the echoes of screams.

The image of that girl, so happy and kind and lovely, exploring Wonderland flashed through my mind. The original Alice was barely a teen when she first arrived. She stayed and she visited often, practically growing up here. Everyone had loved her so much. She was our little darling.

How could any of us have known that giving her a crown would have driven her so utterly mad?

The only thing I was thankful for now was that her love of cats had put the Cheshire in her good favor, giving him lordship over the worst of her beasts. More significantly though, Mau's fondness for *me* had typically kept the demons off *my* tail when we played our ruthless games with each candidate. Apparently he was much too distracted to call off his hounds this time around, however.

Or he was simply getting off on watching me squirm right now. It was impossible to say which.

Not that I could blame him. I'm sure I'd do the same if our positions were reversed.

With another deep inhale, I opened my eyes to my present reality, and I looked up the length of the hole. I knew these sorts of traps well. I'd had to retrieve a number of dead Alices from these holes in order to bring them back to my vault. Well, whatever was left of them. It would be ironic in an annoying way if this was how I met my end, considering how many women I'd chased into these woods to meet the same demise.

More grumbling filled the air followed by the sound of nails scraping on rocks and branches as that awkward beast drew closer still. I wrapped a tight fist around the dead bodies of scattered Jubjub Bird blades, and I braced myself. If this encounter was going to spell out someone's last life in Wonderland, it wouldn't be mine.

Though I'd be lying if I didn't acknowledge how rapidly my heart was beating as I felt that first warm gust of a Jabberwock's breath filling the chamber. In all my feigned confidence, I'd never bested the Jabberwock. *It* had bested me at least twice. Maybe twice and a half. The half was a debate Kitten and I still had fairly often.

I closed my eyes again and filled my lungs with that steam from his snarl and bark. Then I waited.

A long tentacle like appendage extended into the depths of the trap. It snaked down until it was close enough to grab me. Then it shifted into a claw lined with razorblade nails that would be used to slice me into smaller, more easily digestible pieces. Actually chewing was effort the Jabberwock didn't care enough to extend. The claws pierced the dirt around me, digging in deep, then closing in on me until I was secure in its grasp.

I didn't protest as it lifted me from the hole. It was much easier to get out of these things with its help, after all. I waited patiently until the first hint of open air hit my face, and I was able to catch sight of the gaping mouth that waited to consume me. An excruciating routine I'd already been through.

Canines that were several feet in length protruded from the animal's jaw, with a handful of dead birds from a recent feeding skewered along them. I exhaled with relief to see that no trace of Alice was among the Jubjubs or Mome Raths.

Closer and closer. I waited until it opened its mouth as wide as it could. The moment it was content and confident it had won would be the moment I needed. Closer still, and... *There*!

With a swiftness, I drove the sharp beaks of the birds in my fists straight into its flesh, until I was embedding the points into muscle and tendon. Dark green blood splashed from the impact, covering my hands and forearms, and it jerked at the unexpected pain.

I used that window to wriggle from its grasp. I jumped down onto the forest floor and rolled back, creating whatever distance I could between us.

The Jabberwock was otherworldly even by Wonderland standards. It was a large and hulking beast, covered in fur, yet proudly displaying its sinewy muscles in strategic and intimidating bare patches. Large wings protruded from its back that were ironically not strong enough to let the beast take flight, but the heavy blades that jutted out of each wing's apex served as worthy and deadly weapons. Weapons it barely needed between its claws and its startlingly long neck that helped it so easily catch its prey.

In the Commonland, they might call it a dragon or a wyvern, but the reality of it was far more terrifying than anything a human had ever dreamed up. Especially when it was bitter about having missed out on a delicious Alice.

I should run. The foolish thought ran through my head, purely as an impulse of fear. But I knew better. What were my chances of escaping, really? Zero? Less than that? I may have been faster than it was, but if I turned my back on it, I would be its feast in an instant. What it lacked in swiftness, it made up for with swiping range.

My eyes darted around the trees, looking for some sort of weapon that might aid me. I could distract it if I had more Jubjub birds or Mome Raths at my disposal, but they were still conspicuously absent. I could kill it if I had a Vorpal Sword, but last I heard, the Queen kept that locked away in her weapon vault to assure that this was the one and only creature in Wonderland that no one stood a chance against. Not the birds, and not me.

Well, this and the Queen's army. *That* little encounter was the *third* time I'd died. I would feel guilty about how I treated some of the Alices after that incident if not for the fact that guilt had long since vanished from my emotional database.

I stepped away as the Jabberwock reared back with an ear shattering scream. Then I crouched down, ready to dodge whatever swing it might take.

Fucking Cheshire Cat and his fucking games.

Chapter 11

Alice

I approached the home, and like the annoyingly well-mannered person I was, I rapped lightly on the door and waited for an answer. Several seconds passed, then several seconds more. I furrowed my brows. Any more seconds would be way too long. I needed to keep moving, and I needed to keep moving *now*.

"Are you sure you want to go in there?" That haunting, disembodied voice halted me in my tracks again. I searched for the first hint of Mau's magical smile. He appeared beside me, leaning against the wall, so casual and so condescending.

"No, I'm not sure. I wasn't sure I wanted to run in the direction of a giant, Alice-eating beast either," I snapped. I'm sure he knew I'd encounter that thing when he sent me that way. Maybe he'd even done it on purpose. It wouldn't surprise me at this point.

He stared at me with a hint of surprise. Though that clever smile was quick to paint his lips again. "So touchy, Alice."

"If you'd started your day with a roofie hangover, narrowly escaped being a Mouse's sex slave, watched a person get brutally murdered, nearly got eaten by a monster, *and*, to top it all off, spent every moment in between these events fucking *running*, you would be touchy, too." I'll admit that came out snippier than I even intended. I could have probably dealt with all the rest though if not for all this goddamn RUNNING. "Oh, and don't even get me started on the drowning and the badger sharks."

"Slivy Toves, you mean."

"Oh my god, I don't care!" I huffed. *Mome Raths, Slivy Toves, Jabberwocks, Nonsense!*

"Sounds like a good time, to be honest." Mau laughed.

"A *wonder*ful time even." I added with all the snark in my repertoire.

A hitch of a smile danced briefly on his lips, then his expression shifted to something curious, yet still so annoyingly amused. "Do you always try to mask your fear with sarcasm?"

"Yes. Yes I do."

"At least you're honest." The Cheshire Cat gave me that proud expression that made my heart skip without its consent. He was so agreeable, he was oddly hard to stay mad at, despite his otherwise mocking demeanor. I should have been tearing into him some more, but instead, I was letting myself get whisked along with his pace all willy nilly. I couldn't say why. Maybe just because he was good looking. Or maybe it was that smooth, ASMR purr to his voice. Those things usually helped soothe a terrible personality at least a little bit.

"So what's behind this door?" I demanded, not letting him suck me any further into casual or friendly conversation.

"Another test." He responded flatly. "A much more challenging test."

"Challenging how?" I pressed again. Is that what all of this was? A series of tests? That last little incident was the kind of challenge I'd much rather never take again.

He looked up, as if he was searching his mind for the right word. "Challenging *fun*, I suppose. It's a test I've failed before."

"Challenging *fun* sounds a whole lot better than challenging Jabberwock." I rolled my eyes, then added under my breath in a way he most certainly would hear me. "Or challenging *Coello* for that matter."

"That's only because you haven't really challenged Coello yet. He can be quite fun, too." Mau stood from his position against the wall, straightening himself out to a solid six feet or so of height, then he paced over to me.

I took a step back, but only one, and not a single step more. I was getting tired of being intimidated, and he wasn't all that scary, to be honest. He came off more like a psychotic court jester than an executioner. Conversely, the White Rabbit came off as the friendly neighborhood serial killer.

Mau took my lack of retreat as an invite, as he neared enough to place a hand on my cheek. I delved my gaze deeply into the star light flecks in those violet eyes of his, as if I might find the answer as to whether I could trust him or not somewhere in those pools. His irises were like fairy dust: every bit as beautiful and every bit as enchanting.

He continued speaking in a low tone, never shifting from my eyes. "But to be honest, everything starts to become boring after a while when you've lived long enough." His expression lacked its usual amusement as he studied my face. I'm not sure what kind of information he was discerning from being so close, but my intuition didn't fire off the usual danger signals, so I held still and let him slide his thumb gently over my cheek. Traces of dried blood came off on his white glove. "But you're still young and inexperienced. You should try it all at least once if you can."

"So I guess to answer your question, yes, I *am* sure I want to go in there." I said confidently. I wasn't going to be the first to back down on our staring contest, even as he straightened up again and returned his hand to his pocket.

"Clever Little Dove." The corner of the Cheshire Cat's lips upticked. He took a step back. "I should wonder if you'll regret listening to me, or if you'll thank me."

"I suspect both." I added with a raise of my eyebrow.

"We seem to be on the same wavelength." He added before he started to disappear again, slow and one piece at a time. When the last of him faded into the open air, he left nothing but the echo of his hum behind him.

I released the tension I'd been holding in my lungs, uncertain if I was happy or uneasy about being alone again. Though I should be suspicious of any stray thoughts that welcomed the company of a Wonderland creature.

I frowned outwardly then turned my attention back to this suspicious cottage. Not exactly confidence inspiring, but if this was a series of tests, I'd best just get them over with. I'd probably have to pass them all eventually whether I wanted to or not.

Taking a deep breath, having run out of patience for social grace and decency, I grabbed the doorknob, and I forced open the door. It wasn't locked, much to my relief. I took a few steps in, glancing cautiously about all the while. It was a simple place, with roughly built, old timey furniture that resembled a typical and comfortable grandmother's house. Lace doilies under the place mats, white and yellow checkerboard wallpaper, heavy oak furniture, and a tea kettle on the burner—like, full *blown* grandma shit. I wouldn't be surprised if a few Little Red Riding Hoods had been eaten in this place.

Nothing daunting. I exhaled and took a moment to calm the anxiety that had been building unencumbered up until now. As if I owned the place, I walked to the stove and grabbed the now hissing pot of tea. I poured myself a cup, spooned in some sugar, then I swirled the hot liquid around the porcelain until the grains dissolved completely. It smelled nice. Therapeutic even. I certainly wasn't so bold or foolish as to actually *drink* it, but I enjoyed the peaceful nature of the brewing.

The Cheshire Cat, huh? I thought vaguely to myself as I replaced the teacup on the counter. He was probably about as safe as that tea. That is to say, visibly simple and unthreatening, yet likely hiding poison behind the hope of warmth. Or it could be every bit as soothing as it smells, and I could just be paranoid. Betting on the flip of a coin would be equally as guaranteed. So why did I listen to him? Twice now even.

There was something in his eyes that was different from the others, perhaps. Something just as sinister but maybe less detached. More… honest?

That must be the trauma talking…

Not wanting to think on it too much longer, I walked over to a door towards the back side of this homey cottage, and I opened the passageway to the next room. What appeared to be a long tunnel from the outside was a series of different micro environments on the inside. The next chamber looked modern, like a rich CEO bachelor's apartment, complete with uncomfortable black and white angular furniture and abstract art pieces. In one corner, a dancing pole was displayed prominently. In another, a mahogany bar with crystalline bottles of nondescript liquid. Alcohol, maybe. Lines of white powder sat undisturbed atop the glass coffee table along with a spattering of credit cards. But most notable were the splotches of red that sank into the otherwise white couch, punctuated by piercings that looked like bullet holes.

The next room was a green house full of wilted plants. One singular strawberry rested in a central flower pot. It was the only thing ripe and alive in the room.

The next chamber was a classroom with the simple line "I will not try to escape" written repeatedly on the chalk board with increasingly erratic strokes. A collar was chained to the seat of every desk.

There was no obvious rhyme or reason for each new diorama. I wanted to dismiss it all as more nonsense in the overflowing cup of ridiculousness that was Wonderland, but I couldn't help but think there was a story being told by all of these juxtaposed images. Like symbolic snapshots of someone's life.

When I stepped through the door after the classroom, the path I'd come through disappeared behind me, and I found myself standing in a maze of mirrors.

This must be the test he was referring to.

From the moment I stepped into the reflective maze, it was impossible to ignore the fact that I hadn't seen my own reflection since I'd arrived. I knew well enough what my face looked like, of course, but the girl staring back at me in every wall and surface was distinctly… different. She was someone I barely recognized. But not because she was a total wreck. No, quite the opposite.

My hair was neatly styled into dark brown waves. It was a shape that was cute and elegant and youthful and suited the angles of my face. Yet in contrast, my dress hugged my curves perfectly, exaggerating my waist line as the corset cinched me into a perfect hour glass that spoke more to my figure. The fullness of my skirt made my hips look wider, creating the illusion that my legs were slimmer and longer than they were. And that pendant? It really did match my eyes perfectly.

Had I always been pretty like this? I hadn't really dressed up in ages. Daniel never took me anywhere, and I'd gotten used to date nights that never made it past the couch. Any of my old cocktail dresses didn't fit anymore, and somewhere along the way, I'd stopped bothering to put on something that flattered my changing body. But this was actually cute on me. I didn't see the little imperfections that I convinced myself needed to be fixed before I could wear something nice again. Not the extra twenty some pounds I needed to lose or the first traces of wrinkles that I needed to hide. None of that seemed so bad now.

No, I looked like some sort of princess ripped out of a fairy tale. If you ignored the blood all over my chest, my corset, and my face, anyway.

Maybe I was the Devil's princess. I would fit in much better here that way.

I drew my lips into my mouth, running my tongue along them to try to clean some of the vibrant red from their surface. They still tasted of metallic death. Mishka mixed with Coello. I was proud I could injure Coello to the point of drawing blood, however small the wound, even if he'd pretended to be unmoved and unfazed by it.

I hoped he was pretending anyways. A man without reflexes from pain was a dangerous man, indeed.

I licked by thumb and tried to use the moisture to clean the stripes from beneath my eyes, but the redness wasn't so easily washed away. It had dried into my pours and stained my skin. To remove the stripes would have been pointless, anyway, considering the heavy streaks of death he'd run down my neck, from my jawline to my corset. There was no way I'd be able to clean that much blood from me.

My gaze settled on the palm print on my breast. I'd fit so perfectly in his hand, and the dark stains on my bust advertised that point to anyone who ventured across my path. Streaks in the bloodstains showed the way his fingers had slid down the top of my breast, banishing any thought that it could have been simply suggestive spatter. It was a handprint that marked me as a dangerous toy for a dangerous man. Who in Wonderland would help me if they saw this?

Mau, perhaps. I got the impression he wasn't afraid of much of anything, which was probably testament to how little I should trust him. But I saw the fear in the Mouse's eyes.

If there were any decent people here, they still wouldn't be decent enough to want to cross the White Rabbit. I wouldn't be cruel enough to risk their safety for me either.

I closed my eyes and placed my hand on my neck, just remembering the way he'd touched me, both on that bed and right after he'd killed Mishka. The feel of his fingertip slipping inside of me and the way he'd held me, staring into my eyes with a vicious hunger. I resented the fact that it had felt good. That I was so starved for affection, that even a murderous magical bunny rabbit, symbolically killing the man who cheated on me, had been enough to make me damp between my legs.

Pathetic. Pathetic and fucked up.

I sighed aloud, then ran a hand through my hair to calm myself down. My gaze drifted upward, examining my environment to distract myself from unwanted idle thoughts.

The roof was also a mirror. It clearly reflected my cleavage and gave easy view down my top. My nose scrunched in irritation. At least the floor was less reflective. A blessing or a curse, depending on who I might encounter in this maze. Mau had certainly built this place up in my head, to the point I had no idea what to expect from this so called challenge. I was certain it couldn't be as simple as just a maze built of reflections.

I placed a few steps carefully and cautiously into the room, committing to whatever came next. It was near impossible to tell where one mirror ended and another began. I was feeling along the walls, leaving fingerprints on the glass, in an effort to not run straight into something hard. The smudges helped to mark my path so I didn't accidentally double back on the same trail, but still, it was difficult to focus on anything with the way the reflections bounced off each other. It took my best efforts to just read the way the images converged.

Then the lights flickered. Total blackness then comfortable brightness again.

I bit my lip, trying not to let nerves take me. *Just keep working your way through. It'll be safer on the other side.* I told myself what I knew was a wishful lie. I kept inching along when the lights flickered again. It stayed black a touch longer this time, throwing me off of my careful navigation. Another flicker, and the lights went out completely.

A lump hitched in my throat. I didn't want to think about what kind of monsters might be lurking in this maze.

This is fine. It's not like it was easy to read the layout of the land anyway. If anything, my vision felt like a hindrance.

So I closed my eyes, purely using feel to find my path. My steps were careful but sure. I moved slowly, but I didn't worry that Coello would catch me. He'd have the same obstacles to deal with, after all.

I sidestepped the wall, keeping my chest to the surface of the glass…

And then I felt something firm. Like… another person. My eyes shot open, and the lights flickered back on only long enough to meet a gaze that was darker than a black hole and sucked me in just as forcefully. That eerie look was attached to a man with equally dark hair, wearing a black suit and a black tie and nothing underneath but a perfect collarbone and a well-built chest.

"Are you lost, Princess?" He said in a deliciously deep voice that had as much bite as it did enchantment. Still, I knew better than to trust a pretty face in a place like this.

"I'm just passing through." I attempted, batting my eyelashes flirtatiously. If I could disarm him by being cute, I'd use any weapon I had.

"Just passing through someone else's home?" The lights flickered again when he smiled, bearing perfect teeth set in a sharp jawline. It was as if his very existence absorbed light. Maybe it did. He glanced briefly at the ceiling, and my face flushed knowing all too well what he was looking at. "Hmmm, I wouldn't mind just passing through you."

"I bet you wouldn't." I took a step away from him, narrowing my gaze to show my displeasure. The lights went out again.

Before I could react or defend myself, a hand was around my neck and my back hit the glass. He had me cornered as he towered over me. He placed his forearm beside my head to completely cage me in.

I fought my body's need to tremble. I wasn't going to be intimidated. Not outwardly, anyway.

"Where'd you find this?" The man in black softly traced the streaks of blood with his index finger. In the darkness, every movement felt that much more unpredictable and that much more intense.

He danced his fingers back up to my necklace, then he tugged on the pendant until the chain was cutting into the back of my neck. "Did you kill one of my friends, Alice?"

I swallowed as he said my name. Even knowing the Alices in Wonderland were a routine for these men, there was something unnerving about the familiarity. It was unfair for him to know who I was, when I had no clue who he was.

"The White Rabbit may have." It was by survival instincts alone that I was able to speak without my voice hitching. Which was why I chose those words very, very carefully. It wasn't likely that *I* could intimidate him. But maybe if he knew Coello was hunting me, he'd back off. Perhaps that was something that man was actually good for.

He chuckled. "Fucking Mishka." He trailed his touch back down to my chest and hooked a finger under my corset top. He threatened to pull it down using teasing pressure. "This definitely looks like Coello's handiwork. I don't know how many times he's killed that silly Mouse now."

I eyed him curiously in the dark, ignoring the way he was sliding across the rim of my rigid bust. No, that bit of information was far more interesting than his provocations. *People can die more than once here?*

The light flashed again, revealing his narrowed gaze and the cruel uptick of his lips. I barely had time to take it in before his hand was on my neck, squeezing with rapidly increasing pressure. "It would be a shame if this was his last opportunity."

I clawed at his hand, but he was quick to claim my wrist and shove it back against the glass. A different darkness began clawing at my mind; one that was much more real than the visible lack of light. I was fighting to keep consciousness, but I was losing oxygen far too quickly to have a choice in the matter.

"Be nice, Brother." Another voice ripped me back, and the pressure on my neck loosened up until it was gone completely. I choked for air, gripping my neck as I tried to find normalcy again. The lights shot on, and the flickers of darkness ceased. This new figure was completely opposite the other, from his impeccable white suit, to his wispy snow-like hair, to his unusual colorless eyes rimmed in a light gray. But that was where the differences ended. His face, his voice, his height, and his build were otherwise exactly the same as the other. "You didn't even like Mishka. No reason to strangle the Alice just to bring him back."

"I wasn't going to kill her. I just wanted to see if she liked being choked." He smirked at the white haired man.

"I don't." I snapped, feeling somehow emboldened now that there was someone advocating for me. I couldn't say if this new guy would be any better, but at the very least, he sounded less likely to want me dead. Speaking of dead… "What do you mean bring him back?" I glanced to the man in white, thinking he might give me some sort of answers.

"Why does Coello never tell the Alices anything?" The man in black frowned. The one in white shrugged. Yet naturally, they didn't elaborate. *God forbid anyone fix the issue.* Whatever the case may be, I gathered that the dead didn't stay dead here. Though the Alices definitely did. Maybe at some point they could explain how that correlates.

Though before I could ask, the more angelic of the figures was by my side, nudging the more demonic one away. He addressed me while I remained trapped in that corner. "Please don't let my brute of a brother scare you. He's terrible at interacting with humans." He offered a hand. This time I took it. "I'm Finn. This is Tynan." He shared an enchanting smile that unexplainably lifted my spirits. "We mean you no harm, Alice."

Tynan, the dark one, took a step back with a shake of his head.

I shot a look of daggers in his direction. "That seemed pretty harmful to me."

Finn, the light one, waved a hand dismissively. "The line between harm and kink sometimes gets a touch blurry with this one." He shared my expression of irritation toward his brother. "But I'm sure he would have only choked you until he was satisfied."

"Oh, come off it." Tynan scoffed at his brother then returned his attention to me. "I've yet to meet a woman who would take a gentlemen who lets them leave unfinished over a monster who can make them scream. Am I wrong, Princess?"

I blinked rapidly, not even ready to dignify that with a real response.

"Death and orgasms are not the same, brother dearest." Finn cocked his eyebrow.

"How would you know? You've never given anyone either." Tynan snipped back.

"Enough! I don't have time for this." I groaned. These guys bickered like children, and I was not in the mood. Every minute they wasted was a minute I lost to my pursuer. "If you want to help me, great. If you want to hurt me, get it over with. But whatever twisted game you want me to play with you, let's just start playing before I have Coello smearing me with any more Wonderland blood."

Finn lit up, a soothing expression on his face. "Oh, don't worry about that. This is a safe place for you, Alice. The mirror maze changes every few minutes. Only those who we wish to let through can make it to the other side."

"The White Rabbit has yet to meet that criteria." Tynan chuckled in that deep dark way of his.

That was uh… reassuring?

"Do you wish to let *me* through?" I asked with the sweetest puppy dog eyes I could muster. Despite my frustrations with the pair of them, the man in white seemed to be the first person in Wonderland who I had any chance of garnering sympathy from, and I wasn't going to miss that chance.

"I would consider it." Tynan smirked as he eyed me up and down, shamelessly and blatantly.

"And I would do anything for an Alice as breathtaking as you," Finn asserted with a gentlemanly bow. *Quite the charmer.* "Consider yourself our guest, my dear. I have a feeling you've earned a bit of relaxation."

CHAPTER 12

"I've drawn you a bath, Alice." Finn said, sweet as sugar, much unlike his prickly, dark haired brother. They'd brought me through the maze, bickering between each other the entire time, while I awkwardly tried to have no opinion that might make it seem I was choosing sides.

Once we'd reached the exit, they'd welcomed me into the chamber they called home. The walls were still comprised of mirrors, but the rooms were spacious and easy to navigate. There were no twists or turns or wrong directions to take. Just two ordinary kitchens, two ordinary bedrooms, and two ordinary bathrooms with ordinary bathtubs.

The only way each room differed was the color of the floor itself. On Finn's side, the floor was white, which reflected off every surface to create a sense of brightness and open space. On Tynan's side, the floor was black, forming an imposing sense of darkness and of being closed in. They were like opposite sides of the same coin.

"Thank you. I really appreciate it." I said with a shaky smile. It was probably foolish to be going along with this, but Finn, at the very least, seemed like someone I could trust. He was gentle, kind, and had the compassion to realize how badly I must want to wash all of this blood off of my skin. He'd even offered to do my laundry while I bathed. A true gentleman.

He waited outside the room while I undressed, and he gave me time to sink into the perfectly warm bubble bath, hidden from his eyes, before he stepped in to grab my clothing for laundering. I laid back, enjoying this brief moment of respite in what had been a chaotic introduction to this other world. I *knew* they couldn't *all* be evil here.

I hummed a tune while my nostrils filled with the scent of lemon and lavender, and I scrubbed the grime and death from my skin. This peace and comfort surely wouldn't last long, but I deserved to enjoy it while it did. The Jabberwock or the White Rabbit could eat me afterwards, and at least I'd know my last moments were comfortable.

Resting my head upon the end of the tub, I gazed up at the mirrored ceiling. The bubbles hid my naked body completely like a blanket of purple flowers. Another draw of the scent and my eyelids began to feel awfully heavy. When I closed my eyes, it dawned on me that I'd not had real sleep in what felt like an eternity. The rest I'd had while under the influence of Wonder Roofies hardly counted.

If I wanted to outrun Coello, I needed to take advantage of this brief moment of safety and get back to full strength. Yeah, that was what I needed. Then… Then, the race was on.

An unconscious world of calm gripped at my mind, and it dragged me down slowly. I didn't fight it. I was asleep almost instantly. The deepest, most contented, and dreamless sleep I'd had since I found out about all that nonsense with Daniel. About everything with my best friend.

My lack of rest lately had nothing to do with Wonderland in actuality. If anything, these trials felt easy compared to my real life. At least here, there were some semblance of rules. The men were open about their intent, however cruel, instead of hiding behind false lies and promises. Living on my sister's couch just because I couldn't bear to share that space with him anymore had already felt like being displaced and on the run in a way.

If the test was whether or not I could resist being treated well for once in my life, I'd gladly fail and accept the consequences.

I inhaled deeply once more. Another tug of blackness, and I was gone completely.

The smooth texture of satin caressed my skin as I slowly came back to consciousness from my most restful sleep. I stretched out, letting the shimmering material slide over my every movement. It felt so nice and cool against me. My nipples perked, feeling especially sensitive as my chest heaved in a deep breath, enjoying the freedom from my corset. Self-care and simplicity.

Stretching out my tired legs gave me the unmatched satisfaction of smooth threads sliding over my hairless skin, and of satin slipping easily over my bare and waxed…

Shit. I shot up to a seated position with a start, suddenly remembering exactly where I'd been when I'd drifted off. But now… now I was in a bed with smooth sheets, dry and refreshed with my hair already done yet my clothes conspicuously absent.

More conspicuous still were the two men, slowly stirring on either side of me. The sheets were split down the middle, one half black and one half white, as though the previous rooms I'd seen had merged into one. And so too were the men, Finn on one side of me and Tynan on the other. Around me still were mirrors taking up every wall and every surface. In the reflection ahead, I could see my bare back in the infinitely mirrored images. Above me, I could see both men waking up, meeting the surprise in my gaze only via our shared reflection.

"Is something the matter, Alice?" Finn asked with angelic concern, He tugged me by my arm, bringing me back down to the mattress in his general direction. I desperately clung to the sheets that separated his face from my bare breasts.

"Are you always this much of a scaredy cat?" Tynan asked with a devil's bite, while rolling over and placing a hand on my hip. He gripped me and tugged my lower half in his direction.

"Where are my clothes?" I managed, trying to ignore both the way Finn was gently dancing his fingertips up and down my arm and the way Tynan was roughly kneading his palm up and down my thigh.

"They're drying, of course. They were quite dirty. It took an effort to get the blood stains out." Finn's hand climbed up to my shoulder, then he traced my collar bone and slid slowly over to my neck.

"He always overdoes it on the service." Tynan settled his grip on my ass, squeezing a handful like he was admiring how firm and full the muscle was. "I didn't mind you when you were dirty. But Finn is a bit more picky." His deep, low, sinister purr was now directly in my ear. I dared to look at the mirror on the wall in front of me. And I watched as that hand on my ass slowly started making its way around my hips. His fingers slipped over my lower abdomen. The satin separated our skin, but that only meant every movement had rippling consequences as the fabric slipped along my nakedness with the slightest provocation.

I clenched my thighs together, trying not to acknowledge the tingle that his touch was sending through me. Though the dampening sheets didn't hide much.

"Tynan pretends to be cruel, but we both wanted you to have a chance to relax, feel safe, comfortable, and refreshed. You're such a pretty and unique Alice, I don't want to see you fail. And neither does Tynan. He's not so bad when you get to know him." Finn's lips were now brushing the nape of my neck. His hand gripped me by the back of my head, and he pulled me in closer. He spread his tongue on my skin, and licked all the way up to my jawline. "Now that you're awake, would you like us to help you relax in some other ways?"

"I-I…" My whole body tensed, though their touch was gentle and coaxing. I tried to swallow down the confusing mix of fear and wanting that was settling in my gut. What did he mean by not wanting me to fail? Was he talking about this game I was playing with Coello? Or was there more to being an 'Alice' than simply being his prey for sport? I wished someone would explain better what was going on. I must be here for a reason. Or at least I hoped I was. That way, there was some chance of me fixing the problem and getting to go home.

"I bet you're scared." Tynan hissed in my ear, bringing me back to the moment. "You probably wouldn't know what hit you if you were with a man who could actually make you orgasm."

I wouldn't validate that statement by agreeing out loud, but he was… very correct.

Finn sucked harder on my neck, and Tynan bit into my shoulder, sending a yelp and a shudder through me at the same time. Then Finn spoke first. "Watch yourself in the mirror, Alice. I want you to see the expression on your face when you're truly pleased. It's a beautiful sight, I promise."

Then Tynan, "And you can watch the way your pussy stretches for my cock, as I force that pleasure through you."

The gravelly depth of their voices, tugging me in opposite directions to reach the same point, was doing something to me I couldn't explain.

What a proposal. Did I want to let two gorgeous men have their way with me in their bed, while I watched myself come in the mirror? No, that's not something I did. That was something Dinah might enjoy, but I didn't do deviant things like that. I was a one man kind of girl. A committed relationship kind of girl. A nine years of being so in love I didn't even care that I never got to finish kind of girl.

The kind of girl that terrible men took advantage of, leaving at home to do their housework and chores, while they gave their love away at the bar, because I was more worried about being a good partner than if my partner was good to me.

"Have you ever choked on a man's name while he's burying his cock in your pussy, Princess?" Tynan growled as those teasing fingers drew small circles beneath my navel. Just a little further down. A little closer.

Could I say yes? I *was* safe here, right? They were protecting me and taking care of me. Did it matter that this was Wonderland? That I barely knew them? I'd gone to the bar to find myself a one night stand that night, and I'd left unconscious in the grasp of a monster.

Maybe I was still in the grasp of monsters, but these ones were touching me in all the right ways.

Why *not* get what I came for? If this was the test, and getting myself off meant I failed, then I wanted to fail. For the first time in my life, I wanted to be the one who got what *I* wanted, no matter what the consequences were to others. I could die tomorrow in a place like this. The White Rabbit would likely be the one to do it, too. So what was I waiting for? What was I denying myself for? If anything, maybe letting these men have their way with me would make me less appealing to Coello. Or maybe this would just piss him off.

I wanted to piss him off. I wanted him to be mad that someone else got me first. I want to taunt him by saying '*Maybe you should have run faster, Mr. Rabbit.*' Fuck, that would be satisfying. I wouldn't even care if he hurt me after. If he was going to do that anyway, at least I'd have gotten to come first.

I nudged my hips back against Tynan's stiffness. Even through the layer of the sheets, I could tell he was thick, and he could go *deep*. I'd never had anyone who was capable of either. What would it be like to be filled with something like that? He'd be guaranteed to hit my G spot. My every spot.

Maybe that aphrodisiac is still in my system. Yeah, that must have been it. That's what I could blame. I would never in my right mind let myself get caught up in such a feeling otherwise.

"Is that a yes?" Tynan stopped being shy. He dipped his hand between my legs, and he nudged the sheets into my dampness. Satin on my clit was even better than it was on my legs.

"We would never force you if you don't want this, Alice." Finn began sliding the sheet down. I loosened my hold, letting him expose my breasts to open air and open eyes. And then to his wandering lips. He encased my nipple with his mouth, then he gently massaged it with his tongue until it was completely firm for him.

I bit into my lip. Vocalizing this was more difficult than I thought it might be. Until Tynan slid his finger up between my folds. The second that perfect pressure hit the top of his stroke, it was going to take everything in my power to stop me from saying it. And I didn't have any power to waste on such a thing. "Yes." I said through a sharp gasp. "Please." I shoved my teeth back into my lip to stop myself from any possible protesting.

Yes. I deserved this. I deserved to be made to feel good, to feel wanted, to feel *enough* for once. To not be the discarded girlfriend who spent every day questioning what part of me drove him to another. To be someone so desirable that *two* men, at the same time, couldn't hold themselves back from wanting me.

Fuck yes. I smiled to myself, as if I was keeping this small secret—the knowledge that I was the one who wanted *them*, even if they thought they were the ones convincing me.

"That's a good girl." Finn hummed against my breast as he shifted his focus to my other nipple. "And good girls get rewarded."

"I'd say she's much more of a very, very bad girl." Tynan chuckled against me. He finished tugging the sheet down, giving him a perfect view of my pussy as he glanced sidelong in the mirror. "And I love punishing bad girls." He punctuated with a strong slap against my ass.

It was hard to say which side was more intriguing. But it didn't matter, because I didn't *have* to choose. Today, I was going to close my eyes and let myself feel.

I lifted my chin to give Finn better access to my neck. He took the invitation, feathering kisses up to my cheek. I didn't complain as he made it to my mouth. Nor as he filled my mouth with his tongue. He kept me well distracted as his brother slipped his first finger inside me.

Tynan rubbed along my inner walls, as if testing which spots made me moan the most helplessly into his brother's mouth, and what kind of pressure dampened his hand the most enthusiastically. He was good at it, meticulously finding those spots and driving me utterly mad, one rub and rotation at a time.

And then each brother's focus traded places, Finn moving down between my legs and Tynan tugging my cheek back so he could explore my mouth next.

Finn inched down my body, licking and tasting my skin all the way down. Tynan slipped his slickened fingers into my mouth. I tasted my own satisfaction and pleasure as a distraction while Finn's tongue slipped between my folds. He circled my clit with varying pressure, then he sucked on me with irresistible tension.

I bowed my back, pressing into Tynan's chest, and he pulled my lips to his again, sharing the flavor. I was enveloped between two warm, strong, incredible bodies that asked nothing from me but to show them how good they made me feel.

My half lidded gaze followed the mirrors above and beside and in front and behind us. I watched our reflections, from the hands, to the tongues, to the teeth.

Finn spread my legs, exposing me to my own view. In the mirror to the right, I could see his tongue dipping into me, then rubbing careful patterns over every nerve ending I had. In the mirror above, I could see the bite marks Tynan was leaving down my neck, as he roughly nipped and sucked on my skin. My chest heaved, and my breasts looked full in the mirror, especially as Tynan rubbed and kneaded and squeezed them. He ran his hand over my breast, leaving my nipples exposed to view in between his fingers, then he'd pull back, sliding over my most sensitive spots.

My lips were parted and my inner thighs were slick. I watched as my body responded to the satisfaction it had always wanted.

Had I always been this sexy? Or did I just never notice? Never felt like I could be?

The visual alone was enough to push me over the edge.

I cried out when Finn's tongue snaked inside me, then I drew in a sharp breath when he drew a strong line all the way up my center. He created shapes between my legs that sent jolts right through me.

And still, they asked nothing of me but to watch, so that was exactly what I did. I reveled in the image of my body moving with them, my muscles convulsing, and my release wetting the sheets. I was utterly mesmerized, lost in a daze, while these men made me come so hard my vision was filled with stars.

This is what I deserve. If this was the test, I'd be happy to fail it.

Chapter 13

Such a good girl, this Alice was. The best, perhaps. And refreshing, quite frankly. She wasn't afraid or ignorant of sex. She was, if anything, eager and interested and entirely too giving. She lacked the selfishness of someone with enough experience to want, but she also lacked the innocence of a virgin who still found it a painful and nerve-racking task.

She was a bird who had tasted flight before her wings were broken, then she convinced herself that she'd never deserved to fly in the first place if it disrupted the sky. What a thrill to get to please such a woman: one who had given too much and received too little.

If she died at the hands of the Queen, it would be a shame. Perhaps we could keep her. The White Rabbit might complain, but he could always find another Alice. There were plenty of options in the Commonlands from what I knew. Even if the name grew less popular by the year, there would still be one or two out there that could challenge her highness and stand up to Wonderland.

This one, however, needed care. Care only we could provide.

I looked up from my comfortable position between her legs, watching the way her eyes rolled back as she allowed me to send those waves of appreciation through her. Every dip of my tongue and rotation around her clit had such power. She was so very sensitive, as though she'd been starved for true affection or quality touch for years.

Why had no one taken the time to enjoy such a body? Why had she been giving herself to someone that couldn't even make her orgasm? Was that what normal mortal girls did? The Queen would have never put up with such a thing.

And well, even if this might slight Coello, these trials were really to groom a new Alice to take the throne, so what could he say if I proposed to keep her just a little longer? It was necessary to teach her confidence and self-love. I wouldn't want her to become a repeat of the current demon who ruled us. The original Alice had been warped by Wonderland from an age that was entirely too young to understand what this place was. We hadn't given her the care she needed then, and that was why she became the monster she now was. This Alice, however, was already a mature and defined woman. She would surely have a firmer moral compass than the young girl who was jerked around by the games of cruel men, both in her world and ours.

Alice reached down and laced her fingers through my hair, pressing my lips back down to hers. So eager and needy. I teased her with another dip of my tongue between her folds, then I let her push me down further, so I could slip my tongue inside her. The way she writhed against my face was divine. And watching my dearest brother licking the sweat off her neck? Even more so.

With one hand, she grabbed his head, laced her fingers through his black hair and held him down against her chest, begging him to bite at her nipples. With the other, she clawed into my platinum locks, and she commanded her pleasure. Beautiful yet tragic that she had no idea why she was here at all. This must have been so overwhelming. My heart ached for her. Perhaps we could just tell her.

<I know that look in your eye.> Tynan scolded me through the silent channel between us. I met his gaze through the reflection on the far mirror.

<And what look is that, Brother?> I moved my kisses to her inner thigh, spreading her glistening orgasm over her skin.

Tynan ran a hand through her hair, then he gave it a harsh tug, eliciting a soft moan from our Alice. *<That look that wants to protect her instead of doing your goddamn job.>*

I smirked at brother dearest as I climbed back up her body to meet his eyes at parallel. He took my absence from her pussy as an invite to nudge her open with the head of his cock. *<That's funny, because I'm fairly certain doing your job doesn't involve shoving your dick in her either.>* I took her mouth again, sharing that sweet flavor of pleasure. She sucked on my tongue when I slipped it inside her, like the good girl she was. *<I do believe, when we arranged this game, you were only supposed to test her STRENGTH, no?>* We'd all been tasked with gauging a different quality from the trial. The cat was to test her cleverness. The rabbit: her speed, the caterpillar: her resolve, and the Mad Hatter… I chuckled to myself at the thought. Ah, the Mad Hatter.

<Yes, and being able to take my dick requires true fortitude.> Tynan grinned smugly while he pulled her hips slowly against his, watching every inch of his shaft disappear inside of her. *<Fuck, she's warm. It might take some fortitude on my part to take it back.>*

I resisted the urge to laugh out loud. *<The sacrifices you make for the good of Wonderland.>*

<I'm glad you're finally starting to recognize them, Brother.> Tynan used a firm grip to guide her hips at a tempo that he could stand without coming too quickly. She deserved slow play, and I could feel through our shared connection exactly how close he was. His pleasure was my pleasure, and my pleasure was his, and I was palming my own cock to try to relieve the pressure.

Tynan shoved into her with increasing power, connecting her hips to mine in small bursts. I took the initiative to slip my cock between her wetness, and rub it over her clit. She was so aroused and compliant, it was a battle to keep myself from smearing come all over her stomach.

<I'm not that afraid of Coello. Are you?> My brother offered with a slight upturn of his lips.

<I am, but… I suppose she could still use some more care. Before he comes to retrieve her, anyway.> Her moan into my mouth was the final straw before I was crashing over the edge. I lost myself against her body, as Tynan lost himself inside her.

And now she really *was* ours, so long as we chose to keep her.

Chapter 14"

Alice took charge now. She pushed me down onto the bed with a hand on each shoulder, and she climbed atop my lap. The look in her eyes was fierce—perhaps even a bit angry. She was a woman who had no interest in games, and only interest in what pleasure she could get from us. That was a typical side effect of taking our semen. My brother was always a smooth talker, but there was a reason she was mounting *my* cock right now and not his. Women don't always want to be treated like delicate flowers. Sometimes they just want to get fucked by the biggest, hardest dick.

Though between the image of her body covered in my brother's come and that expression as she bit into her lip and lowered herself onto me, letting me reshape her pussy again… I was beginning to wonder which one of us was falling under whose spell. She was certainly enticing, and she was something unlike anything I'd ever had.

Finn positioned himself behind her. He placed a hand on each breast, and he rolled her nipples between his fingers while he lapped at her neck. So soft and gentle. That's not what she needs. *<Put it in her ass. Let her take us both at once.>*

She rocked her hips on me, and I was fighting to keep it together. Finn chuckled against her neck as he picked up on every signal I sent. He knew perhaps even better than I could admit that I was coming undone in that perfect cunt.

He ran his hands down her body, settling one on top of each thigh, and he began guiding her movements on me. Fuck, he knew how to drive me insane.

<What, there's not enough room for one more?> He teased as he directed her hips in a circular rotation. Alice was gasping through each bounce, enjoying the ride so much that she must have been completely under our enchantment now.

<There's always room for one more.> I shot him a wicked grin, and he took that as his perfect cue. He moved his grip back up her body, then he placed a hand on her back, and he shoved her down onto me. Her soft breasts pressed into my hard chest, and Finn dampened the head of his cock on the abundant fluids I'd worked from her. He rubbed himself against me as he pressed into her pussy just enough to communicate his intentions.

The little slut gripped my shoulders, and she nodded against me to give Finn her approval. Fuck, I *do* like this Alice.

Finn nudged a little bit at a time, not wanting to cause pain. Carefulness I rarely employed. He entered her slowly, stretching that tight pussy with the utmost care until we both had room to move inside of her. I gave her a moment to brace herself against me, then we both moved in perfect sync.

"Come for me, Princess." I growled into her ear. Though she was already drenching my lap in arousal. She dug her nails into me hard enough to leave a mark, and she bit into her lip to muffle the little gasps and squeaks that escaped her throat on each shared thrust. Her eyes were watering as she took both of us over and over again. That angle hit just right, and I couldn't help how exquisite that fullness felt on my dick. Then the feeling of Finn releasing inside her hit me, and I was careening off the edge of sanity.

God fucking damn. Coello can get his own Alice.

Chapter 15

Mau

"The Cheshire Cat"

I rebuilt my body in the room of the twins, but I'd not even fully formed before I found myself smirking widely. Though I'd followed Alice into the Hall of Mirrors to observe, thankful that a long history of good will meant these men always allowed me passage through the maze, I'd not quite expected her to be such an enthusiastic participant in the twins' little game, and it was still quite a scene to behold. The new Alice, hot and blushing and completely naked, visible from every angle thanks to the mirrors. She was lying on her back between them now, and her breasts were flattened against her chest, bouncing up towards her collarbone every time Tynan pulled out of her very wet pussy and slammed back in. Her hands were over her head, jerking off Finn to the rate of his brother's thrusts. As if they were fucking each other through the conduit of her soft and nicely curved body.

Seeing her in this light, she wasn't flawlessly muscular with the lithe build of a young athlete like we usually ended up with. Nor was she a perfectly defined model without an ounce of fat on her body like the original Alice had become. She beget none of the perfection I'd come to expect of Wonderland. And somehow that was… so much more interesting.

She looked like she would feel good in my hands. Soft to the touch and easy to hold, with thighs I might not mind being suffocated by. And watching the way she so effortlessly took Tynan's cock, deep, hard, and while soaking it in her natural excitement…

Yes, I might be willing to get behind this Alice.

"Just can't get enough, can you?" I said, drawing attention from at least deux of this ménage a trois.

"Cheshire." Finn addressed me first. Then as if he was too busy to acknowledge my presence any longer, he returned his attention to Alice, who was gasping louder and louder as Tynan found her sweet spot. Finn gripped her wrists and pulled her hands away from his hard dick. He repositioned on his knees, and he pulled her chin back until her lips were in line with the tip. "Will my good girl suck me off?" He asked her in a sweet yet condescending voice.

Alice responded by tipping her head back enough that she could take him inside her mouth.

"You're such a dirty little slut." Tynan purred, using his rhythm to help his brother face fuck her more efficiently. "How many times are you going to let us paint you with our come, Princess?" He punctuated as he circled her clit with his thumb. Her moans were muffled only by the cock in her mouth. "What do you want, Cheshire?" He at last acknowledged me, lifting those pitch black eyes to mine.

"You know how Coello feels about magically enslaving the Alices." I raised an eyebrow.

"She came of her own free will." Finn shot me a look. "Then she came again, and again." His words hitched as she sucked on him just right.

"And I'm guessing you came in her… and *on* her again and again, until she was enchanted by the spell of Tweedle Dee and Tweedle fucking Dum." I made sure my tone was adequately severe, even if I was, admittedly, rather amused.

She was a puppet for them now. It would be near impossible for her to break this enchantment on her own. I'd yet to see that sort of mental strength from anyone, let alone a human. I'd even been prone to falling for their trap a few times, when I was in the mood. It was all fun and games with the twins until they tricked you into swallowing.

"I hadn't meant to but—" Tynan cut himself off as he hit climax inside her. He fell forward, holding her hips to support himself as he let the pleasure ripple through his body. He breathed heavily, while Alice gasped and choked on Finn's orgasm as it hit her throat. *Fucking heathens.* "If you'd felt how warm and perfect her sweet little cunt is, you wouldn't have let her get through the woods in the first place."

I shook my head while each of the twins pulled out of her, one leaving semen on her inner thighs, the other dribbling traces on her forehead. She rolled over, eyes closed, breathing heavy, total contentment in her expression, covered in a mess of sex, and looking terribly vulnerable and fuckable.

I've seen plenty of beautiful Alices before though. This was nothing noteworthy to me. If anything, I was far more interested to see how Bunny would react when he came upon such a sight.

"I think you've had enough fun." I tapped the mirror behind me. "Is it this one?"

"Like we'd fucking tell you." Tynan growled as he began getting dressed hurriedly. So shy. *As if I'd never seen his cock before.*

"Which one is it, Finn? I'd rather not completely destroy your beautiful home." I appealed to the kinder of the twins.

"She asked for it prior to the enchantment." The white haired brother avoided the question as well. Curiouser and curiouser. They must really enjoy this one, too. *What is it that has everyone so in knots over another disposable human girl? I can't understand it.*

I kept my eyes on the little dove, watching her breathe steadily. A crack in the mirror was all it would take to break the spell. I shouldn't be helping her along, but if she'd made it past my sweet Jabberwock, this was the least I could do. Though, to be quite honest, getting taken in by these two only confirmed my suspicion that she was just as weak as every other.

The more I thought about it, the less I wanted to do anything about the situation. If I just left her here, they would owe me one, and having them in my debt never hurt.

I contemplated for several moments, when I noticed the vaguest twitch of Alice's expression. My eyes narrowed with a curiosity. She furrowed her brow, then cleaned her lips with her tongue. Strangely normal movements for a puppet. Usually under enchantment, the Alices were barely allowed to breathe on their own. I'm fairly certain that was Tynan's favorite part.

I shot a look between the panicked men, who were still dressing in their suits, then back to the girl who scrunched herself into a tucked fetal position, slipped a hand between her legs, and smiled softly to herself, before nuzzling into the sheets.

Not enchanted. At least not entirely. She's just… content and tired out.

How is that even possible?

Though, I didn't think either man had actually noticed in this case. She was in their bed, writhing, getting off, having a wonderful time, and she was *consciously* choosing to do so from beginning to end.

Would you look at her, just showing up in Wonderland and hopping right into a threesome. Why, that kind of perfect deviance may just make her an Alice after *my* own heart.

I noticed my unconscious grin too late to stop it entirely, but then I shook it off, not wanting the twins to question why I was looking so pleased in her direction. Whatever their assumption, it would be wrong anyway. I wouldn't be so easily charmed by her like the others, regardless of these little things.

Still... *Your secret is safe with me, Little Dove.* "Have it your way." I raised a fist and tapped lightly on the mirror behind me, still going through with the theatrics of it all. Partially to hide the fact that they hadn't been able to put her under their spell, and largely because I chose violence today and every day.

"Wait—" Tynan called from the other end of his outstretched hand.

"You don't have to—" Finn started at the same time as his dark haired brother.

That was enough to confirm which mirror I needed to break. I cast them each a wide smirk before my knuckle hit the glass hard enough to make it split. The crack splintered along the surface rapidly. I gave it another hit.

In an instant, accented with a loud thundering crack of the glass, the whole room vanished. The walls crumbled away, and the illusion disappeared, leaving us all standing outside in the open field just a few hundred yards from the forest entrance. No longer was there a bed. Only a field of flowers, where Alice lay disheveled and used.

"Dammit, Cheshire—" Tynan began to scold me, when Finn raised a silencing hand.

"We apologize for our transgressions, Mau."

"I'm sure you do." I shook my head. "But you should already know I'm not the one you need to be afraid of." I glanced sidelong at the forest exit. Still no sign of Coello. The Jabberwock must be having his fun with him.

I couldn't help my wicked smile at the thought. I was sure he'd be fine. If he somehow wasn't, I'd just kill this Alice and start over again. It was no bother to me either way. She was interesting, but nothing I would sacrifice Bunny for. Mishka or Tynan, maybe, but not Coello.

Speaking of Alice…

I paced over to the girl on the floor who was completely unconscious now, resting peacefully in the flowers. The lavender and cobalt looked nice against her flushed skin. Her post coital high had her glowing, and those pretty and parted pink lips were an enticing invite.

Though I must say, she looked so different without blood smeared all over her. So… ordinary. I might even call her delicate. Yet, if she survived the Jabberwock and rode the twins for fun, she was anything but.

Maybe *this* is the woman that Coello sees. A fiercely fuckable little dove.

"Fetch her clothing for me, will you?" I spoke absently towards the twins, who half grumbled and half flitted off with apologies, while I kept my eyes on Alice. I crouched down and gently brushed the hair from her forehead, giving me a better view of her face. I took off my glove and used it to clean traces of their antics from her skin.

I frowned. *If she really is something special, and if she might bring about the end of the Queen, am I ready to end these games for good?*

At this point, I didn't know what else life could be. I'd gotten too used to the Queen's Wonderland, perhaps. It was ruthless, and it was dark, but so were all of us these days. I think I might have been the only man in the Alice cycles who hadn't yet been killed, so perhaps my point of reference was skewed by sanity. Or I was worse than them all by design. It was hard to say. But if everything went back to how it started before the original Alice stumbled down that rabbit hole, would we even know how to exist in that kind of peace anymore?

What a curious thought. I shouldn't let myself get sucked in so easily. There was still no reason to think she'd succeed.

When the twins returned with her costume—an outfit customary of all Alices in Wonderland—I took the time to dress her, while they both watched completely dumbfounded. I was partial to the pink. The original Alice had been obsessed with a powdery baby blue, which was likely why this became the color of the opposition. It was a powerful color. Commanding in its softness.

Alice was compliant as I dressed her. She laid limply in my hands like a doll as I tightened down the ribbons of her corset. Some of their magic must have gotten to her after all to be able to be handled without waking. Not even I was completely immune to their puppetry, but for a human to have any power to resist was certainly fascinating. Would she remember any of this though, I wonder?

"Do you want this too?" Finn asked as I tugged the last row of ribbon tightly. I glanced up at him to see a jeweled necklace in his hand. Mishka's control necklace. It was quite exquisite in decoration when it wasn't forcing women into slavery. Though it was powerless now, wasn't it?

"I'd say she's earned that trophy." I nodded, receiving the necklace from Finn and latching it behind her neck.

"I think she's someone who has earned more than anyone will ever give her." Finn said with an unusual fondness as he settled his gaze on her.

"We could have given it to her." Tynan scoffed. "But not when we're always so focused on running these women through some bullshit test course. It's no wonder these trials never succeed."

"Now now, we've all seen what the Queen has done to the Alices who showed up under-prepared." I tossed Tynan a look that had him turning away. Finn fidgeted on his feet, so obviously recalling the scenes that his eyes may well have been projectors. We'd all been witness to one too many beheadings, I suppose. Among… worse things.

Even I shuddered to recall the time she subjected an Alice to a 52 card shuffle, having her run through by each soldier in her personal guard, one at a time, continuing even after her death. Whether I questioned the path of Wonderland or the value in replacing one ruler with another, there would certainly be no love lost for the current Queen of Hearts.

"So then, what will you do with her? To say she passed our test is a bit of a stretch." Tynan spoke with a tentativeness that felt far removed from his usual confidence.

"To say she failed it isn't entirely fair either." Finn added with a lift of his finger. "She didn't give in to us out of fear. She gave in out of honest desire. I think there's a strength to that that's worth considering."

I nodded silently to the twins. "I think we can all agree that's a fair and reasonable assessment. But I wonder if our dear rabid Bunny will see it that way."

Finn and Tynan swallowed down their dread in unison. It was the bright one that spoke first. "We held up our end of the deal." He muttered, more for himself than me.

"Whether you did or you didn't isn't up for me to decide. I'm not the one who designed these games." I bared my fangs in delightful cruelty, before I settled my attention back on our guest, leaving them to look between each other with a hint of panic. Once I assured her costume was well in order, I hoisted her up over my shoulder and addressed the Tweedle Brothers one more time. "Let me know what Coello says when he finds you." I said in a way that dripped with both amusement and violent threats. "Assuming you're still able to speak after he rips your collective throats out."

I savored that wide-eyed horror that pinged in their expressions as I pulled Alice into my alternate space time. It was my favorite way to travel, and likely the reason I'd yet to be felled in our many Wonderland Rewinds. Here I could exist invisible to the rest of the universe. I could be a spy or a fly on the wall, but I could also avoid the swinging of axes or the blade of a guillotine when the Queen got uppity and started removing heads. A trick I may have used more than once.

Stepping away from the twins, I carried Alice towards the next segment of the woods that ordinarily she would have to fight her way through herself. I trudged through the bog, and I sidestepped the Bandersnatch who swam through its muck. It would listen to me if I asked it to back down, more or less, but walking about with an Alice who smelled of sex and satisfaction on my shoulder was like wearing a suit of raw meat in a lion's cage, and that wasn't going to end well for anyone involved.

So I kept up my cloak, and I climbed from the swampland into a densely packed forest of mushroom trees.

We were at the edge of my territory, now. Quite frankly, I shouldn't have been venturing here at all without good reason. Though maybe this little dove was reason enough on her own. Apparently she intrigued me enough that I'd let her skip the Bandersnatch, which I *absolutely* shouldn't have done without a borderline divine reason. And Finn and Tynan would think I'd saved her from their spell, which was acceptable under no circumstances. All decisions I felt hard pressed to explain at the moment. If I were to analyze it all more deeply, I'd likely conclude it was more about making Bunny happy than myself, and it had more to do with him than this Alice.

And if I were to analyze deeper still, I'd more likely conclude that I was lying about the above assessment. But whatever the case, I found this next chapter of the Alice trials was often the most telling of them all, and there was something about this Alice that I needed to be told.

The massive shrooms towered overhead, creating comfortable canopies that were thin enough to let in the sunlight, but thick enough to keep out the rain.

I travelled swiftly through the realm of fungus before I came upon a particularly wide and plump mushroom. It was hollowed out and modified to resemble a home. Well, maybe it was more accurately described as a hideout made to blend in among the mushrooms. The roof was bright red with small white spots, the body had small, half-moon shaped windows that contained no glass, making them useless to actually keep out the abundant bugs in the mushroom forest, and the door was an overly vibrant scarlet that was painted to appear as if it was made of wood.

It wasn't wood at all, but I appreciated the attention to detail as I knocked lightly against the squishy entrance.

"I have something special for you, Bruco," I called through the door, knowing the sound would carry through the pane-less windows.

The little red door flew open, and Bruco stood in the entryway. I greeted our dear friend the Caterpillar with a bow, partially because I'm wonderfully and exquisitely polite, but also to show off the prize on my shoulder.

Bruco eyed me up and down, settling his gaze on my unconscious Alice. Those emerald eyes flashed with curiosity. He placed a hand on his slim hips, and he tucked flyaway strands of his blond braided hair behind his ear.

Bruco often reminded me more of a fairy of sorts than an insect, with his ears that pointed just slightly at the tip and his youthful, boyish features. He had none of Coello's masculinity or the twin's muscle. I'd oft thought him frail. Likely that was why he ran the Wonderland Apothecary instead of playing along with our violent delights.

"Since when do you take care of your toys? I thought the whole fun of it for you was to push them to the point of near death, and see if they can escape before the *near* becomes *here*."

I snorted at the suggestion. "You think me such a brute, Bruco?"

"A brute would be an improvement." He shook his head and threw up his hands.

"So dramatic." With a roll of my eyes, I pushed past the Caterpillar, and I dropped an unconscious Alice on his patient bed. "Well, Coello seems to have a thing for this iteration of Alice, and after seeing how she handled the twins, I'm not completely closed off to the possibility that she could be worth something."

"You? The *Cheshire Cat* aren't closed off to the possibility?" His mouth was agape. *Annoying*. "I thought you despised the games at this point."

"I simply find them a touch repetitive. A pretty girl, Jabberwock teeth, another, and she drowns in the bog. The last few Alices have offered about as much mental stimulation as burning ants with a magnifying glass." I shooed his smug tone from the air with a wave of my hand.

"Is she different somehow?" Bruco eyed me as if he might find an answer if he stared long enough.

"I wonder." I spoke without betraying any details. "If only there was some sort of doctor who could give her a test and find out."

"Point taken." Bruco snorted. Though when he took a moment to study her features, now that she was laid out on the mattress, his eyes seemed to sparkle with delight. He drew his gaze up and down her body. "If I must, I'll test her." He said, shooting me a devious smile. "But know that this is rarely a stop the Alices can survive."

"I'm well aware." I waved a hand dismissively. "But that's hardly my problem."

With that, I turned on my heel and freed myself from Bruco's mushroom home. Whether this was the best course of action or not, I couldn't say. But this was the way of things, and I would do best not to disrupt the order further. If she couldn't handle someone like Bruco, she couldn't handle rebelling against the crown.

Besides, I had more important things to do than to keep watching after some human girl.

My eyes drifted back to the forest. Coello still hadn't surfaced. *I suppose I should go check on him.*

Chapter 16

"The White Rabbit"

The Jabberwock's battle cry shattered that calm before the storm, and the beast swiped and clawed at me with violent swings. It was only thanks to my rabbit reflexes that I was able to dip and sidestep around every attack. But I couldn't keep this up forever.

Another swipe of the Jabberwock's claw, and a tree came smashing down directly in my path. I jumped back, narrowly missing the ricochet of splintering branches and scattering twigs.

Another quick hop, and I was running into the felled canopy, where the tight branches made it difficult for a beast of that size to follow me. I dipped in as deeply as I could get, then I used my boot to break free a branch that had enough of a splintered point to function as a makeshift harpoon. I gripped the spear with both hands, and I brace myself as the Jabberwock reached blindly into the trees. As that tentacle-like claw neared, I lifted my weapon high, then I came down hard, skewering his claw and pinning it into the trunk.

The Jabberwock roared out a note that could only be described as a bellowing death rattle, and I knew I had my opening. I'd learned a few of its tricks the last time it ate me whole, and I had foolishly clung to consciousness the entire process of being digested alive. Not something I ever planned to do again, but the memory did a mighty job of inciting my most deep felt rage.

I ripped another branch from the canopy, taking a flurry of leaves with me, and I hoisted that sharp point into the beast's forearm. A third, I shoved into its bicep, nailing down each point in rapid succession in hopes that the pain would immobilize it long enough to get where I needed to go. The shriek every time wood tore flesh was near ear shattering, and the roar that followed was so deep and vicious, it served as a weapon all its own.

Fear, that is. That sound was fear embodied in an audio frequency. The greatest weapon of any beast was making its prey cower in helplessness just long enough to do as it pleased.

I smiled to myself, picturing that same paralysis on Alice's face. I smiled wider recalling the feel of her teeth sinking into my hand.

That's right. *I* was the predator in Wonderland. I wouldn't be eaten by a simple puppy who thinks itself a wolf.

In the brief window I had, I broke off one more branch, and I ran at the beast's open mouth, ready to plunge the stake into its throat.

I was milliseconds from victory when the beasts other claw hit me broadside and swept me into its grip.

Fuck. I underestimated this stupid fucking thing *again. If I just had a Vorpal Sword, I could—*

I hadn't even finished the thought when a flash of light appeared like a ring, circling the neck of the Jabberwock. With the briefest delay, that ring turned to a fountain of gushing blood, shooting out of the severed artery in its neck like a fountain, painting me from head to toe. It stared at me with lifeless eyes and its mouth agape, as if the shock of the matter was the only thing keeping its appendages attached to its body. Then the neck of the beast slammed into the forest floor with a thundering thud, sending all the Jubjub Birds, Mome Raths, and loose leaves scattering in a wild whirlwind of force.

The leaves settled. The last birds flew away. And the whole forest went dead silent. More dead than the monster itself.

"Well that was quite a show you were putting on, Bunny." Mau smiled at me from atop the bleeding and headless corpse. He retracted his claws, and he flexed each blood coated finger. "I legitimately feared I might have to watch you die, *again,* if I didn't intervene soon."

I relaxed my guard and tossed aside my weapon, then I rolled my shoulders with a nonchalance, as if I hadn't just been desperately fighting for my life but a moment ago. I didn't need the Cheshire Cat seeing me shaken, after all. I'd prefer if he only ever saw the wicked sides of me.

Though, as I glanced at the neck still periodically pulsing and wiggling on the floor, I couldn't help but think that now I *needed* this Alice to survive. That way, the Jabberwock would stay dead as well. "You know what they say: Murder me once, shame on you. Murder me twice, shame on me…"

"Murder you three times, and you're simply an idiot." Mau added with a smile and a slight tilt of his head. "It's good to see you're learning, Bunny."

"I wouldn't have to learn if you could control your beasts." I raised an accusing eyebrow in his general direction.

Mau threw up his hands in surrender. "The Jabberwock only listens to me in *theory.*"

"That theory seems pretty sound, considering you told it to hunt me down, and it did exactly that." I cocked my eyebrow, not at all falling for any such excuses or nonsense.

And the Cheshire Cat laughed. "I suppose you're not an idiot after all. I do enjoy that panicked look on your face entirely too much, I'll admit. There aren't many ways left to scare you." The way his lips twisted befitted his name.

"Uh huh. That's what I thought." I added with a very unamused roll of my eyes.

"In my defense, I told the beast to hunt down Alice. It's not my fault she was faster and better at escaping than you." He glanced up at the sky while playfully tapping his chin. His taunting was more effective at getting under my skin than I was going to admit. "You know how easily we all get bored here. You were simply a victim of circumstance. You should just be happy that this little dove actually passed the trial. Even I was impressed, if I'm quite honest."

I paused for a moment at that acknowledgement. "I suppose she did," was the only praise I offered openly, before I snapped my fingers to manifest myself a smoke. I think I'd earned one at this point. Another snap and I lit up and took a drag to calm myself down.

He did have a point. The test course for Alices to get through Wonderland intact had many pitfalls, and few were more unreasonable than crossing the Cheshire Cat. But if Mau didn't go easy on her, and she legitimately made it past the Jabberwock on her own resourcefulness, that was certainly a good sign.

"Such a dirty habit." Mau interrupted my thoughts as he shook his head. With that perfect feline grace, he hopped down from his mount atop the monster and walked over to me. He grimaced before he yanked the cigarette straight from my lips.

I glared at him with every ounce of hate in my bones, but the Kitten, as always, was completely unmoved. He instead placed that same cigarette between his own lips and took a long, slow toke. He stood there for a moment, turning the flavor around on his tongue, before he exhaled and handed me back my dart.

"Tastes like something you rolled yourself. Bruco's smokes are much better." He waved a hand in the air dismissively. And that was the most offensive thing he'd said so far.

"This one's from Commonland. They like the taste of actual fire there for some reason." I shrugged. I liked that it wasn't sweet for once. Everything here tasted like candy, and sometimes I didn't mind crossing over to the mortal realm for the Alice hunt just to cleanse my palate. "They have a lot of strange flavors there."

"You'll have to open the portal and give me the tour sometime." He placed the cigarette back between my lips, letting his fingers linger for an extended second.

"Yeah?" I turned away as I took another puff. "Maybe if I didn't almost get murdered every time I entered your forest, I'd be more inclined to extend an invite. But I'm not sure the mortal realm would survive a guy like you."

"This from the man who kills Mishka every other week just for sport?" Mau taunted. He moved closer.

"*To* the man who delights in licking his blood off my body afterwards." I pushed back without missing a beat.

"Fair point." The Kitten took that as some sort of an invite to step into the last inch of my personal space.

Though I didn't flinch. I was used to that too. "What can I say? I'm a cat who likes the taste of a dead mouse."

"Really? Is that what you like about it?" With a slight lift of my chin, our gazes were level.

"I like a *lot* of things about it." Mau grabbed my cigarette and tossed it aside, then he placed that same hand on my waist. A sharp tug, and my body was against his, connecting us at the hips. There weren't but inches between our lips. "I found your new toy playing games with my old toys."

I grinned at the mental image, paying no mind as Mau undid the top button on my shirt. "Was she winning?"

"She certainly didn't sound like she was *losing*." The Cheshire Cat shared the vibration of a laugh before he moved that hand up to the back of my neck. He held me still as he closed the distance between us, then he sniffed lightly along my jaw. He let the tip of his nose follow the line of my cheekbone upwards, tracing my face shape with the lightest contact, until the angle had his lips brushing my skin. "I'll admit that I find her curiously more fetching than the last Alice." His warm breath trailed moisture on my face then inched down to my neck again. "I've not met many women who can get a mouth full of Finn with a smile." His hand on my waist slid down my side, until his fingers were lightly brushing my ass. He nibbled softly on my neck. "There are quite a lot of things I find interesting about her, actually. I think I might invite her over for some tea."

"Maybe I'll join you." I lifted my chin as his kisses climbed back up. Though he stopped short of my lips. He hovered there, tempting me to make the connection for him. But I wouldn't. It was more fun to watch him beg. "If she makes it that far."

"Oh, my sweet, sweet bunny," Mau ran a hand through my hair, pushing it out of my eyes and removing the only barrier between our gazes. "Please do come either way. I'll fuck you on the table whether she makes it or not."

"Is that a promise or a threat?" I knew full well how this game worked.

"Fucking you is a promise." At last, his lips nudged mine. "But the Bandersnatch you'll have to outrun in order to get there? That's a threat."

"Son of a—"

In an instant, Mau vanished again, leaving behind nothing but his devious laugh and the trace heat of his body. I stood still for several more seconds, before a tremor through my body shook off the sheer intensity of his presence. *The Cheshire fucking Cat.*

Sometimes I wondered why I so easily trusted that guy, and why I kept getting tangled up in his rhythm. Of all the creatures of Wonderland, we all knew he was the most dangerous and the most deceitful. Maybe that's what I liked about him.

I rolled my shoulders again, and under the fading influence of adrenalin, a slight ache radiated from where I'd impacted the ground. *I should probably get some salve from the Caterpillar.* I'd need to be in top shape if we were going to stop in to a party in the Queen's court.

And even more if I had to cross the Bandersnatch to get there. I might need the Twins for that part.

Why must he always make *my* life more difficult?

The Cheshire FUCKING Cat, indeed.

Chapter 17

Alice

Fog. Pink fog, purple fog, green and blue. I blinked my way through blurred vision, trying to figure out where I was. It was difficult to discern whether this was a dream or reality, whether I was alive or dead, whether this whole Wonderland debacle had been an actual thing, or if it had all been purely in my imagination.

I stirred slightly. My body coming to life as slowly as my mind. I was sore. My nipples had a phantom pain, as though they'd been handled roughly and extensively, and I could still feel the size of Tynan's cock between my legs. The last thing I remembered was waking up in their bed, giving into them, and giving into the most satisfying orgasm I'd ever had. Or like, ten of them. One for every year I wasted with my ex, and one more as a blessing for future fucking. *What a pleasant thought*, I mused silently with a shit eating grin on my face.

But as to where I was *now*, I couldn't begin to say, and I was willing to bet that was going to be a bad thing. There were no mirrors here. Gone was the image of my naked writhing body, and gone were all the pretty visuals of hard cocks making my pussy cry happy tears.

I drew in a sharp breath—one I'd planned to release in a dejected sigh—only to find I was back in my costume. Back to snug corsets and frilly skirts. They must have dressed me after they were done. That would have been the polite thing to do, even though there was nothing actually comfortable about a corset. Still, they were definitely the best people I'd met since coming here. The kindest anyway. Whenever I make it back to the real world, I'll be happy to tell Dinah this part of the story.

Though as I reminisced so lackadaisical, I realized I was filling my lungs with another round of this colored smoke. Smoke that could do *anything*. Yet… any sense of panic that I probably should have had never manifested. The air smelled of gum drops and cherries. I smiled to myself and closed my eyes, considering sleep's invitation again. This wasn't so bad…

What the hell am I thinking? This is Wonderland. This wasn't my room or an amusement park or a party. I couldn't let my guard down to such an extreme. I opened my eyes again with my remaining will power. My vision was still filled with those vague clouds of color. They were really there. This wasn't a dream or illusion.

Thinking quickly, I grasped the satin sheet beneath me and pulled it to my face. I breathed through the material, trying to keep some of this smoke from my lungs. Surely, there was *something* wrong with it.

"Oh, you *are* more clever than the average Alice." A soft voice, gentle and not terribly deep, drew my attention. On the other side of that sound, blurred by smoke, was a thin and fair man dressed in a doctor's coat. He looked young… early twenties, maybe. Though I'm sure he was hundreds or thousands of years old, considering the nature of this place. I didn't really know much about Wonderland. How old it was or how it worked or why everyone was so obsessed with having a woman named Alice in its depths, but I at least knew that the men were immortal-ish, and that most everyone had been around long enough to bore themselves into rampant sadism.

This man seemed oddly gentle though. He reminded me more of Finn than Coello. Maybe he wouldn't mind filling me in on how this all worked.

I wrenched myself upright, but I still kept the cloth to my airways, just to be safe. "Who are you?" I asked.

"Who are any of us?" He responded as he rubbed his chin. "I know who I think I am, and you know who you think you are, but is that the same person as who *I* think *you* are and who *you* think *I* am?"

"Jesus fucking Christ." I groaned, dropping the sheet so I could dramatically place my forehead on my raised knees. "Does this never end?"

"The riddles? Or your exploration of self?" He said, sitting beside me with a relaxed posture, as if trying to come off as safe and casual. He sucked a breath from something that resembles a vape pen, before puffing out another round of blue smoke. "Not that it matters which. In this place, neither will ever end." He said as he offered me his pen.

I took it for no logical reason other than the fact that I didn't fucking care. Maybe the smoke I'd already inhaled was doing that to me, but whatever. The thought of getting a little high made this whole situation less annoying. I held in the button and took a pull. Then I took several moments to choke that mango whatever-the-fuck tasting liquid back out of my lungs.

"So trusting." The elf-ish doctor stared at me, wide-eyed.

"Obviously. I wouldn't be here if I had any sense." I retorted, not feeling terribly patient. Though my words had none of the edge or bite that I'd intended. They were just kind of there. Bland and toneless. The smoke probably helped a bit with that too. Honestly, I didn't even care at this point if the smoke was some horrible drug, and I made another mistake by breathing it in. What was this guy going to do? Kill me? Fuck me 'til I screamed? *Jokes on Wonderland: I'm starting to like that shit.* "So what's your deal? Wait, no, don't tell me. Let me guess. You're a green bean with a choke kink."

The man snorted. "What the hell?" he shook his head while unable to contain his laughter. "What kind of Wonderland have these guys been subjecting you to?"

"An annoying one." I rolled my eyes. The smoke was unexplainably relaxing the more I inhaled. It didn't seem to be doing anything other than that. No unwanted arousal or nausea. Just good old fashioned getting high.

"Well, let me try and improve that then. You can call me Bruco. Others know me as the Caterpillar of the Mushroom Forest. I serve as the Wonderland doctor and apothecary."

"Cool." *Caterpillar, green bean—same thing.* I didn't bother offering so much as eye contact. I'd long since lost interest in being polite. "So how did I end up here?"

"You need to be more specific, Alice." He said with a smile. "*Here* is so many things. It's your life decisions. It's your path. It's Wonderland itself. It's that gentle high of breathing in the smoke of Fire Berries. And it's the collective people who have shaped you. Here could be an infinite scope and a narrow one at the same time. So where, exactly, do you feel you are?"

More philosophy. I sucked down another deep breath of smoke, then I handed him back his stick. "Here." I pointed at the bed. "In your house. How did I literally end up *here* here."

"Oh. Do you not remember?" He had this weird, glowing, almost puppy-dog-esque expression. It was too cute for a place like this. "The Cheshire Cat brought you *here* here."

Mau did? That's strange. Was he saving me? From the twins? I wondered if he killed them. No, he wasn't Coello. I didn't know much about the Cheshire Cat other than the fact that he made it very difficult to know anything at all about anything, but I didn't get the impression he was a senseless killer.

"Why?" I asked as if he might ever give me a straight answer.

"I wondered the same." Bruco shrugged, predictably giving me nothing of the sort. "But for whatever reason, he wanted you to heal, and as the doctor, that's what I can provide."

"Finn and Tynan didn't injure me." I raised an eyebrow. *If anything, they were the only ones who made me feel any good.*

"Why don't you get up and walk across the room then." He snickered as he spoke.

He did have me there. I could walk, but likely not in a way that wasn't embarrassing. "Okay, well, whatever. I'm not actually injured though. I don't see how you're going to help me."

"For you, I think you need more of an emotional healing." Bruco took back the pen and huffed it.

"Because Wonderland is so goddamn traumatizing?" I rolled my eyes, blatantly and with intent for him to see it. "Or are you actually good for something else?"

"There's always something else. It's easy to blame the environment to avoid analyzing what's actually inside."

I raised an eyebrow. "If you're supposed to be the Wonderland therapist, I'm not impressed with your work so far." I nudged my chin towards the general outside, hoping he'd figure out I meant literally every fucked up person here. "But by all means, *fix me*, Doc."

"In order to fix you, I first must know what ails you, Alice." Bruco nudged in closer to me. I turned my head to face him, just in time for him to tap our noses at the tips. He stayed close, keeping those emerald eyes locked as he teetered the vape from his lips to mine. "Take another taste." He whispered as he nudged the piece into my mouth.

I didn't flinch. I showed no fear. I don't know if I had any fear left in me at this point. No, I just stared him square in the eye, and I drew in the smoke. Then I blew it back in his face, creating a powdery veil of purple between our gazes.

"You're not my type." I said bluntly, annoyed by how close he remained. I'm not sure why I'd felt the need to tell him that, but I did.

"So honest." The Caterpillar grinned. "Take another puff."

"Do all of the men here need drugs to get laid?" I mocked him, but I didn't hesitate to huff in more of his smoke. Quite frankly, I didn't give a fuck anymore. Again, probably the smoke talking, but the sentiment was becoming grounded in me. "I'm not scared of you, just so you know. Coello, maybe, but I bet I'd beat you in a fight." I didn't mean to keep expressing my conscious thoughts verbally, but I couldn't seem to help myself.

Hmmmm… A truth serum? That must have been what this smoke was. That would make sense from the

Wonderland Psycho—ahem—Psych*iatrist*. Whatever, I was done hiding my feelings anyway. I didn't need drugs to give him a piece of my mind. That was something the meek, easy, gullible Alice would need. But that girl died in the White Rabbit's bed.

"Why are you so defensive? You can be as blunt as you like with me, Alice." He kept repeating my name. I'm sure there was some manipulative marketing tactic that told him it would make people bond to him better or something.

"I'm not defensive. I'm just tired of being a pushover." I scoffed, then I pulled back from his position that was entirely too close to my face. "I spent most my life trying way too hard to fit in, spent my entire adulthood compromising and jumping through hoops for some guy who didn't care about me, and then I ended up in Wonderland, surrounded by freaks who call themselves animals and bugs, and I've gotten to the point where I don't even care if I die or get captured or whatever the hell the end game is for you people." I couldn't stop. The frustration just poured out of me like someone had broken a water line.

"How sad, Alice." Bruco frowned as he placed a comforting hand on my shoulder. He kneaded my muscles, calming my nerves. "Do you not understand why you're here in Wonderland?"

I blinked several times. "There's… an actual reason?"

The Caterpillar took a huff of his own drugs, then he laughed. "Has no one told you why you're here? Has Coello been threatening you while the Tweedle Twins have been fucking you and the Cheshire Cat mocking you and the Jabberwock chasing you, and not one of them had mentioned your purpose?" He seemed to find that awfully funny, which was also annoying. Fuck, I really didn't like this guy.

"Not. Even. One." I drove home the point.

"How funny." He cooed. Seriously *cooed*. "It sounds like that's all you need to be fixed, my dear. Why what a frabjous day for me that I get to direct someone to their whole life's purpose. How very lucky!"

"I'm listening." I snatched back the pen, and I sucked down all the flavor I could. I didn't care if this thing was lowering my inhibitions. It was getting me high as fuck, and I needed to calm down. "Get on with it. Start fixing."

"Well, it's simple, really." He swept his hands around the room, as if that line meant anything on its own. "But in order to understand the present, you must first understand the past."

"Your past or my past?"

"Wonderland's past." He nodded along. "You see, once upon a time, long, long ago, a young girl named Alice followed a rabbit down into his hole, not realizing she was chasing Coello into Wonderland."

"And?" I nudged, hoping that might help him find the point of his story faster.

"Back then, Wonderland was a wonderful place. A peaceful place. A beautiful place. It was a land of—"

"Wonder. Got it. Yes. Continue." Apparently when I was on truth serum, I became a pushy bitch. I wouldn't be apologizing.

Bruco's brows furrowed, but he continued. "Long story short, she loved Wonderland so much, she chose to return year after year to visit us all. We showed her our games and our magic and treated her to our delicious treats, always begging her to stay. When she reached adulthood, she finally listened, and we made her our mighty Queen."

"The Queen of Hearts?" I asked, now genuinely interested.

"The Queen of Hearts. Our hearts." He nodded. "Though we soon discovered that she, possibly, didn't have a heart herself. Alice was warped by both her time here and her time away. None of us knew what her life was like outside of Wonderland, except perhaps Coello, but we hadn't realized she'd chosen to stay here in order to escape where she'd come from."

"Which was?" I waved my hand as if I was physically prying the words from him. Sure felt like I was.

"A hard life. One where she'd been locked in a cage of darkness and depravity and sex, with no say in her future, her partners, or her destiny." The heavy frown on his face as he said it actually made me frown a little too. "She'd had to kill her master to get free, then Coello brought her back here through the looking glass, where she could finally be safe and happy."

"I'm guessing that didn't work out quite as you imagined." I thought back on the rooms I'd ventured through on the way to see Finn and Tynan, and I couldn't help but wonder if those had been snapshots of *her* life. Strippers, drugs, bullet holes… it made sense now.

"No. Sadly, she'd been wounded deeply by the horrible men in her ordinary life, and she shared that pain not through compassion and discussion, but through the rule of her iron fist. Upon becoming Queen, Wonderland came to reflect her soul, and everything here became a very different place."

"I see." I blinked a few times to process what I was hearing. So many questions popped into my mind. Like

144

why hadn't they put a stop to her once they realized things were wrong? Why did she turn her refuge into the same horror she was running from? "You guys must be stronger than a 'normal human girl' though, right?" I added with a tinge of mockery, considering how many times I'd been called that so condescendingly thus far.

He shook his head. "She wasn't a normal human girl anymore once she accepted Wonderland's crown. She'd grown up here on our games and our eccentricities, and just like that necklace around your neck, the crown was far more than just an ornament."

I glanced down at the pendant that still rested in my cleavage, shining so bright and blue. If Coello was to be believed, this necklace would have given the Mouse total control over me, and I would have become his hopeless puppet. But without Mishka around, the pendant held no power at all. It was just a charm on a pretty silver chain.

"Her crown is enchanted?" I asked. "By who?"

"By the land itself." He said. "So long as Wonderland remains, so too does her power. But, the problem with that is, the land is shaped by whoever rules it, so if a woman who is deeply disturbed should place the headpiece atop herself, so too will Wonderland be deeply disturbed. And if a woman who is pure of heart claims the crown—"

"Whoa, wait stop." I threw up a hand, creating a barrier between myself and what he was about to say. "You guys keep hauling Alices to Wonderland in hopes that one of them will take the crown from the Queen. Am I understanding that correctly?"

"Yes." His face lit up with delight.

"And they have to be named Alice for some reason?"

"The crown is enchanted to her name." He nodded along. I grimaced at the realization that not only was I putting this together nicely, but I had the vague thought flash through my mind that it made *sense*.

"And you need them to be 'pure of heart'?" Except for this part. This part was all sorts of nonsense.

He tilted his head back and forth like a see-saw. "Pure of heart-*ish*."

"Ish." I repeated with a roll of my eyes.

"All humans get a little warped over time, so unless we started kidnapping infants—select infants at that— beggars can't be choosers, you know."

"Have you considered that the humans also get warped when you have a psychotic rabbit threatening to fuck them to death, a cat sending them into a forest full of man eating monsters, some hot brothers fucking their innocence away, and a fucking *caterpillar* giving them drugs?"

Bruco pondered for a moment, looking up at the ceiling while he did it. "Why no, I hadn't considered that."

My palm met my face. "How is anyone supposed to remain pure of heart while you guys all try to kill us?"

"You don't understand." Bruco nudged closer to me again. I had no room to retreat, so I allowed it. "Our games may seem cruel, but they're nothing compared to what the Queen will do to you once you stand at the foot of her throne. If you can't maintain your strength of character throughout these trials, then you would either be tortured far worse by the Queen, or you would end up just as depraved as she is when you acquire her crown."

"What makes you think that any woman could survive this if she wasn't already depraved?" I pushed back. His logic was severely flawed.

"Well that's where I come in." His pretty face seemed to warp as it smirked. It could have been an illusion, it could have been the drugs, or he could have been more a monster than I realized. "I'm the one who tests the Alices for their resolve."

"How exactly do you test—" His hand was on my neck, and my body was pinned to the bed so fast, I had no time to argue or react. He clenched down his fingers on my airways, and he clenched harder still over my pulse, almost immediately cutting off circulation to my brain.

I couldn't fight it. I was gone in an instant.

Chapter 18

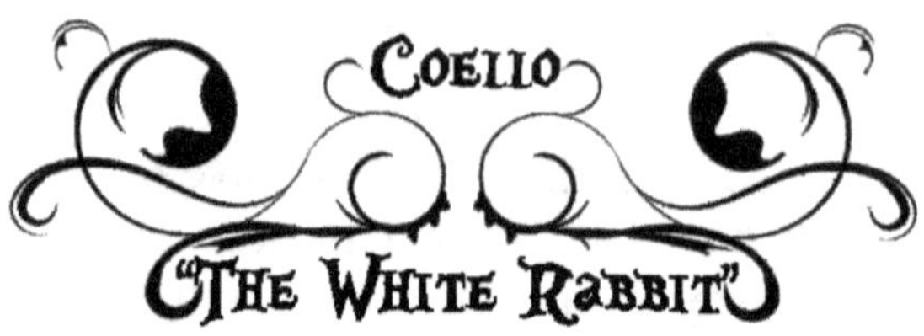

Getting to the other side of the trees was a desperately needed freedom. My body still ached from the impacts and wounds the Jabberwock had left. Though it was hard to say if I was more annoyed by that thing trying to kill me or that Kitten had facilitated it. Alice was lucky she was getting such a lead on me. It would be a minute before I caught up, and I was starting to think that was by the Cheshire Cat's design more than it was my own. He'd possibly gone a bit rogue on this one.

Though it hardly mattered. As long as I found her before she met with the Queen, it would be fine. I was certain Mau wouldn't rush things. We were more or less in this together precisely *because* we were all in it for ourselves.

First, and foremost, it was much more important I checked in with the twins. Mau hadn't specified whether or not she'd moved on, but there was still an entirely likely chance that they might still have her in their bed. While I'd never been twisted in their sheets, I'd heard enough from Mau to know it could be… a hard place to leave.

But that was part of the test. Many an Alice had been left a broken, weeping pile after the Twin's magic degraded their minds into empty sex dolls. I'd seen enough Alices end their journey there, and the punishment for that was sometimes more than even *I* could take pleasure in.

When I surmounted the hill to the Hall of Mirrors, the building itself was notably shabby compared to its usual cottage-like charm. It was falling apart, with boards over the windows, overgrown yet browned ivy snaking around the walls, and holes and splinters in the door. Odd. If they were switching up their illusions, I couldn't understand why they would pick something like... uh... this.

I opened a door that was barely holding onto its hinges, expecting to walk through the usual montage of the Queen's shame, with the short vignettes of her fucked up life, but instead of drugs, blood, chains, and the Hall of Mirrors... there was nothing behind the door at all anymore. On the other side, I was back where I started, with no trace of the illusion to spare. Even the dilapidated cottage I'd originally entered had disappeared.

"Finn. Tynan. Where the fuck are you?" I snapped, immediately annoyed by this confusing turn of events.

"What took you so long?" An irritated voice answered back. I turned to face Tynan, the darker of the two men, who stood against a lone Tumtum tree in the meadow. I preferred him to his more delicate and over-sensitive brother. Tynan had been killed one too many times, and Finn hadn't been killed enough, in my opinion.

"I'll let you guess." I rolled my eyes and placed a hand on my hip. It wasn't like there was ever any question as to *who* had it out for me in Wonderland.

"The Cheshire Cat really will be your undoing, Coello." Finn approached next, and he leaned against the opposite side of the tree from his brother. I resented the statement. "All of our undoing, most likely." He motioned widely, as if to imply Kitten had been the one to shatter their illusion.

That was... an odd accusation.

"Did Mau do this?" I eyed him suspiciously.

"It certainly wasn't Alice. She was occupied." Tynan scoffed. "Even double occupied at times."

"I like this one." Finn added. "She doesn't have a gag reflex at all."

I raised an eyebrow in both of their directions as we stood in that open field. "And yet she's not here." I said with an annoyed sweep of my hand.

"Yes. We *just* told you Cheshire broke our mirrors. He dispelled our illusion, then he hoisted her over his shoulder and left. What part of that is confusing?" Tynan said. Both men stared back at me, as if that was an acceptable explanation as to why they'd lost track of the Alice.

What was *confusing* was the fact that Mau had shattered the illusion *for* her instead of making her do it herself. Being able to break free of magic of her own power was the whole point of the twin's trial. Since when did Mau just hop along and help out? I've watched him skin a woman alive *for fun* after she disappointed him at this stage, so why...

"And he… helped her?" I echoed the question as if to verify I was registering that right. I couldn't be registering that right.

"Considering the world hasn't reset, I'm guessing he isn't off somewhere *punishing* her." Tynan grumbled.

"And considering he vanished with her, I'm guessing he didn't feed her to the Bandersnatch, either."

"Wait, he vanished with her?" I wasn't sure what to make of this. Even if he carried her away from these buffoons, he didn't have to drag her into his alternate time-space. He never shared that with anyone without a good reason.

"Yes." Both men said in exasperated unison.

"For someone so fast, you sure can be fucking slow sometimes." A growl from the dark one.

My eyes narrowed in his direction. "You want to say that again?"

"No, he does not." The light one said, shooting his brother a scolding look. "We don't know what kind of game Mau is playing, but to be honest with you, Coello, I'd say it was rather suspicious that he saw fit to override our control. I've never understood that man's games, but I understand them even less now."

"He just killed the Jabberwock for me, too." I trailed off as I parsed all of this together. In hindsight, Mau had *never* killed his own Jabberwock. That's precisely why it had killed *me* so many times. I thought back on my last conversation with him, piecing together everything he'd said. He'd expressed he was fond of her, but I didn't think that meant he was helping her in some way.

I glanced up at the twins who were staring at me with wide eyes.

"The Cheshire Cat killed the Jabberwock." Finn uttered in disbelief. "What will the Queen say?"

I bit my lip, not answering the question. He had a point. I'd been so distracted by the usual chaos that it hadn't even occurred to me how far off that behavior really was for him. I knew Mau was on *my* side, if no one else's, but he was never one to openly betray the Queen of Hearts. No, he played her very well, always pretending to be loyal when it served him. When Wonderland decided to rebel against her rule, he kept all outward interactions entirely neutral, to the point that the Queen had entrusted him with her favorite pets. And yet today, he specifically murdered the Jabberwock without so much as a second thought. If she found out about that kind of betrayal, to save *me* no less—the person the Queen now blames for all of her problems in life—then she'd execute him on the spot.

So what *was* his game?

"The Mad Tea Party will be starting soon." Tynan interrupted my train of thought. I glanced at him briefly before shifting my gaze to the clock set into the ticking sun. "I'm sure he expects us to attend."

"Right." My eyes remained fixed on the sky, and I spoke absently. "If he's planning something different for this cycle's showdown in the Queen's Court, that would be the place to discuss it."

"Need some help with the Bandersnatch?" Finn asked with a raise of his chin.

"I haven't gotten to kill anything in a while." Tynan cracked his knuckles and rolled his neck.

I nodded to both men, then I redirected my attention toward the bog. Creating a Wonderland without any of the Queen's monsters sounded impossible. *But what if...*

Chapter 19

Like seemed to be a running theme in my life lately, I came back to consciousness in complete and utter darkness. But this darkness felt different this time, and it was hard to explain how. It was warmer. Somehow more confining. Or maybe just more… complete.

I tested the use of each of my limbs, wriggling my fingers and my toes. I wasn't paralyzed, but that was the extent at which I could move. Everything else was wrapped tightly against my body. I tugged at my arm, bound in some web-like strings that stuck to my skin and left behind a slimy residue. Something organic.

Gross.

But it was even worse than just that. Not only was I tied up, but as I slowly oriented myself to being conscious, I also started to realize my whole body was upright. Not laying in a bed, but I also wasn't standing on the floor. I was… suspended to a wall of sorts?

I drew a deep breath and closed my eyes for a three count. Then I jerked my arm in its restraints again. The sticky threads gave just slightly. Enough that I felt like there was hope. Such a fleeting and rare thought in a place like this.

I jerked again, and they gave more. I could feel the mucus-like silk starting to tear and separate under every show of force. One more hard jerk and my right hand was free. But it didn't get far. The momentum of tearing the threads had me hitting bluntly into the wall beside me.

Wait…

Frantically, and hoping with everything I had that I was wrong, I followed the rounded wall with wide palms, hitting into every inch. I had to verify I was feeling what I thought I was feeling. That wall wrapped in front of me, behind me, to my left. There were but inches between my body and the tightly enclosed shell I was in.

"No." I heard myself utter out loud. A word of disbelief that was barely audible over the pounding of my own pulse. My lip quivered, and my eyes started to water. I thought I'd seen all the horrors they had here, but this was something worse. So much worse. "No!" I shouted louder, my voice breaking with the exclamation. I used my free fist and started banging on the barrier.

A cocoon. It had to be. *A fucking cocoon?!* "Let me out of here, you fucking Caterpillar motherfucker!" My screams only bounced off the wall that was entirely too close to my face, shooting back in my ears with all the shrill terror they contained. I wasn't ordinarily claustrophobic, but I also wasn't ordinarily tied up inside a dark void in a world full of happy murderers, and this was a level of trapped I wasn't mentally or emotionally prepared for. I'd rather be stabbed while Coello looked me in the eye or drowned in the twins bathtub or eaten alive by the fucking Jabberwock, but not this. Not suffocating in a dark box with no way out. *Not this. Not this. Not this.*

I tore the remaining threads that bound me, possessed by my own horror, then I pounded as hard as I could on that enclosing shell. But my fists just thudded on tightly woven walls. "Don't fucking do this to me. Please. You can't! I… I can't…" I pounded again, harder and more desperate. I wanted—needed—that wall to give at least a little. I needed some proof that I had a chance of getting out. In all the madness I'd been subjected to so far, at least before there had always been hope. But in this tightly confined darkness, any such thought was quickly sinking.

"This isn't funny. It's not cute." I was trying to sound provocative, but words were becoming a struggle. I couldn't help the tears from building. From spilling. From dribbling down my cheeks, following the contours of my face until I could taste them on my lips and feel them splashing on my chest. "Let me out! Please! If you need to test me, test me. But not like this."

Full break down. My voice was broken by deeper and deeper sobs. My heart pounded in my chest at the near speed of a heart attack, and a sweat started forming on my brow. My breathing only grew more and more shallow. I was going to suffocate. I beat the Jabberwock, I out ran the rabbit, I had the twins wrapped around my fingers, and I'm going to die by fucking suffocation because of an effeminate worm.

I used both fists to bang on the wall at once, timing the hits in perfect unison, as if the combined force would suddenly be enough to break through. Still nothing gave in the slightest. "Fuck you! Fuck you fuck you fuck you!" My yells devolved again into incoherent sobs, which devolved into hyperventilating hysterics. I was swimming through my panic, trying to find some logic to latch onto to calm myself down, but it felt near impossible the more it sank in that I couldn't move. That this space was so, so very small.

But I *needed* to calm down. I needed to slow my breathing. How much air would I even have in a place like this? Was that his *delightful* little game? Fucking suffocate the 'Alice' in a cocoon? How was this even fair? Who could survive this?

But there had to be a way to win, right? If what Bruco said was true, then they don't want me to die. They want me to succeed and take down the Queen and be the new Alice. So… so there's a way out. There has to be a way out.

My bitter sobs burned in my throat, while my rage and my fear mixed to the point that my stomach started to retch. I swallowed down bile in a desperate bid to not cover myself in it in the little space I had, but the taste of shoving it back down hardly helped that cause. It was everything in my power to keep it down.

My legs were still bound by threads, but with how tightly this cocoon encased my body, giving me barely enough wiggle room to even lift my arms and pound against it, I wouldn't have been able to do anything with them anyways. I couldn't kick my way out of here.

Think. Think. Think. Find a solution. Don't let him win. More sobbing interrupted my thoughts. I couldn't seem to help myself. I felt like I'd been buried alive, and I was drowning in dry air.

"Why are you doing this?" My voice cracked in half mid-sentence, no longer hiding any amount of my distress. "Why?" I heaved heavy sobs between every word. I didn't bother to try and stop crying anymore. I couldn't get a handle on myself at all. This was so hopeless. So unfair. "You said you were supposed to help me." Shameful was the only way to describe the last words that dripped from my lips.

"I *am* helping you, Alice." My eyes widened as his muffled voice was barely audible through the walls. "To become a butterfly, you must first undergo a metamorphosis." That condescending piece of shit worm said.

"I'm a human. I can't become a butterfly." My pure anger was the only thing that allowed me to continue speaking at all. I gave in to that rage until it slowly overrode my fear. Though in all my anguish, my voice had lost any bite or agency. It was more flat and pained and hopeless than it was mad. "Just… just let me go. Please." I resented the words. I sounded so pathetic, but I *was* pathetic. I was whatever I needed to be to not die here, quietly suffocating in darkness. "Send me home. I'm not the Alice you need. I'm not a butterfly. I'm not anything. I'm just a pathetic, normal, human girl. I'm a disappointment who can't help anyone." My pleading dipped darker and darker. "I can't even help myself. So what good is it to test me like this? I'm a waste of your time."

"I don't think that's true." His voice through the weaving of his cocoon sounded like a verbal frown. "But I have to ask, Alice, why do you think that's true?"

"I just want you to let me go." I barely managed the words. My voice was hoarse and dry after all my crying, screaming, and heaving.

"No. That's not why you're saying that." His voice circled the shell as though he was pacing around it as he spoke, "Why don't you search a little deeper, Alice. Tell me, what makes you think you're not what we need?"

"How could I be?" I snapped with unexpected vehemence that came from far deeper in my belly than I even understood. "What makes me any more special than anyone else?"

"Wrong answer. Try again, Alice." The way he repeated my name so constantly was starting to get to me. It was somehow both grating and deceptively sweet.

Is that how I'd get out of here? Playing a game of trivia? Was this self-worth bingo? Fuck this. "Because I'm an idiot." I said more calmly now. "Because I'm the kind of girl who people take advantage of, because I don't have a spine. That's why my ex cheated on me, that's why my best friend betrayed me, and that's why I fell for the White Rabbit's advances and ended up here in the first place." I nearly hissed out the last words. "And worse, how I got *here* here, in the first place!" Slowly, some bite came back to my voice. "Because I thought I'd be doing myself a favor for once by fooling around with Finn and Tynan, but no! That was a trap too. Because I always fall into every fucking trap you guys lay out for me."

"And what does that mean, Alice?" His voice, still so calm, only fed my frustration.

"It means I'm a waste of your time. Because I'm a waste of everyone's time." That line sprang from my lips like a hiccup that I could neither predict nor stop. And my eyes widened in the darkness, just hearing myself say it out loud. *Is... is that what I really thought about myself?*

Who am I kidding. I knew that's who I was. I had more than enough proof in all my relationships.

"Is that who you are then?" He asked, as if trying to lead a response.

"Yes." I said stubbornly, not interest in being led through a maze of psycho-analytics with him. It was bad enough what I was saying to myself. He didn't need to be in on my self-admonishment any further. "That's who I am. And that's who I'll always be."

"Good." His tone carried a smile. "That's wonderful, Alice."

"How so?" I dragged fingernails down the wall to no avail. *Why won't it break?*

"Because it means, no matter how cruel and violent and awful the world may be to you, you still cling to your own sense of morals. Even if those morals hurt you, you won't compromise doing what you feel is right. Imagine if everyone could do such a thing."

"Then the real world would almost be as fucked up as Wonderland." I spat with a roll of my eyes. Though to be honest, it was… a nice sentiment. Maybe there was truth to it. My resolve didn't do me much good, since it was clearly my downfall, but it was a pretty way to paint my stubbornness and stupidity as an asset instead of a defect.

"Isn't it already?" He chuckled. "Or are you trying to pretend the world of humans is so kind and good and just? Because it sounds like your problems started long before you arrived here, no?"

"Well that's…" I didn't have a response for that. I just rested my head back against the barrier behind me, and I stared blankly into the darkness. The initial shock of this confined space was starting to wear off as we held this casual conversation. "Those problems were less life threatening."

"I wonder if that's true. Because it sounds like they were killing you in a different way."

"In a less permanent way." I corrected.

"I might disagree. The death of a person's soul is far more permanent than the death of a person's body. One will carry into eternity, the other will begin a new cycle."

A new cycle? My ears perked "What does that mean?"

"It means exactly what I said."

"Are you saying I'll be reincarnated when I die?" I pressed. Finn and Tynan had hinted at such a thing. But no one had confirmed anything. Perhaps I was fearing this whole place needlessly.

But then, I saw all those Alices in Coello's dungeon. So…

"Oh no, not you. I forget sometimes that death for Alices is more permanent. It's only the rest of us who get to come back on every cycle."

Wait… what? "What do you mean by a cycle?"

"An Alice cycle. Your lifetime, Alice. Every one of you starts a fresh beginning for Wonderland when you arrive. And we start over again when you die."

I shook my head silently to process the thought. "So if you kill me, Wonderland… resets?"

"Yes, of course."

Yes, of course. I repeated in my head mockingly. "Of course, why?"

"Because the Queen's kingdom will always remain as it was at her peak moment until someone else takes over and creates a new snapshot of the world." He implied that it was obvious, and somehow, by Wonderland rules, it seemed reasonable to me. "So if the new Alice dies, we return to the time before the Alice arrived, and everyone comes back anew."

Interesting. "Do you retain memories when you die?"

"Why wouldn't we? Like I said, it's only our bodies that must be revived. The spirit will always remain."

"I guess that explains why you don't care if you kill each other." I spoke absently, while my attention drifted down to the pendant still around my neck. The Mouse's pendant. The Mouse who Coello had apparently killed more than once. I wondered if Coello had ever died? Mau? Finn? Tynan? "Have you ever died in one of these cycles?"

"Me?" He seemed surprised by the question. "Many times. I've lost count, to be honest."

"What does it feel like?" I nudged while still jostling the pendant around in my palm.

"It's not fantastic."

"It must be traumatizing." Now I was the therapist, turning this whole thing around completely.

"Perhaps. We never come back quite the same after. You lose a touch of your… for lack of a better word that you would understand, *humanity* each time. Things that were unthinkable become thinkable. Things that were scary become normal. Death is a great evolution of perspective."

So thoughtful and deep, this Caterpillar. Though that somehow made sense to me. No wonder everyone was such a psychopath. I could only imagine what kind of evil the Mouse had in store for me when he placed this pendant around my neck if Coello killed him on the regular. Maybe the White Rabbit really did save me in more ways than I realized. It would be nice if he could show up and do that now.

No. I wasn't some damsel in distress. I wasn't about to wish for the same man who kidnapped me to come to my rescue. This wasn't some Stockholm Syndrome love story. I'd save myself. Somehow.

"Don't you see a problem with locking your only hope in a small, tight space though?" I turned the pendant over in my hand again, this time feeling along its edge with my thumb. It was a smooth wedge that came to a rounded point at the end of the necklace. "How long do I have before I run out of oxygen?" I asked, trying to keep his attention. Talking both kept me distracted and kept my mind moving to anything that wasn't my predicament. Keeping the conversation going as long as possible was helping me clear my head.

"It could be minutes. It could be hours. It's impossible to know." His voice implied a shrug. "It really all depends on how quickly you're breathing in there. Fear wastes so, so much oxygen, so please, Alice, hold strong to your resolve."

I tilted my head and tugged the pendant up and over using the limited space within the cocoon. "Wouldn't it be a waste if I died over something this unnecessary?"

"Everything is necessary, Alice." A hum followed the statement.

So annoying. I sighed at the response then gripped the pendant in my hand. The decorative gemstones cut into my palm as I squeezed it tightly. *Maybe…*

I slammed the pendant into the wall of the cocoon, and the whole cocoon shifted slightly. The closest thing to a notable impact I'd managed since I'd begun.

"What are you doing in there, Alice?" Bruco asked with a curiosity. A curiosity I wouldn't be entertaining.

"You would know if you hadn't trapped me out of sight, now wouldn't you?" I taunted back before slamming the pendant into the wall again. The woven tapestry of the cocoon seemed to shudder slightly again. It wasn't much but it was something. I squeezed tighter and hit harder. Then again and again until my hand was bleeding from the impact and scraping of metal and gem stones in my palm.

"Force won't be enough to break the silk." He said nonchalantly. "But I'll be here to continue our conversation once you tire yourself out."

Like he would admit it if it would. I ignored him and kept hitting the edge, knowing somewhere in my gut that I was onto something. Each strike just caused my hand to bounce back over and over again, but there was movement in the chamber, and that had to be good. Maybe I could knock myself down from wherever this cocoon was mounted, and maybe that would be enough to shatter it.

I drove the pendant into the wall again, and again, and again. I didn't seem to be making any actual headway, but I had to keep trying. He'd just about confirmed he would let me die in here, and I really didn't want to die yet. If I did, they'd do this to another poor girl, and I'd be another one of the White Rabbit's trophies.

I slammed the necklace into the wall again. Clutching the pendant hurt. It hurt so badly. It was grating at my palm and making me damn near cry as the gems tore skin. But I just wanted out of here. I'd learned some useful things from Bruco so far, but they meant nothing if I let him suffocate me in his silk coffin.

I could feel my blood starting to drip down my wrist, but I kept pounding. The liquid splattered against myself and the cocoon walls from the momentum of the impact. I licked the metallic flavor off my lips and kept pounding.

"Sweet Alice, you're going to use up your oxygen much too fast if you keep straining yourself like this. Please just talk to me. I promise I'll consider letting you out. You just have to do as I say." Bruco pleaded with unexpected sympathy. I didn't want his sympathy. He didn't get to have all the power when he was the one causing me pain in the first place. I'd given that kind of agency away too many times already. Not today. Not to him. Not to Wonderland.

I was seeing red in all this darkness now. I hit harder. The pendant nearly slipped from my hand it was so

163

wet with my own blood. Another hit, and it did slip. The whole necklace tumbled to my feet. In such a tight chamber, it would be impossible to bend down to retrieve it again.

"Fuck!" I screamed, and the word echoed back to me as it ricocheted off the walls.

"Are you finished now?" He prodded. So smug. So *fucking* smug.

"No." I gnashed my teeth together, now too angry to let the fear settle in me again. I was onto something. I was getting somewhere. I know I was. I slammed my palms against the wall out of sheer frustration.

And that was when I felt it. The weaving of the cocoon seemed to… shift. Under the dampness of my blood, the threads lost some of their firmness. They softened. They squished.

My eyes widened at the realization.

My blood.

Was that the secret? Did I just need to get the cocoon wet?

I smeared my red hand over the surface, feeling threads separating under every stroke. The solid texture turned to something more akin to raw meat, and the muscle like surface was easy to sink my fingers into.

I drove in one digit at a time, using the point of my fingernail to concentrate the pressure in a single spot. I latched on, then I tore the flesh-like wall with every ounce of strength that I could.

The threads tore like snapping sinews, one at a time, making wet squelching noises as I squeezed and separated each handful. Sticky globs clung to each other as I removed chunks from the wall, stretching silk threads like gooey strings of fat that gave only when forced. I dropped the heap of cocoon on the bottom of my casing then I squeezed my hand into a fist to assure the blood kept flowing. Another bloody handprint and another portion of cocoon ripped away. Another and another and I saw my first hint of light. A single pin hole, complete with the fresh oxygen that flowed in freely. I took a deep, relieved breath, then I grabbed another handful.

"How did you…" Bruco's voice was distant in my ears. If he said more, I didn't hear him. I didn't have time to listen. I didn't have time for anything or anyone but saving my own life. I ripped another chunk, forming a slit down the center of the barrier, one fleshy inch at a time.

When my first hand's wound started to dry up, I put my thumb to my teeth and bit hard enough to break skin. I didn't give myself the time to contemplate whether it would hurt or whether I had the gumption to maul myself for survival. There wasn't time for that.

I squeezed blood from my torn flesh, and I smeared a line down the center of my cage. It was just enough fluid to finish the job, as my finger broke through into the open air.

I clawed through the shell until I created a wide enough slit, then I tore the bindings from my legs, and I shoved myself out of the opening, using every muscle in my arms to pry that shell open and set myself free.

The Caterpillar stared at me wide-eyed as I climbed from his prison. His lips dropped in surprise, and sweat decorated his forehead. I must have been quite a sight, climbing from a fleshy membrane, covered in the spatter of my own blood. Maybe this was what it felt like to become a butterfly.

I wrenched myself from the pod, and I hopped down onto the solid ground of his soft mushroom house. Then with a swallow and a breath and an overwhelming sense of relief, I lifted my eyes to my captor.

I stood up straight and tall, and I dusted myself off.

The look in his eyes could only be described as horrified. Shocked. Incapable of words.

Seeing he wasn't going to offer his own words of congratulations, I walked over to him, and I glared with all the daggers in my soul.

Then I struck him as hard as I could across the face with a wide open palm. "How. Fucking. Dare you." I screamed at him, then I smacked him a second time with all the remaining strength in me. Both slaps left behind dark red handprints. "How *fucking* dare you do that to me without so much as a heads up."

"Oh, would it have been okay if I warned—"

"No! Don't you start this play on words bullshit. It is *never* fucking okay to do that to someone." One more scream, and I'd gotten out the brunt of my rage. I took a deep, deeeep breath, then turned towards his door. "I'm done with this. So fucking done with all of this. Where does this Queen of Hearts bitch live, so I can go over there and demand she send me the fuck home, and leave all of you assholes to deal with her wrath for the rest of your infinite days?"

Bruco swallowed, clearly not used to anyone standing up to him. He rubbed his cheek with his palm, then he looked down at his hand to take in the amount of blood I'd painted his face with. The squiggly expression across his lips made me think he might cry.

Good. I hope he's offended.

"You… you were supposed to pass the trial by answering my questions and keeping calm under pressure. This isn't…" He was a jumble of thoughts and I was a volcano of impatience.

"Well, sorry I couldn't become your precious little butterfly." I scoffed before returning to the hanging cocoon. It was a grotesque thing when visible in the light. It looked like a coil of spider webs and mulch, hanging like a sad ball sack in the middle of his tiny doctor's office. And he thought it was okay to put me inside of this thing? He probably made it himself with some fucked up caterpillar excrement. And he made me *touch* it. Fucking disgusting.

I shook my head before climbing back up to fish out my pendant. It took some effort, but I was able to just barely grip it with my fingertips.

Triumphantly, I held up my necklace, then I hopped back down from the bulbous pod.

"You cut your hand on the Mouse's pendant." He said, dumbfounded. "How did you know your blood would dissolve the cocoon?"

"How could I have missed that point when all your dumb questions were making my ears bleed?" I scoffed with a roll of my eyes before storming to the door. Just to be dramatic, I kicked it as hard as I could, sending my foot right through the unexpectedly squishy wood.

My expression flattened as I yanked my foot back out of the new hole, then I proceeded to open the door by its knob like a normal, civilized person.

"Serves you right." I grumbled before I made my exit.

I pounded my footsteps away from the good doctor, assuring he heard my rage as I walked… somewhere. I was in the middle of some weird mushroom forest, and truth be told, I had no clue which way was where, but at this point, I didn't even care.

"Come get me, Coello!" I yelled into the open air, hoping he might hear me. I wanted everyone to know how done I was with their shit. After that stunt, it was hard to be scared of much of anything. Let alone some guy who identifies as a rabbit. "Come on! Hurry up! I'm not running anymore!" I shouted.

But nothing. No answer.

Of course there wasn't.

Chapter 20

I sneezed then rubbed my nose as we traveled into the bog. Someone must have been talking about me.

"Coello." Finn called my name, drawing my attention back to the path between their Hall of Mirrors and the Mushroom Forest. He motioned toward the mossy edge of the grass before it plunged deep into the Bandersnatch's swamp. The ground disappeared completely under the black water. "You've crossed this bog several times before for previous Alice cycles, have you not? How did you do so in the past?"

I glanced between my companions, then back at the bog itself. My eyes darted from one set of tall brown reeds and overgrown grass stalks to the next. No movements. Even the most subtle would be enough to betray the Bandersnatch's location in the water, so either it was resting, or it was preparing to pounce. "Mau was usually working *with* me instead of *against* me in the past, so it was rarely an issue." I gave Tynan an accusing bit of side-eye, "and most the Alices who got past the Jabberwock didn't make it out of your bed, so it's not like I have to do this often."

"Not my fault bitches like being choked." The dark one shrugged with a chuckle.

"They usually don't like being choked *all the way* though." The light one rolled his eyes at his brother. "Though I'll admit that most of them don't have much opinion anymore once we get that first round of enchantment into them. This one actually…" Finn paused. He lifted a finger. "She was… quite active the whole time actually."

Tynan blinked a few times. "She was. She even gave consent when we… uh… ahem."

"Double penetrated her." Finn added nonchalantly, like that was a completely reasonable way for the day to go.

I raised an eyebrow. "How am I the least fucked up of all of you?"

"You literally keep a room full of corpses, and I'm not convinced you've never gotten off on one. Or in one. Double pussy penetration is a pretty well-adjusted good time by comparison." Tynan noted with all of his snark. "But that's not the point he's getting at. The point is that if she was participating actively, then she wasn't under our enchantment at all."

"You just thought to mention that now?" I was befuddled as I stared at the two of them. But also… intrigued. "How did you not notice?"

"I mean… we were a little caught up in the moment." Finn mumbled.

"It was hard to think about anything but her when she was riding me like that." Tynan shot his gaze to the floor. "That means Mau broke our mirrors for no good reason. That bastard."

"The nerve." The Tweedle Twins went on to bicker with each other over their shared annoyance with the Cheshire Cat, and I went on to lose myself in that realization.

The Alice was completely conscious as she got in bed and stayed in bed with both of them? She bit me, outran the Jabberwock, and she resisted their enchantment? Mau must have noticed, even if these two dunces hadn't. That must be why he helped her. *Oh Alice, my dear, this bodes well.*

"What does it take to resist your enchantment?" I interrupted their arguments.

Finn stopped to contemplate the question first. "Security, I suppose?"

"Confidence." Tynan added.

"What does that mean?" I pursed my lips at their predictably obtuse answers.

"Let me try to explain this a bit better." Finn began. "You used to always whisk away your Alices as soon as they turned eighteen, no? They're usually quite young and still figuring out how to build boundaries and self-worth. None of them truly know quite what they want in life or a partner yet. As such, they're often rather thrown off by the over stimulating and oft chaotic rhythms of Wonderland." He thought on it for a moment. "This Alice is how old?"

"Thirty."

"And how jaded?" Tynan asked with an amused snort.

"She just got fucked over by some guy she was partnered to for a human decade." I answered mechanically, reciting the information I'd gathered before I approached her. "So… pretty mad at the world, I'd say."

"Fascinating. But apparently useful." Finn nodded. "Why did you pick her?"

"Because the definition of insanity is doing the same thing over and over again and expecting different results?" I said with a shrug. "Something about her drew me in. She's got some fire in her eyes." I struggled to articulate what exactly that *it* factor was though. Perhaps I didn't even understand it myself.

It was difficult to pick an Alice for the trials time and again. I never knew what was going to work, so I generally shot for women who were at peak physical performance. There were always a modicum of Alices on my list of candidates, but the Commonland was a difficult place in many ways. So many were as bad off as the Queen, herself, coming from lifetimes of being broken down, abused, and scarred. Initially they came into Wonderland thinking it was an escape or a dream no matter how bad it was. They didn't take it seriously. I had to up the ante substantially to get them to all start taking it seriously.

Some made it fairly far, thanks to the armor they'd built from the years of pain and defending themselves, but others were quick to resign themselves to their fates, feeling undeserving of power even if they achieved it. None of them had the ability to roll with the punches and stand up for themselves against any of us.

Maybe that's what I liked so much about this Alice. She was prickly and demanding and taking up space, and not one of us had overshadowed her yet. Even when she was losing, she made sure we knew that she was going to go down kicking and screaming and cursing our names. Perhaps if the Queen had half of her fight, we wouldn't be in this predicament right now.

But while all of this spoke to great promise for the tasks at hand, none of it solved the current issue of having to cross the bog.

Tynan commanded darkness, which wasn't helpful when you were dealing with a swamp monster. Finn commanded light, which was equally unhelpful when that same monster was also blind. And all I had going for me was my swiftness. I glanced at the sun again, ticking ever closer to the Mad Hatter's Tea Party, then I frowned outwardly. "A boat will get us across. But I can't promise we won't have a fight on our hands."

"Then let's fight." Tynan said casually.

"If we remove the Bandersnatch, the Queen will be that much weaker." Finn spoke with a hesitant but hopeful confidence. "She's come to rely so heavily on her monsters, I don't know how strong she truly is herself anymore."

I nodded to them both, then I got to putting together a boat.

The trees in Wonderland were compliant. Much easier to work with than the personality-less plants of the Commonland. With a little convincing and a promise of brighter skies and happier days ahead, they lent me their branches and bent them into convenient shapes. Each piece held together by their wills alone, and before we knew it, we had ourselves a simple row boat. All three of us boarded the little craft, and the branches formed oars that paddled slowly across the deep bog.

I kept my eyes peeled for any burbles or sways that would indicate we were getting closer to wherever it hid beneath the water. The black surface of the bog made it deceptive of its depth, and it was hard to know what portions were but knee deep, and what were deep enough to hide an entire beast. The Bandersnatch wasn't a tiny thing, after all.

Still we floated along, and my mind drifted back to Mau as we passed.

His behavior had been truly strange. He'd sealed himself as an enemy of the crown the moment he murdered the Queen of Heart's Jabberwock. While we reset the world on a regular basis with each new Alice's death, that didn't mean that we all forgot what came before. The Queen would recall what he'd done, and that would likely mar his status as her favorite pet in all future cycles. Which, while his status in her court was certainly more treacherous than it was faithful, his loyalty to our side of the rebellion, paired with his ability to play both sides, was the one, single advantage we had in these games. To cross her now meant he either had a plan, or he wanted to throw the entirety of Wonderland into chaos. And to be honest, you could never tell with him. Both plots were equally as likely.

I glanced between Finn and Tynan, who both scanned the water for the first sign of our adversary. They also seemed to have a different view of this Alice. She had resisted their spell, after all: something no one else has ever done before. It was strange to see everyone else getting on board with her potential. I was the one who picked the Alices every time. It was always on my shoulders to find the one, single girl who would lead us to liberation. Which is probably why it felt kind of nice to see everyone appreciating my efforts for once. The failure to find a good Alice, time and again, had built some thinly veiled animosity between us all, more out of frustration than anything else, really, and it was unexpectedly pleasant to be getting along and working together again.

The boat drifted past some rocks, then it entered the forest of reeds. That was when I detected the first hint of movement. I tensed, wishing I had some Jubjub Birds at hand that could be used as weapons, but I knew we'd be on our own here. Three against one should have been fantastic odds, but there was no such thing as favorable odds against a Bandersnatch.

Bubbles of an animal releasing breath pushed to the surface of the water and popped in small explosions of black liquid. We all froze in stance, no one wanting to be the first to say a word. Maybe if we were lucky, it wouldn't notice us. It might mistake our vessel for some wayward branches drifting through the bog, and let us pass safely.

The growl that followed created small vibrations that radiated outward from our boat. A sonar of sorts was the only way it knew how to find prey, since it had lost its eyes all those cycles ago. But it was good at it. I had no doubt he'd figured out our situation.

Silently still, Tynan swept his hand horizontally in front of his chest. The darkness of the black water started to bounce from its depths, and it all gathered in a line in front of him. The shadows of the muck twirled and wove themselves together until they'd created an intricate sword.

Finn struck his hand vertically, drawing in the sparkle of the ticking sun. Another blade began to take shape. I stared at both of them skeptically. That was… new. Where had this power come from?

Tynan and Finn both closed their hands around the hilt of their magic blades. The water's surface was clear now, having had all of its darkness drawn away. And like a curtain had risen on the stage, we all stared into the open mouth of the Bandersnatch as it lined up its lion-like jaws to clamp around our tiny boat.

"Jump!" I shouted but milliseconds before mighty white fangs crushed the boat beneath us. All three of us scattered into the water. I splashed through the thin veil of surface tension, and I was engulfed completely by the bog. Now in its lair, the vision of that monster came fully into view.

Part lion, part whale, part gator—it was a conglomeration of beasts that could swallow someone whole, topped with the attitude of a robot programmed only to kill. It had no eyes, but its mane was scaled, and its claws were sharp, while its large tail gave it the power to propel itself quickly and forcefully through the water. It swiped at Tynan, but he managed to deflect the claws with his blade. It bit at Finn, but he swam backwards, using his own light sword to keep the thing at arm's length.

The Tweedle Twins kept it well distracted, and I used that moment of respite to dart for the surface. I stole a quick lung full of air before its mighty tail came smashing down on me, forcing my head back under. I'd have been crushed by it completely if Tynan hadn't come to my aid.

The dark sword pierced through the Bandersnatch's tail fin, and Tynan met me with his pitch black eyes in the water. He motioned with his chin towards the other end of the bog. I shook my head. I wasn't going to abandon them both and risk losing them. Ordinarily that wouldn't have bothered me. I'd see them again after the reset, after all. But today, there was a real risk of them being permanently erased from Wonderland, and I wasn't willing to take that gamble.

Before I could protest, a sword of light sliced clean through the tail of the beast. The Bandersnatch roared, and every Slivy Tove in the bog went darting for cover. The beast thrashed as its blood bloomed in the liquid bath, and all three of us shot up for another quick gasp for air.

"We've got this handled, Coello. Go on ahead." Finn said before he dove back down.

"He's right." Tynan insisted next. "The Bandersnatch has no heart, so your magic won't help here. But ever since that last encounter with Alice, I think *we* gained strength more than we tested hers." The smile on his face reflected genuine appreciation. It was an expression I'd not seen from the dark one in ages. "We'll survive."

I nodded my head. I wanted to ask more about when they'd realized they could now turn their darkness and light into weapons, but there was no time for casual show and tell. If their encounter with Alice had made them stronger, then it was all the more reason to assure this round ended in victory. I had to trust them. They'd never failed me in the past, and there was no reason to think they'd start now.

And if they died here? Well… it wasn't too late to kill this Alice just the same. I didn't want to, but if I had to choose between a vague chance at a successful revolution or the men who I'd shared Wonderland with through tragedy and hardship, I would still choose them. All I could hope was that I wouldn't have to.

Against an unexplainable tight pang in my chest, I turned my attention to the shore, and I swam with everything I had. The gnashing of teeth, the roaring of mighty vocal chords, and the splashing of battle raged behind me. When I made it to the grass, the twins were still fighting, and if I didn't know better, I might even say they had the upper hand. Tynan had removed a claw. Finn was deflecting the remaining one.

I hesitated to run for only a moment, then I shook my head and turned sharply on my heel. Yes, I would trust them.

Chapter 21

Alice

It felt like I was stomping about for hours, and the mushrooms never seemed to cease. I'd been making a scene of my frustration for so long, in fact, I'd gotten too tired to keep at it, and I resolved to just walk like a normal person for a bit. The Caterpillar wasn't chasing after me or anything, and Coello was nowhere to be seen.

When the Mushroom Forest finally started to wane, I found myself upon a small house, this one more normal than the mushroom shacks or Finn and Tynan's Hall of Mirrors. It was just an ordinary home of an ordinary size. Too ordinary for Wonderland.

Dare I enter it? I sighed and ran a hand through my hair. I wanted to sit down and think and collect myself, and it might have a bed or a sofa or a table at least. But it also might have another test or a psychopath who will lock me in an enclosed space for fun.

And if I paused too long, it might also mean the time Coello needed to catch up to me. Which… did I even care at this point? It had been so long since he'd been on my heels that I struggled to be afraid of him anymore. Not with everything else I'd seen anyway. At worst, he might show up and have his way with me, which I might even enjoy at this point. He wasn't bad with his fingers, and I could use a way to ease some tension.

It's a bad sign for my mental health when such a thought is even allowed to cross my mind.

I sighed and yet I still approached the house. I didn't bother to knock. If someone was there, I wanted the jump on them. I needed the upper hand for once. So I attempted to force open the door with a hard kick. In my mind it looked as cool and smooth as when a cop busts through a door in a movie, but in actuality it took about five attempts and some huffing and puffing, only to have me giving up. I settled for taking a seat on a bench swing that was mounted to a mushroom tree outside.

Fortunately, despite my commotion, nobody answered the door. It was genuinely empty. Not an ideal situation, but at least I could take a breather.

The ambience was that of total silence, other than the foreboding and suddenly extremely noticeable ticking of a clock. Where this clock was, I couldn't say. But it was a soothing tick, and I didn't care to seek it out, lest I ruin that peace for myself. All I cared was that I appeared to have found a place where I could be alone for once.

"Oh what's this? You saved yourself?" A voice popped into my ears so suddenly I jumped. Like magic, Mau appeared beside me on the bench with his always wicked smile, his always enchanting violet eyes, the complimentary dark hair, and that annoyingly attractive and put together purple suit. "Fantastic work, Alice!"

"With no thanks to you." I huffed, crossing my arms in spite of his enthusiasm. I stood to leave without so much as offering eye contact. I didn't know where I was going to go, but I wasn't going to stay here and be mocked by a cat. Certainly not when he was the one who left me with the Caterpillar in the first place.

But Mau caught my wrist and tugged me back down onto the hard bench. I should have fought him more, but it was right when he enveloped me with his arm that I realized exactly how mentally and physically exhausted I was at this point. So I gave in. He wasn't here to kill me, I was certain enough. So I could at least entertain what little comfort he offered.

"What do you mean? I brought you there in the first place. You *couldn't* have saved yourself if not for me." He… sounded perplexed. Genuinely perplexed! This fucker…

"That's because I wouldn't have been in danger if not for you! I can't save myself from danger if I'm not *in* danger!" *Christ, I've been here too long. I'm starting to talk like them now.* Everything was a play on words and bullshit and repetition and riddles.

"Oh, that's not fair, Little Dove." He wrapped that arm more snuggly around my shoulder, and he pulled me in.

I squirmed in his grasp, pointless as I knew it would be, and I used what little energy I had left to direct my anger where it belonged. "Stop calling me that! I'm not your *Little Dove*. You're not my friend. You're not my lover. You sure as fuck aren't helpful. You… you're just as mad as the rest of them!" The more I tried to wriggle free of him, the more firmly he held me. I don't know if that made me more angry or if that kind of strong secure grip was actually weirdly comforting. Whatever the case, my face was hot with some kind of intense feelings.

"Alice, *my dove*," He said for catty emphasis as he stroked my hair, "we are *all* mad here. The only difference between you and I, Coello and I, or the twins, or Bruco is that I am the only one who is honest enough to admit it."

I shook my head. "*I'm* not mad."

"Does that not prove my point?" Mau chuckled in a low purr. "If you were anything but mad, you never would have ended up here in the first place."

"I was drugged." I shook my head in fervent denial. "It's not like Coello asked me if I wanted to go on a happy little jaunt through Nonsense Hell, and I followed him willingly down the hole."

Mau snorted. "Really? Because I'm fairly certain Coello is *required* to get an affirmative answer before he can take you here."

"W-well…" I was absolutely *not* going to say that Coello was ridiculously hot, I had been desperate, and I agreed to go home with him. I definitely wouldn't be mentioning that I was going to do so under the context of sleeping with him. None of that was relevant, considering he roofied me shortly afterwards. "I mean, technically, he asked me to come with him, but he didn't exactly specify he meant to his murder dungeon."

"Hmm. Murderers usually don't." Mau shrugged, as if that was the most reasonable statement in the world, and it was totally fine that the White Rabbit killed people. I mean, he was right, technically. No good murderer would tell you that's their kink. But of the many things I was not saying to Mau, I'll be damned if I was going to say *'yes, you're right about something.'* "But you still agreed to follow a man with eyes like Coello, that are so clearly and distinctly inhuman, and that can only be a sign that you were rightly chosen, based on our very specific criteria."

I raised an eyebrow. "And what criteria is that exactly?"

"That you were mad." Mau added in a noncommittal response that revealed nothing, yet so many things at the same time.

"Really? Because I thought the *criteria* was just being named Alice, so I could save your whole fucked up kingdom from the evil queen by stealing her crown." I shot him that *'oh look who isn't so ignorant anymore'* glare of irritation.

"I see the Caterpillar still likes to talk." Mau nodded. "That's the other criteria that we use. But madness is still an absolute imperative."

"Whatever." I huffed, while the Cheshire Cat continued to rub my shoulder with something that almost resembled affection. "So what's next? Have I passed all the tests yet? Or is there some other horror-scenario I need to survive before I can go home?"

"The second one." Mau chuckled to my disdain. "But only one more, and then you're free."

"Free to be slaughtered by the Queen of Hearts?" I asked. Even if I passed all these trials somehow, I had a feeling the reason Alices kept dying here wasn't because the Queen threw them a congratulatory dinner in the end.

"You? Slaughtered? Come now." Mau's tone was unexpectedly comforting. "You not only outran the Jabberwock and escaped the Caterpillar's cocoon, but you made the twins get you off *how* many times without falling under their spell?"

Huh? I scrunched up my nose. "What spell?"

"Exactly." His smile reflected in his eyes in a way I won't dare call cute. "You will be just fine, Little Dove. You are the toughest and most prickly Alice I've ever met, and I personally would put my bet on you in a fight any day. And that's not confidence easily won." He said as he gripped my chin lightly with his thumb and forefinger. I complied as he lifted my gaze to his and held my attention completely captive. "You may want to wash up first though. You seem to have a knack for ending up covered in blood." He mewed. That kind of confidence, even if I felt it may be undeserved, made my heart skip a beat unexpectedly. I fixated on his long, pretty eyelashes as he inched closer to my face, then I froze completely as he neared enough that I could feel his careful breathing on my skin.

He sniffed softly across the spattered drops that painted my cheeks, as if taking in my scent. He was so careful and thorough, it was almost as if he thought he'd need it later. The movements and the heat of his breath dancing along my jaw felt innately animalistic, yet also… intimate. My heart pounded in my chest in heavy beats that I'm sure he could hear as well as I could. Why his closeness made my heart race so intensely, I couldn't say. But… I didn't think it was fear I was feeling. Though I'm not sure I could separate fear from excitement any more.

"Do you like it, Alice?" He whispered against me. "Being covered in blood, I mean,"

"It's my own blood this time." I managed. Though I couldn't help holding my breath in between my words. "I had to cut myself to get free of the Caterpillar's cocoon."

"That's not what I asked." I could feel the slide of his lips pulling into a smile on my cheek. My pulse pounded harder, but I didn't pull away. His intensity was hard to break. To resist.

Mau's broad tongue touched my skin, and I held perfectly still and perfectly tense as he licked the blood from my cheek in slow, savoring strokes. I let him clean me, closing my eyes to focus on the gentle caress instead of the harsh reality in front of me, while a swirling mix of confusion settled in my chest. And an equally confusing hint of curiosity between my legs.

"So this is what you taste like." He purred. I flushed. "The real, honest, unequivocal taste of Alice."

That heart beat had climbed to my ears, where it was moving at a pace I think might kill me. I had to force myself to turn my head from his touch. "You're not going to try to clean all of it with your tongue." The words were tentative and nervous and uncertain. Maybe even a bit questioning in a *'I might be okay with it if you did, but let's talk about it first'* kind of way.

His eyes dipped slowly down the trail of blood spray as it disappeared beneath my bust line, having spattered and dripped down from the bloodied pendant around my neck. "Only with the lady's permission."

I swallowed. I hesitated to give or deny any such permission. So instead, I simply said, "Maybe this house has a shower."

Mau cocked his head back, and he examined my face as if he was trying to read my intentions. I don't know that *I* even knew my intentions at this point.

"I'm certain it does." He purred.

Chapter 22

With a twirl of my fingers, I revealed a key to the home on the hill, eliciting eyes wide with surprise from the little dove.

"Is this *your* home?" She said through her otherwise agape lips.

"Something like that." I responded with a mischievous smile. I'm sure the White Rabbit wouldn't mind if I borrowed his house. Certainly not if it involved getting Alice naked. Ahem, *innocently* naked. He'd given me the key a long time ago, after all, and why else would he do such a thing?

I opened the door, though first taking a moment to acknowledge the slight cracks in the wood where Alice had tried to break her way in. Adorable. She was a bit more spunky than I was used to, no doubt.

Which is probably why I didn't mind welcoming her into Bunny's lovely home.

"The shower is upstairs and to the left." I tipped my chin towards a dual staircase that wrapped around the foyer. Coello's home was quite nice, and I knew it well. It wasn't what I might call modern, but it had a Victorian elegance that suited his rough yet discerning taste. It was a shame he wasn't here right now. He might have made this much more fun. Though for her sake, it was probably for the best that he was still tangled up with my Bandersnatch. As long as he made it to the Tea Party, I wouldn't stress on it. If I had to personally slay yet another of the Queen's monsters, it would be intensely difficult to explain it all away if a new cycle had to begin.

My ears perked at the sound of a turning faucet followed by the running water of a shower. And then the shriek of a very startled Alice.

"Do you need some help in there?" I asked with an appropriate level of mockery as I approached the second floor master bedroom.

"Why is it so hot?" She whined.

"Why would a creature of hell, in a world hand-crafted by the Devil himself, have such hot water?" I reworded the question for her, and she sighed in response.

"I guess that's the most logical thing that's happened since I got here, in hindsight." Her voice was the equivalence of an eye roll, and I couldn't help the small chuckled that escaped my lips.

"You seem so baffled by the logic of Wonderland, but I think if you really paid attention, you'd find this place makes perfect sense. You just have to look at it in context of here and not your Commonland." I stepped into the bathroom, where she stood in a shower as far from the running stream of water as she could be, and she gasped before clutching a towel to her bare body. I shook my head. "I've seen you with the twin's orgasms smeared on your skin. You don't have to be so bashful."

"O-oh." She squeaked. Though she still clung desperately to that towel. Precious. "R-right, you're the one who brought me to the Caterpillar." There was a pronounced bitterness in that statement. But then her gaze lifted to mine with a less bitter curiosity. "Commonland. Is that what you call the real world?"

"*Real?*" I raised an eyebrow. "What makes this world less real than your world? I promise you can live or die here just the same as you would there."

"You can't though." She stood her ground on the statement. "No one dies here, do they?"

"Only the Alices." I pursed my lips. Bruco really did talk too much. "For the rest of us, death is but temporary inconvenience."

"Have you died before?" She was so curious, this Alice.

"Me? Of course not." I emphasized the point by disappearing before her eyes, then reappearing behind her in the shower. She jumped when my hands braced her shoulders. "I'm very, very challenging to get a hold of, even for the Queen's army."

"I-I suppose you would be." Her voice hitched. Being naked and at my mercy seemed to make her feel incredibly vulnerable. I liked *that* expression on her, too.

"Any other questions for me, Little Dove?" I dug a touch more pressure into her shoulders, to assure my presence was fully felt.

"Just how do I turn down the temperature of the water?" She forced the subject.

"You can't." I drifted those fingers down to her biceps, reveling in the way she shook in my hands. "Do you want me to stay in here and help dissipate some of the heat for you?"

"N-no. I'll just clean off with a washcloth." She shot back

"Oh nonsense." I mused, pulling her back a step until the water was drenching my coat. Though she didn't argue as my barrier between her and the showerhead lessened the temperature of the stream that made it to her skin. She was unexpectedly compliant as I pried her hands from her chest and held them up at either side of her head, letting her towel drop to the floor. "Your hands are injured, after all. You'll only make it worse if you scrub too hard on your own." She remained perfectly still as I pressed my chest against her back and whispered softly into her ear: "Let me clean this blood off for you. You've earned a little rest and pampering, Alice."

She swallowed in my hold. Her eyes shot down to her chest, as if confirming for herself how fully on display she was. The water beat down against me, running streams down my shoulders and over her skin. The warm liquid followed every curve and contour of her softly shaped body.

Her cheeks went hot. Hotter than the water, and hotter than the blood in the veins of a Wonderland beast. Then, without another word, she nodded to give me the okay.

"There, there. I'm not going to hurt you, you know." I chuckled against her. Her body shook just slightly as a result.

"I *don't* really know that, to be fair." She whispered.

I released her wrists, and she kept them at shoulder level, not bothering to cover herself again. *I'll take that as an invite.* "Maybe you don't in here…" I placed a finger on each side of her head, rubbing soft circles against her temples, then I drifted my hold downward to her shoulders. I ran pressure down her back, eliciting an involuntary moan at the soothing massage of her sore muscles, then I slipped my hands around her waist, so I could pull her back against me. Those fingers wandered up to her breasts, which were still painted red with her blood spatter, and I settled one hand over her heart. "But you know it in here."

"Y-yeah. Maybe I do—" She cut herself off with a gasp when I cupped a breast in each hand and softly pinched her nipples between my thumbs and forefingers.

"Sensitive here, are you?" I purred against her neck. "I'm just trying to be thorough."

"Keep going." She whispered in a way that betrayed her innocence and betrayed the reservations in her tone. "Clean it all."

"Of course." When each of her nipples was completely firm and clear of crimson, I continued downward, tracing light pressure along the contours of her abdomen, down to her navel. I slipped a finger inside, and she pressed back against me. I trailed that same finger in a steady line, drawing down her center. I slipped lower and lower, until I was but millimeters from entering her folds. "Where else do you feel dirty, Alice?"

She bit her lip. A most appealing expression. "Lower."

I couldn't help the chuckle that I shared with her body. "Oh? Do you mean here?" My middle finger dipped in slightly, until I was pressing gently on the top of her clit. Rubbing small circles made her tremble against me. Her breathing was short and nervous. I took that as an opportunity to lick the blood flecks still speckling her shoulder. I continued a long stroke of my tongue upward, cleaning her neck, nibbling on it along the way, until I was touching my fangs to her smooth jawline. "Or do you need me to go lower?"

"C-can I have both?" The words shook from her throat, but not due to a lack of confidence. No, quite the opposite. She was very sure of what she wanted. I smiled involuntarily. *Absolutely adorable.*

"You can have whatever you desire in Wonderland, *my* little dove." Emphasizing possession effortlessly made her wetter. A little fact I couldn't help noticing as I used my free hand to round her waist, slide down the enticing curve of her ass, then slip between her legs. I penetrated her with the tip of my finger, while I continued to rub those careful circles into her clit.

"I want this then." She moaned, now supporting her weight against me completely. Occasionally the full heat of the water would slip past me, but her body seemed to be getting used to the temperature the longer she shared my body heat. She pressed her ass against my clothed cock. A subtle move to see how much I was enjoying this. *And Alice, my dear, I am very, very much enjoying this.* The taste of her blood on my tongue was enough to drive me mad, but the way she was riding my fingers, the heaving of labored breaths as I worked her near climax, and the water running over her naked curves was everything I could ask for.

It was by the most desperate and wise reaches of my willpower that I wasn't freeing myself and pounding her into the wall on my cock. But I didn't want to take her just yet. I would wait.

"M-Mau." She whispered my name through a husky breath, dripping with so much sin that my willpower nearly snapped. "Keep doing that. Please." I gave in, just a smidge, when I drew my fingers from her pussy, and I slipped those same fingers into her mouth. I tested all of my resolve as I smeared the fluids across her cheek. That scent was ecstasy.

Mmmm, I can take just one taste.

I had her flipped around to face me and her back against the shower wall in a split second. Her gasp was little more than a squeak as I held her by her chin, keeping her head firmly in place, and I licked her own pleasure off her cheek. Divine. She was absolutely divine.

More.

I trailed my lips to hers, and I at last connected our mouths. Her head hit the tile as I pressed into her, forcing her lips to part with my tongue, and tasting every bit of her flavor. She gave in easily, moving with me, and letting me control her mouth. A commanding kiss. One that gave her no quarter. I only broke that bond to allow her to breathe.

Humans, you know.

She was still panting as I dropped to my knees, I braced her hips against the tile, then I tossed her a sly smirk before I pressed my lips against the apex of her thigh. I sucked on her skin, only enough to leave the lightest marks as I made my way back up to center. I wanted to leave only traces of my presence, but enough that anyone inspecting her closely enough couldn't help but notice. *Little love notes to Bunny.*

I slipped my tongue between her legs, first teasing at her entrance with the tip, before sliding up her folds to take a long, savoring taste. And what a taste it was. This Alice was most delectable.

"Oh—" She was no longer capable of words or complete thoughts as I licked, nipped, and sucked every inch of her pussy, rubbing moans through her lips and shudders through her legs. She gripped my hair for support, as her shaking thighs clamped around my ears. She drove her nails into my scalp as I dipped my tongue inside of her again.

I wanted the edge of her sanity. I wanted to find the spot that made her scream, and I wanted to watch her give in completely to the madness of our world. How better to do that than to be lost on my tongue.

Her fingers dug in harder and harder, and I tasted her more deeply, creating a suction mixed with careful rubs and flicks. Her tension turned to trembles turned to shakes turned to the picture of a woman giving in to a full body high. I could feel her release as she cried out. Her voice was an exquisite melody when her knees buckled and she melted against the tile. I stood and I caught her from dropping to the floor, sweeping her into my arms, and sharing her own flavor with her in a deep and probing kiss.

This Alice was perfection.

When the little tremors through her body started to settle, I stepped away and let her find support on her own two feet again. She was breathing heavily, with her lips red and swollen from my kiss, and her breath wildly erratic. Those gorgeous blue eyes found mine, and she stared into me like she was trying to process who I was and what I'd just done to her.

What had I done, indeed.

"Thanks for your help." She said sheepishly. "I can finish up—I mean, I finished but—I mean—"

My smirk was involuntary. "I'll be downstairs if you need me, Little Dove." I shook my head with a laugh, and I stepped from the shower, where she seemed now much more comfortable in the water that bordered on molten. Slowly she was becoming accustomed to Wonderland.

With a snap of my fingers, I was dry again. She nodded, and I left her alone in the room to clean up her mess.

Her flavor still lingered on my tongue as I leaned back against the door and caught my own breath. *What HAS gotten into me?* I asked myself with a heavy note of amusement. I can't wait until we arrive at the Hatter's.

Chapter 23

Alice

I found it exceedingly difficult to think about much of anything after my shower. Or more precisely, after I let the Cheshire Cat play his games between my legs. I hadn't intended to do any such thing with him, but he was… difficult to resist. Even if I ignored his flawless face, that smile of his, and those irresistible violet eyes, he had a way about him that was domineering, yet reserved. Cruel yet playful. Secretive yet somehow honest at the same time. He was a flag redder than the blood he licked off me, yet I kept imagining that phantom sensation of his tongue inside me again.

My mind flashed back to the way it had felt as he slammed me against the wall. The thud against the back of my head. The pressure of his fingers digging into my body as he took me, forcefully and desperately, like a drowning man who had been taunted with air.

Is that what it feels like to be wanted? To have a man actually desire you above all else? To want you to feel good and to get off on your pleasure instead of only his own…

This whole situation was… foreign. Possibly the most foreign of every wild and unexpected turn I'd seen since I got pulled into this alternate reality.

I frowned to myself as I gripped my clothing, trying to build up the desire to actually put it on. How sad that I had to step into an entirely different universe just to know what that felt like. But also... I had never been more happy to have left that old life behind. Maybe Daniel cheating on me had done me a favor. Maybe this was where I belonged.

Wonderland, indeed.

Why was I so adamant on going back anyway? Fight my way through Hell, surviving all manner of horrors, so I can go back to... work? My mundane office job that existed only to make me enough money to live, while offering little more fulfillment than that. To my fake friends and horrid dating? To bills and killing time until I made it into old age with nothing to show for my life?

What if I stayed here? What if I was the one who could take down the Queen in a realm of immortality? Would that really be so bad? To live in a castle as long as I wanted, doing what I wanted, when I wanted, while surrounded by men who wanted *me*. That was a fantasy at best. But it could be my reality, couldn't it? Anything seemed possible here. In all its nonsense, it was also a place of possibility.

When I thought about it, I'd gotten off more in the last few hours than I had in my entire lifetime. Not to mention from more different partners. But these guys all seemed to have a magic touch that my mortal ex-boyfriend had never even tried to replicate. Was it weird though, to be getting off on just about every guy I met, when I knew they all knew each other? Some of them probably even got along. The Cheshire Cat seemed to have oddly positive things to say about the White Rabbit, anyway. What had this place ignited in me?

If you give a girl an orgasm, she's going to want to do it with all of your friends.

I tightened down my corset, wrapped my injured hand in a fresh bandage I'd found in the bathroom, and I stepped back into the master bedroom. That large, luxurious, white comforter looked like heaven. Though not knowing who it belonged to, it would probably be foolish to risk taking a nap in it. Especially if any of these blood stains might rub off on the white fabric.

A stroke of wickedness flashed through my mind, and I considered it entirely too heavily. But no. In all the death in Wonderland, I wouldn't let clean blankets be a victim. They deserved better than that.

I rubbed at my hands absentmindedly, letting my mind drift back to my last conversation with Mau. I guess he was right. Perhaps I really always had been mad.

Should I even be offended by such a thing? I'd learned to survive in a place like this. I've let men ravish me, I've fought monsters, I've even gotten weak in the knees when Mishka was murdered in order to save me. In all my denial, I had to admit… there was a certain appeal to such an accusation. If madness was accepting my own desires instead of fighting for what's right and decent, maybe I wanted to be mad. Maybe I could be selfish and look out for myself and embrace that form of "madness" without having to question whether I might be judged for it here.

With a sigh, I walked down the stairs, and I peered out the front door, where I found my dark haired companion sitting comfortably back on that bench swing. I approached him and took a seat down beside him.

"Feeling refreshed, Alice?" Mau asked me sweetly.

"In so many ways." I blushed as I smiled at him. *Harmless.* The word drifted through my mind briefly. *To me, Mau was harmless.*

"Wonderful." He responded without any hint of irony. "Because it's almost time." With a quick circle of his wrist, Mau gestured toward the sky. In it, the sun shone down in a way that was muted enough for me to stare right into it. And within the shining orb were… the hands of a clock. Hands that ticked slowly. There were no numbers, and there appeared to be far more hours on the face than the twelve I was used to. I could only imagine that same orb would turn into the moon once the hands reached a certain, likely nonsensical, hour. It would fall in line with the rest of Wonderland's logic at this point.

"I don't understand." I remained fixated on those ticking hands, while a man in a small green coat, who vaguely resembled a frog more than a person, entered the yard's white picket fence. Before I could panic or judge him as an enemy or a friend, he pulled a small envelope from his messenger bag, and he handed it to Mau. With a nod, the man wandered off, disappearing as quickly as he'd appeared.

I just stared blankly at the letter. "What just happened?"

"We've been invited to your next test, Alice, my Dove." Mau cocked his head to the side slightly. "It's time for the Mad Tea Party, of course. And you still have to meet the Mad Hatter before we arrive at our final destination."

"Why should I want to meet a man who calls himself the 'Mad Hatter'?" I scoffed at Mau's clearly awful suggestion. "I've seen enough insanity for a lifetime. I would much rather not meet anyone else at all in this horrid place."

"And that's why he's the last person you need to meet."

I sighed, and he laughed again. I'm glad Mau found everything funny, because I wasn't bringing much cheer to this day.

"So what is his test supposed to be? I don't know how much more you guys can put me through at this point."

"What fun would it be if I spoiled the surprise? This is like a training course. If I were to tell you, that would defeat the purpose. But I promise you'll be glad you attended."

"Wait, so these tests are actually supposed to be helpful to me somehow?"

"That would be crazy if they weren't, no?"

I wasn't going to even validate that statement with a response. So instead, I moved on. "Who all is coming? Is this Mad Tea Party going to be dangerous?"

Mau placed a palm in my hair and ruffled it gently. An unexpected gesture of affection. "No one will harm the Cheshire Cat's Little Dove at the Mad Tea Party. Not even Coello would dare."

I stared up at him, eyes wide and unblinking. Was he… protecting me now? Why did that make my heart beat just a few paces faster?

"So the White Rabbit *will* be there."

"I doubt it." Mau shrugged. "But I certainly hope so. He's much more enjoyable company than the March Hare." His hand drifted down to my shoulder and squeezed it gently. "But you don't need to worry about him either way. Wild as it may seem, we're all in this together."

"I'll trust you." I said, giving him a nod of approval.

"And *that* is how I know you're mad." Mau smirked, before placing a kiss in my hair. The first touch that had felt truly right since I'd arrived. Mau was a charmer. A dishonest one, perhaps. Or the most honest one, it was hard to say. Yet somehow, I didn't mind his company. I could only hope this so called Mad Hatter would be as pleasant.

Chapter 24

Alice

The clock ingrained in the sun's face ticked past daylight, and like a piece of cloth absorbing a colored liquid, it slowly transformed into a full moon. A moon that was bright enough to cast shadows in a night that was dark enough to make those shadows terrifying.

"Welcome, my dove, to the Mad Tea Party." Mau bowed deeply as he opened the large wooden door that lead into the courtyard. I entered through the passageway with an uncertain step, and I took it all in.

A long, elegant table of deep brown oak was outstretched before me, already covered in a feast of fruits and pastries. The floor beneath my feet was comprised entirely of small red flowers that blanketed the ground like a red carpet, so dense and so soft, it was impossible to see what lied beneath their petals, and the stone walls surrounding this room were covered in dense ivy that bloomed flowers of aquamarine.

The moonlight sparkled on the fine china that was placed at each table setting, on what appeared to be a dinner set for thirty or more people. But I couldn't help but notice, as that same moon drew my gaze, that the clock had stopped.

Six o'clock, the orb in the sky now said, and no longer did it tick.

Despite the substantial size of the table, and the equally substantial place settings, the only seats occupied were by one man at the foot of the table and one at the head. The one to the foot end was of a very muscular and well-built stature. He sported a burgundy tailed tuxedo coat and a fedora over soft blond hair that highlighted a masculine, rugged face. He appeared to be a man in his late forties, with defined features and knowledge in his eyes.

At the head was a man in similar garb, but he was younger, maybe in his late thirties. And he sported all black instead. Well, other than the metal accents and his messy red hair that was tied loosely behind his head. He wore face paint, of a sort, or he was just very, very pale, and dark rings nearly swallowed his eyes with a gothic style. The man at the head stood from his seat as I entered. The man at the foot remained seated.

The door to the courtyard slammed behind me, making me jump from the sheer noise of it. Mau was nowhere to be seen. Alone again. This must be part of the trial. I should have figured as much.

"Alice, I presume?" He said, with a bow and a tip of his hat, revealing more of that fiery red hair. Decorative chains on his black suit, in the form of belts and fasteners, caught the light as he stood back upright. The design was a combination of goth and steampunk, and his face and build were a combination of powerful and gorgeous. His jawline was smoothly cut from diamonds, his eyes were an irresistible royal blue, and his smile was eerily friendly, even despite the face paint. Surely this isn't the man who had been labeled a "Mad" Hatter.

"You presume correctly." I nodded in confirmation, though I felt like I should have been curtseying with how formal and sophisticated this whole thing was.

"You can call me the Mad Hatter, or you can call me Jacan. I will answer to either." He casted me a winning smile as he replaced his dark fedora atop his head. I was used to these dual names by now. Or perhaps they were more like roles—as though everyone in Wonderland had been cast to fill a specific character rather than be allowed to exist as themselves. "And this is Arlen."

Arlen shook his head in disapproval. "You are to refer to me as the March Hare." His voice was gruff and deep and gave off the fatherly tone of *'and that's final.'* He didn't strike me as terribly friendly or welcoming. "You may *not* call me anything else."

I resisted the urge to roll my eyes externally. He was like a less scary version of Tynan, while Jacan struck me as a more scary version of Finn. Though I had a feeling this tea party would play out a touch differently from the Hall of Mirrors.

"Why don't you have a seat, Doll? The party is about to begin." Red flashed through the Mad Hatter's eyes, so quick I couldn't say for sure I'd seen it at all. I drew in a breath, trying to keep myself calm and un-rattled. I fell back on the mantra I'd been pretending to believe, noting that the men of Wonderland *needed* me to survive these trials, so really, there was little to be afraid of. More or less.

Which was an odd thought, really. I couldn't say if the reason I felt little fear was because I knew this and somehow had fooled myself into thinking these men weren't all killers, or if some unexplainable instinct told me that Mau would step in and keep me safe if anything were to escalate. At what point had I come to have faith in such a thing? This must be what they call trauma bonding. Or Stockholm Syndrome. It certainly wasn't a healthy line of thinking.

But still, I approached the table, and I took a seat dead center, with Jacan on my right and Arlen on my left.

"So what tea do we have today?" I asked meekly, feeling terribly awkward and out of place. The March Hare was staring daggers at me, while Jacan was smiling pleasantly.

"There are so many flavors. Don't you want to try them all?" The Mad Hatter said with a wickedness to his tone.

"I think she's tried quite a few already." Arlen said with a pronounced sniff of the air. I flushed deeply. I suppose between Finn, Tynan, Mau… even a touch of Coello, I'd tried a couple flavors of Wonderland's uh… Tea. But I had no reason to assume that was a euphemism other than my own internalized slut shaming and insecurity.

"I've not tried any of yours." I smiled sweetly at the Mad Hatter, before I tilted my gaze to the March Hare. "I have a feeling *yours* isn't very good though."

The Mad Hatter loosed a laugh that seemed accidental. The Hare scowled. *Good. If I could pit them against each other, all the better.*

"You're clever for an Alice." Jacan smirked. He stared directly into my soul, then he snapped his gloved fingers. "But are you *brave* for an Alice?"

Like magic, a cup of tea appeared in front of me, positioned daintily on a small saucer. A light wafting of steam trailed upwards from the presumably hot, deep brown liquid. I stared at the cup with tentative suspicion. Then my attention was drawn elsewhere as a cup appeared at the seat beside me as well. Then a third at the seat beside that.

"What are you waiting for? You said you wanted to sample all the teas, no?" The March Hare said mockingly. "Are you going to let the tea get cold?"

I scrunched my nose and glanced between them. They'd both already sipped through their cup and were moving on to the next seat in a clockwise direction. There were but four seats now between me and the Mad Hatter. The March Hair was rotating away from me.

"Quickly now Alice. You'll regret it if you get caught." The Mad Hatter added with a grin. "We won't. But you certainly will."

And like someone had just fired off the gun that started a marathon, my brain kicked into gear and I reached desperately for the first cup. I downed it like I was taking a shot. The way it burned down my throat, I may as well have been chugging cheap vodka. For all I knew, this tea was exactly that. But something told me there would be consequences if I didn't play along. I downed each cup as the next popped up.

It was hard to explain the flavor. Cinammon, tumeric, peppermint, tomato sauce? Each drink was scalding yet soothing at the same time. They would burn in my throat just enough to make me hesitate upon lifting each new cup, then they would cool my esophagus with a pleasant coating after each swallow, just enough to make me forget the previous pain and commit again.

I downed a fourth cup, and waited impatiently for the fifth as I neared the March Hare's original seat. But this time, the place setting didn't manifest a new cup like the rest. Instead, words appeared on the small saucer. A riddle. One I'm guessing I had to answer in order to get my next cup.

"What comes once in a minute, twice in a moment, but never in a thousand years?" The March Hare recited the riddle for me. He'd memorized the game, I presumed. And if every day was a repeat of the last, I shouldn't be surprised that it never changed.

"Me?" I said with my tongue in my cheek. Based on my recent exploits, that should have been correct, but I knew it wasn't the answer that the magic tea saucer was looking for. The Mad Hatter laughed. March Hare rolled his eyes. My wrong answer brought both of them one seat advanced.

"Delightful answer, but not quite correct, Doll." Jacan lifted the next cup and swirled the tea inside of it, taking care not to spill a single drop. "Though be careful what you wish for, or we may have to test the theory." *A man who looked like him and sipped tea like that could test that theory all he wanted.* Rank that right next to all of the other thoughts I shouldn't be having. Wonderland was fucking me up.

Both men waited patiently for me to make another mistake and advance the board. I wouldn't be obliging them. I'd actually heard this riddle before.

"The letter 'M.'" I said plainly. And the cup appeared.

Onto the next place setting and the next. "How many of these must I drink? Is it possible for me to win at all?" I asked between gulps. The seventh cup popped up, and I reached for it. If these drinks were spiked, enchanted, or drugged in some way, my body hadn't yet had time to process how. I'm sure that was coming still.

"Once around." March Hare said.

"Then once back." Mad Hatter said.

"Then the game begins again." They both said.

"It is always tea time here. Until the clock regains time, it always *will* be tea time here." Jacan added for dramatic flair.

"Then how can I *win*?" I emphasized again. I didn't know how to make the moon start ticking, but there had to be some goal to this.

"A better question might be how can you lose." The Mad Hatter said, downing two cups faster than I could down one. He was only three seats away from me, but the more I drank, the more full I felt.

"Or a better question than that might be what happens when *we* win." The March Hare said in his grumpy drawl, as if correcting his table mate. His pace was slower than the Hatter, but still faster than mine. The sound of teacups clinking on porcelain made a symphony in the courtyard, nearly resembling music as we downed the next cup in perfect time with each other.

"I didn't ask what happens when you win, because you're not going to win." I snapped back immediately, not letting them see me flinch. I couldn't help but catch the brief grin that appeared on Jacan's face. A smile that caused him to hesitate just long enough to gain back a place setting's worth of distance on him. The game moved quickly and chaotically and I was beginning to feel gorged on so much fluid. But as I glanced around the table, I was only half way through the seats, and then I would have to go all the way back the other way. And even if I did that, it wasn't clear if this had an end, or if it was simply nonsensical chaos like all the rest.

"You simply have to outlast us is all." Jacan answered my question, like that was a possible standard.

I shook my head and downed another glass. Whatever. I'd puke it up if I had to. Or I'd piss myself and ruin my stupid frilly skirt. I didn't give a *fuck* anymore. I was going to win. If this was the last test of Wonderland, drinking fucking tea wouldn't be what was my undoing. Not a fucking chance.

At the tenth seat, immediately opposite where I started, I got my second riddle.

"What flies without wings?" I read the riddle aloud.

"Your head, once you confront the Queen of Hearts." Arlen, the March Hare, said smugly. His wrong answer knocked him back a setting. Good. He deserved it.

"Your heart once I catch you." Jacan, the Mad Hatter, added as he dropped himself another position.

I shook my head to toss off their distractions. I closed my eyes briefly, listening to the silence of the still clock. *What flies without wings?*

Easy.

"Time." I said definitively. The cup appeared. The riddle receded. I grinned and downed it and moved to the next. "Except for here." I said as I glanced up at the no longer ticking moon.

"Time stopped here long ago," Jacan confirmed. His melancholy slowed him. "I'm surprised you noticed. They never seem to notice."

I considered that statement for a moment. While the sun and moon no longer ticked in this courtyard, had time *really* stopped? How could we be moving, and moreover, *racing* without the passage of time? This wasn't a void. But then again… if we were racing, and time didn't exist here… "Please correct me if I'm wrong, but if time is stopped, than it's impossible for you to say you finished faster than I have, even if you do catch me." I challenged him.

"I wonder." The corners of Jacan's lips curled upwards. The Hare just snorted with displeasure and returned to his task.

"Is that the real answer to this game? That no one can actually win." I stared Jacan in the eye, then I drank the next cup of tea while never breaking that gaze. This one tasted like raspberries and chocolate. It was quite nice, honestly.

"You *are* a clever, clever Alice." He seemed pleased as he met my stare. He drank his own cup much more slowly than he had done with the others.

"And you're both predictable idiots." I shrugged then stepped aside clockwise to the next space. Now at the Mad Hatter's original seat, my saucer gave me another riddle.

"Why is a Raven like a Writing Desk?" The Hatter recited the words for me, a taunting glint flashed red in his eyes.

I froze in my tracks, suddenly feeling much less confident than I did before. "Wh-why is a raven…" What did that even mean? What's the difference between a writing desk and a regular desk for that matter? Are those somehow different?

"Tick, tock Alice." The Mad Hatter took another place, closer and closer.

"There's no such thing as time, here." I shot back, ironically to *buy* time in this evil merry-go-round. But sassy words weren't going to fix this predicament, regardless of technicalities. *Why is a raven like a writing desk?* First of all, shouldn't it be '*how*' is a raven like a writing desk? No, this wasn't time to play grammar police. Not in Wonderland. If there was one set of rules they did abide by, it was definitely not the sanctity of the English language.

I ran the question through my brain as quickly as I could. A raven is a bird. It's black. It's a scavenger. It's got a sharp beak. It's got feathers. What of that applies to a writing desk? Desks are wooden, stationary, bulky, heavy. You get work done at them, I suppose. There has to be something deeper than that. A word pun of sorts, surely. Riddles are always some sort of dumb play on words.

At a writing desk, you create. A raven kills and devours. That's not it. A writing desk is… brown? You can write with a quill pen made from feathers. Ravens have feathers. But that makes a raven like a writing instrument not a writing desk. That's not a real connection. So why? *Why* is a raven like a writing desk? Why…

It was hard to think straight even despite the difficulty of the riddle itself. My fear that the tea was more than tea had started to manifest as a fog in my brain. A dizziness caused me to sway and to falter. I caught myself on the table's edge, using both hands to steady myself as I squinted at that riddle. I needed an answer. Any answer at all.

"A raven is like a writing desk because neither one exists in Wonderland?" I managed the words with frustration, while a dark haze crawled into my vision.

"A respectable answer. But also a wrong one." The Mad Hatter's voice was directly in my ear. My eyes widened as I felt the heat of his breath brush against my neck. "*Time's* up, Doll." He said as his gloved hands braced my shoulders. I may as well have taken in a breath of pure chloroform with how hard that tea was now hitting me.

How many times has this happened now? These men seemed to like to drug me or knock me out. It kept me helpless. They probably knew they couldn't handle me when I was at my best.

Weak. *They* were the ones who were weak, not me. Fucking cowards.

But my consciousness didn't fade away completely this time. I could still see. I could still hear. I could still feel. But I couldn't quite seem to move. My body went limp, and the only thing that held me upright was the Mad Hatter himself.

Chapter 25

Jacan

"The Mad Hatter"

"Because it can produce a few notes, though they are very flat. And it is never put with the wrong end in front." Arlen, my dear March Hare, answered the riddle for the paralyzed Alice in my arms. "They never guess that one for some reason."

"I can't say I understand the answer either, to be quite honest." I shrugged, then I repositioned our warrior princess, so I could lay her down gently on the table. Defiance still sparkled in her half lidded eyes. Not fear. Not even animosity. Just the vague glare that said she didn't consider herself having lost yet. Interesting. So very interesting.

"What I find confusing is that we still make them play this pointless game when we know they'll never get it right." He was as grumpy as always. "Not one of these women has ever found a way to get the moon to start ticking again."

"And yet, I still want to believe one might find a way." I placed a palm on her forehead and dragged it downward, closing her eyelids for her like I was performing a kindness for a corpse, then I removed my gloves and tossed them aside. Our tea wouldn't kill her. It would simply immobilize her temporarily enough to let us do as we pleased. And I was pleased to do so very many things.

I touched my finger to her lips, drawing the natural venom from her muscles. "You may speak now, my flawless little doll."

"What did you do to me?" She spoke, but the shake in her voice made it clear she understood that she could move no other muscle until I gave her permission.

"You already know the answer to *that* little riddle." I smiled and wagged my finger in disapproval. Not that she could open her eyes to see it. I hadn't granted her back that sense just yet. "Why not use your lips for words that are more useful." I trailed my fingertips down her jawline, then down her neck, releasing her ability to swallow down her fear and dread.

"Then how about 'what are you going to do to me?'" A bite of her lip to stop it from quivering. Noble but hopeless. She was quite cute when she was scared. Perhaps because that seemed a rare treat compared to the simpering messes that were all the others.

I touched my fingers to her chest, where I could feel her speeding heartbeat. The heart and the lungs were the only muscles that remained unaffected by the spell—only enough to keep her alive. The heart and breathing patterns, after all, betrayed the panic that words often refused to acknowledge, and *that* was impossibly satisfying. "I'm simply going to let you taste my tea, Doll." I climbed atop the table and positioned between her legs. I dragged my fingers down her thighs, driving my fingertips into the muscles to return feeling to her lower body.

Her quad muscles tensed as she realized what I'd done for her. "I… I can feel that." She spoke absently.

"Yes, I'm sure you can." I inched my touch back up, slipping beneath the tulle of her skirt. An involuntary squeak escaped her lips as I drew a circle over the lace of her panties. "And I have a feeling you can feel that, too."

She nodded and she blushed, and I was glad I had given her back that use of her neck just to enjoy that confirmation.

Arlen shook his head, no fun ever on his agenda, then he positioned himself at her other end. He lifted her head into his lap and placed flat palms up the sides of her neck to steal back my healing touch and any power or sensation I'd granted her.

She seemed to pick up immediately on that, too. "So with him I'll feel everything, and with you I'll feel nothing. That's about what I thought." She said with a taunting boldness. I snickered, to Arlen's dismay. But I couldn't help it. This little doll was so amusing. She was really getting under his skin.

He scoffed as he covered her mouth with his numbing fingers to silence her again. "I don't know why the Hatter saw fit to let you talk."

"She has a point though." I smirked, daring him with a cruel grin. "There's a reason I'm the popular one and not even the most demented of us wants to play with *you* anymore, Arlen."

I nudged her panties to the side, and I slipped a finger inside her, assuring she'd have sensation where she needed it. She tensed around me as I slid back out of her warmth, then I ran my hands up her middle, staying over the clothes, yet still radiating enough of my heat to bring her to life. Her body shuddered as I returned sensation all the way to her naval.

"I could do without the Cheshire Cat's games, if that's who you mean." Arlen snorted before he met my hands along the length of her upper body. He interlaced his fingers with mine, clamping over her breasts, giving her only half sensation to her already hard and sensitive nipples that I could feel through the cup of her bust.

"Do you want me to fuck you on my tea table, Doll?" I drew my hands from his, and ran them now along the sides of her waist, bringing back more sensation. I slid my grip around to her ass. I took a handful of each of her rounded cheeks, then I spread them just a touch in my hands. "So many ways to make you scream, and yet with your lips paralyzed, I won't get to hear it. You're so unfair, Arlen."

I pushed her knees wider, then I crawled up her body. I took each of her limp hands and placed them over her head. I locked my fingers between hers and held her hands against the table, pinned under my weight, returning sensation to her fingers but not her arms. I wanted her to be able to squeeze and claw at me, but I wasn't interested in her actually fighting back. That wasn't the point. That wasn't any fun.

I craned my neck to meet Arlen's gaze, who was so very close to mine, while he still had her head situated so gently on his lap. "What do you think? Can I let her speak again? I know how much you like to listen to a lady cry."

He ignored my question, and instead he scooted back, creating distance between us. He even placed her head back on the table in a careful way that implied he didn't want to hurt her. He really was a softy at heart.

Then he rested a hand delicately on my cheek. The tingling sensation of numbness absorbed into my skin then was dissipated back into him. The man whose touch brings death was cancelled by my touch of life. He climbed that hand upward, dancing his fingertips up my face, leaving those same tingles with each tap. Then he flicked the hat from my head, swiftly took a cup of tea, and he dumped it down through my hair. The warm liquid splashed over me and dripped down on the doll beneath me. It dampened her cheeks and stained the lace of the corset that was wrapped around her unmoving body.

"How very rude." I smirked, as he stood on the table and paced around behind me. Though the image of Alice drenched in warm tea, helpless beneath me, was anything but unpleasant. She was quite lovely even when so messy and stained and broken.

"I'll tell you when I'm ready to listen to her talk again." He snapped as he moved into position behind me and between her legs. He never was much for vocal women. Though I never dared ask if he'd simply prefer a corpse. I might become one if I did, and I'd already died at least six times to date. I'd rather not add another to my count.

"Which tea are you going to offer her today?" I asked. She squeezed my hands with what little power she had, and I chuckled at her desperation. Feeling merciful, I leaned in, and I kissed her eyelids, one at a time, slowly and with the softness of a butterfly. She opened those eyes cautiously. Irises that matched the necklace she wore like a trophy of the mouse long dead. I'd never met an Alice who kept such a thing, but it really did look good on her.

I climbed over our doll, and I took the March Hare's original position, with her head placed on my lap. Feeling came back to her neck and her cheek muscles as I massaged gently up her face. I freed everything but her mouth.

She blinked up at me. A look that reflected a mind desperate to appear calm. She communicated so well through those pretty orbs. Maybe when we were done with her, we could keep them.

"I've not yet decided." Arlen said as he tipped his hat. Then like the magician he was, he pulled a series of toys from its cavity. On the table before him, he spread out a multi-pronged vibrator, a dildo, and a series of blades of different lengths and curves that would only heighten the experience. Some of his tools gave pleasure, some gave pain, and all of them would make a pretty doll cry before he deadened their senses again.

I lifted her up by her shoulders, returning more of her strength, though still without giving her full use of her arms. I wanted her to watch. And with how much her eyes widened as he ran the broadside of the blade down her inner thigh, I had a feeling she wouldn't be looking away.

Mmmm, let's see how brave you really are.

I leaned down and whispered, ever so gently in her ear, "I can't wait to taste your tea, Doll."

Chapter 26

Alice

I thought by this point, I didn't know what fear was anymore, but every test in Wonderland managed to be more horrifying than the last. My pulse was absolutely pounding. I'm sure the Mad Hatter could feel it as he absently traced the veins in my neck, like a serial killer lovingly preparing to bleed me out. I think I would have preferred he'd kept my eyes closed. Or that he had left me entirely unconscious for this. The thought of being sliced up before my eyes and not being able to so much as scream was a nightmare I didn't know I had.

I might cry if I was capable of it. But somehow, I couldn't seem to manifest tears anymore. Maybe I'd finally become numb to it all.

The Mad Hatter rubbed my temples as though he was trying to sooth me, but the way he propped me up so I could watch as the March Hare used what I assumed was a vibrator to nudge my panties to the side, implied he was offering no such kindness. Arlen didn't want to touch me, lest he take away my feeling again, so the toy acted as a buffer. He placed the head of the largest prong on the vibrator against my opening, and he pressed it in just a touch.

I jerked my hips in the little way that I could, but I didn't have enough use of my legs to kick or thrash.

"Normally I need to use some tea for lube, but your body is unexpectedly ready." His voice was deadpan, as if

218

this gave him no pleasure. I was glad I couldn't speak, or I might admit that it did give me some. Which was almost offensive, in both directions, to be honest. If he was going to torture me, he could at least get off on it. And if I was going to be tortured, my pussy could at least be on my side. I was almost more annoyed by the contradiction of it all.

But maybe it was because, somewhere inside of me, I still knew they wouldn't go all the way. The one small bit of power I had was that they needed me alive more than they needed me dead. And sadistic as they all might be, they wouldn't risk losing their precious 'Alice' over something so senseless. I *kept* chanting that mantra in my head, because the viciousness of it all didn't reflect the hopeful revelation.

Though where the limit was for a man known as the *Mad* Hatter, of all things, it was impossible to say in the worst possible way.

"I think this one likes it." Jacan moved his hands down to the base of my neck. He braced me as that vibrator came to life between my legs. One prong rested inside me, the other was placed just right on my clit. Waves rippled through every inch of my body that had been granted feeling. And fuck, what a feeling it was.

"I wonder." The March Hare took the dildo, and he dipped it in a cup. It was dripping with tea when he held it up at eye level. I watched on, wide-eyed, as he positioned it against my ass. The liquid, to my relief, provided a hint of numbness, much like I'd experienced when the magic first hit me. I was thankful for that kindness as the large head of the silicon cock pressed into my rear, while that vibrator kept pulsing against my front. I felt so full. So completely full.

I wish I could say I hated it, but he was skillful with the way he moved that dildo inside me. He seemed to know what spots to hit, and they didn't seem to be maliciously chosen. On the contrary, he was hitting *all* the right spots.

My breathing grew more and more erratic as he was pushing me, helplessly, towards orgasm. I drew in heavy, loud breaths through my nose, and I trained my eyes on those movements. I didn't want to come for him, but it was going to be impossible not to if he kept that up. I felt the subtle shake of the Mad Hatter's chuckle as he watched my expressions through my battle to not give in.

Arlen danced those fingers up my inner thighs, leaving a trail of numbness in their wake, then he placed the tip of a knife in the same place, knowing I couldn't feel it as he twirled the blade on its point until I bloomed red. I watched as he placed that blade on his tongue, and he tasted the blood he'd drawn.

"She's quite flavorful, Jacan." He said before tossing the knife to the Mad Hatter. Jacan caught the knife by the blade, not fazed in the slightest by the way it cut his hand. Nor by the way his blood dripped down onto my face. "You should take a taste."

"I'd love to." He stared down into my eyes, and he rested that blade on my cheek. This time, I could feel the cold sharp steel against me. There was no numbness to protect me from the pain.

The pulse of the vibrator seemed to find a new rhythm as that blade drew up the side of my cheek, leaving a trail of fresh blood behind it. I winced at the pain while I was subsequently quivering from the pleasure. It was everything in my power to keep my wits about me, while the contradictory sensations rippling through me were drenching my mind in madness.

Jacan followed that cut with his tongue, lapping up the blood and… healing me as it travelled.

His tongue healed? Wait, so this wasn't just simply the give and take of feeling. It was the give and take of… life. Which meant my nerves weren't numb, they were *dead*.

The Mad Hatter trailed his blade along my other cheek now, drawing the same line of pain and comfort from point to tongue. Then he cut a line down the center of my face, slicing the line of my forehead and down my nose, which he followed with kisses until he settled on my lips. He slipped his tongue inside my mouth, bringing sensation back to me, and I wasted no time before I bit down hard to state my intentions.

Jacan reacted quickly. He pressed his fingers into the side of my jaw, forcing it back open, then he shoved his teeth into my lip in immediate retaliation, deep enough to get another taste. The pain was brief and temporary as another flick of his tongue healed me again. He drew back and locked in eye contact.

"You are superbly feisty, Doll." He smirked as he returned to gently massaging my shoulders. He inched his hands down my biceps, returning feeling and power to each muscle. "Maybe it *would* be more fun to let you fight me, after all."

"Who said I'm going to fight you?" I wanted to provoke him, and I had a feeling I knew exactly how. Though keeping my words steady was challenging as the varying frequency of that vibrator forced a high pitched gasp.

"Heh." Jacan placed his hand beneath my chin, and he held my face in line with his own. "I want to see it. Look at me as you lose yourself. Let me savor that expression."

I held his eyes, steadily and refusing to falter in front of him, and I let those waves take me. Orgasm washed that euphoria all the way through my body. I reached over my head with my newly freed arms and gripped the Mad Hatter's coat. Then I bowed my back completely into the feeling, while those eyes that flickered blue and red watched me unravel.

I shouldn't be getting off like this, but *fuck yes* did it feel good. What the hell was wrong with me? Had this place warped me that much?

Jacan laughed again. "Did you like that, Doll?"

Arlen punctuated the question for his team mate by sliding the dildo from my ass. Then he removed the vibrator that was hitting my clit and my G-spot so expertly. It was through half lidded eyes that I watched him lick my juices from the vibrator. He smirked then tossed it to his companion. "This flavor is even better."

"Is it?" Jacan pressed the vibrator to his lips. Then he pressed his lips back to mine. That combined flavor of me and him… I very much didn't mind it. I didn't mind it one bit. I slipped my tongue along his lips, and tasted as deeply as he'd let me. Jacan withdrew only a few millimeters, and he whispered against me. "Your tea tastes like *power*, Alice."

The corners of my lips twisted up slowly. Satisfying. Why was that so satisfying? I moved my hands to his hair, and I pulled his lips back to mine, using the freed muscles in my body to push myself against him. I'd started enjoying myself more than I'd ever admit out loud. More than I'd admit even within the safe confines of my mind. In all their big talk and thinly veiled threats, these men were as harmless as they were depraved. I felt stronger than ever, accepting pleasure from those who thought they were going to break me.

Foolish boys.

Or so I thought, until I felt the deadening hold of the March Hare on my hips. And then the cold steel of a knife on my throat.

"Don't get too bold." Arlen snapped as he teased my arteries with the flat side of a blade. "You still lost the game. We just showed you this mercy for our own pleasure." My eyes shot open as that knife was twisted to rest the sharp edge on my throat. He slid it along my skin, not enough to draw blood, but just enough to cut a single layer. "We're still going to kill you."

Jacan released my lips and he sat up straight. He lifted my chin back towards him, allowing his companion better access. "He's not wrong. But I'll admit, I would rather we didn't have to do this. Sadly, I don't make the rules. Please do forgive me in your after life, Doll."

"Wait. Wait, no—" I felt the tension of the blade bare down. I braced myself at the realization that I'd been wrong. That this was finally it. I was helpless, trapped, and there was nothing left I could do to save myself. I closed my eyes tight, not wanting to see the world fade as I bled out.

Then the knife stilled. The pressure released.

I opened my eyes as hot blood splashed down on me, only to see Mau standing over us. "I think she passed your test just fine."

Chapter 27

The grip and pressure of the blade loosened until it dropped. Jacan still cradled me in his lap, but the March Hare, who was once holding that knife to my throat, was now hovering over me, his eyes near bugging out of his head, as a clawed hand penetrated his back and came all the way through his chest. His blood continued to gush down onto me while Mau flexed his claw and retracted it back through Arlen's body. Then the Cheshire Cat kicked him hard in the side, sending his now lifeless corpse off the edge of the table.

Mau stood tall and unflinching as he licked the blood from his fingers, cleaning the March Hare off of his hand. His nails returned to a normal size, no longer needing the killing daggers he'd used just a moment ago.

The Mad Hatter looked up at Mau, a most quizzical expression on his face. Not stunned or horrified. Simply confused. "This is most unusual. To what do I owe the pleasure of *your* company, Cheshire?"

"I'm here as the lady's escort." He said with a look that could only be described as vicious. "And in the event that you cross a line with her, I'm also here as your executioner."

Jacan's eyes bounced to the crumple of his companion, then he returned them to Mau with clear suspicion. He twitched near imperceptibly. If I hadn't still been on his lap, I might not have noticed it at all. "The *line*? As the Queen's pet, does such a thing even exist for you?"

"I am *Alice's* pet, not the Queen's." He dropped down to a squat, now level with The Mad Hatter. "And the line is in the senseless murder of an otherwise very capable Alice."

I fixated on the Cheshire Cat, and he shared with me the most reassuring upturn of his lips. A subtle and small gesture that placed him firmly on my side. I think I trusted him much more than I should have.

"I just wanted to scare her. See how she would react when actually faced with the very real threat of death. I'd have healed her before she bled out, you know." He shrugged so nonchalantly. "That's how the test of bravery works. Have you forgotten that we have a job to do here, Cheshire? I don't fuck the Alice's for fun." He stroked my hair, softly moving disheveled strands from my forehead. "Well... not *only* for fun."

"Were *you* having fun, Little Dove?" Mau addressed me, ignoring the Mad Hatter's attempt at reason. I shook my head, feeling a touch vindictive. I didn't entirely mind the Hatter's healing, but I very much minded the Hare. "Well fancy that. She wasn't impressed, Jacan."

"I'm fairly certain she had no issue finishing, so I think that may be a bit of a misnomer." Jacan threw up his hands in his own defense.

"*Fairly certain*." Mau scoffed. He playfully caught my eye. "Free the rest of her body. Let's be *certain* certain."

Wait...

Jacan grinned wickedly down at me. "As you wish, Cheshire."

The Mad Hatter did exactly as Mau commanded. It was curious the way no one seemed to be able to defy the Cheshire Cat. Why that was, I couldn't begin to understand. Was Mau more powerful than the others? Or *was* he truly the Queen's pet? What was it about him that kept the other men of Wonderland so firmly in check? He seemed to have more pull than Coello even did.

I knew no one would ever answer me if I asked, however, so I simply accepted that so long as he was on my side, it barely mattered.

Jacan ran a firm grip down my calves, to my ankles to my toes, at last freeing my legs completely. I stretched out on the table, letting the blood flow to each of my limbs. I still felt a bit dazed from the tea, though the shock and the terror had done a good job of waking me up despite. But to say I felt strong enough to get up and run wasn't entirely accurate.

I locked in my gaze with the Mad Hatter, whose black suit of chains and buckles was still so impeccable, despite his pretty red hair that had been soaked in tea, and the flecks of his companion's blood that spattered the metal. The rest was absorbed in his darkness.

"So this test was about my bravery?" I asked him, as if he was deserving of casual conversation. Perhaps because I'd figured out this was all a game, I was more quick to forgive their transgressions. *How very like me.* I internally rolled my eyes at the thought.

Jacan nodded. "Only if she's proved she had the speed, strength, resolve, cleverness, and resourcefulness required to stand before the Queen of Hearts does an Alice make it to my party. But you, Doll, have it all."

I'll admit that I smiled at that. I deserved some sort of praise for all I'd endured.

I hugged my knees back to my chest and looked to Mau who had hopped off the table to get himself a cup of tea. Both men were beautiful specimens, but both were so terribly evil. How much worse must the Queen be if these are the morals of the resistance? For all I knew, the Queen could be sweet as honey, and I was actually getting swept away by the villains. "So you all work together?" I asked Jacan while still watching Mau.

Jacan casted a wayward glance toward the dead March Hare. "More… or less. We have our spats at times, but trauma has bonded us together most powerfully."

"Is that why you try to break the women you claim are here to help?"

He chuckled. He shook his head. He beamed a smile in my direction. "We're not here to break you, Alice. We're here to see if you're already as twisted as we are."

I blinked. Several times. "I'm not… I mean, I'm…"

"Of course not. None of us think so." He assured me with that mocking nod of his. Rude. He had a point, but still rude.

Though now that the March Hare and his death touch and mean glares were out of the picture, I'll admit I felt unexpectedly at ease. I was drenched in still warm blood, and this man who had just placed a knife on my face was now rubbing my feet, and I was… okay with it. Content even. It was like the high of adrenaline and terror that had been pulsing through me had dissipated to the point of a practical sugar crash. And now everything just kind of *was*. Maybe I'd learned enough about their games now to understand it wasn't personal, but I resented myself for not holding it against them.

The Mad Hatter used his thumbs to massage my arches. Feeling had long since returned, but he was going the extra mile by continuing to knead and relax my muscles. I wasn't going to be the one to stop him. Not after all the running, the swimming, the near dying, and the sex. A girl could use a little care between the bouts of brutality.

He continued back up my calves, my thighs, my hips. He nudged my knees apart, and I let him. He rubbed circles up my abdomen, and I let him do that too. He reached my breasts that had never gotten the attention I'd have liked, and I let him touch me there as well.

And while I knew I should have stopped it all once I'd regained enough of my nerves, I couldn't help but think what a soothing, healing touch like his might feel like in… other places.

Healing, self-care… oddly, I'd never had those words in my vocabulary until I'd arrived and survived. Of all the things I would have to give this place, I deserved to take a bit too.

"You heard the man." I propped myself up on my elbows, and I drew Jacan closer to me by wrapping my legs around his waist. This time, I pulled his lips to mine, and I savored *his* flavor for a moment. I spoke softly against him. "Best to be *certain* certain."

"Brave and naughty? My compliments to the White Rabbit who found an Alice like you." He pulled away from my kiss reluctantly, then he drew his touch back down my body, where he speckled kisses down my thighs. The small knife prick from the Hare was healed completely, though the light marks from the Cheshire Cat were still there. He didn't seem to mind. He might have even liked the symbolism. Jacan's touch actually had me feeling stronger than I ever have. It was almost disorienting to go from feeling so awful to feeling so good.

As Jacan's lips neared the apex of my thighs, Mau knelt beside me and took my lips. His claw dug into my hair as he whispered against me. "It's only fair that you be at your best before you see the Queen, Little Dove."

He took a sip of tea, then he transferred it to me through another kiss. I swallowed. I was willing to play with that high of numbness and feeling for these two men. I was willing to play all sorts of games with Mau, in particular. He was stunning and he helped me, and I felt unexplainably safe as he pulled me against his chest, securing me there between his arms. I lifted my chin to give him more room to place kisses on my skin, and I closed my eyes to focus on the feeling.

That tea felt nice as it slid down my throat. Nice, but… different. It wasn't paralyzing like the last cups. No, if anything it was amplifying the intensity of touch, and amplifying how much I wanted it. I pushed back into Mau harder, wanting to feel more of his body against mine so snuggly. I needed more of his touch.

I heard Jacan's chuckle at the same time I heard footsteps. I peeked just enough to catch a glimpse of a face I'd not seen in what now felt like an eternity. The one person in Wonderland who still made me nervous.

The Mad Hatter stood and turned to face his gate, which Mau had destroyed in order to save me. He spoke with characteristic excitement. "If it isn't the guest of honor. I was wondering when you'd show up."

Chapter 28

Coello

"The White Rabbit"

I'd come to the Tea Party after a quick stop at Bruco's for some healing salve, where he had been in… quite a state of distress. Then I dipped home for dry clothes, where I shouldn't have been surprised to see my door partially broken. There were enough blood stains in the bathroom to easily deduce who had been there, considering Poppet's penchant for getting drenched in death. Though I'd given Mau a key precisely to *prevent* the need for repairs. but this Alice had been one to bulldoze her way through Wonderland, whether we helped her along or not.

But I digress. That all seemed like expected chaos in comparison to the state of this Tea Party. If I were to make a list of everything that was so terribly wrong, I'd first of all address the broken gate I'd just walked through: Most unexpected. What had required such a forceful entry be used, I couldn't quite guess. The dead March Hare: Somewhat expected, though usually I had to kill him myself. The scattered teacups and a wickedly pleased Jacan: Completely expected, other than the fact that, for once, that image wasn't accompanied by an Alice who just had her throat slit and healed and was consequently crying and traumatized in his arms.

Then there was the Cheshire Cat… I had no idea what to expect of *him* anymore. He wasn't supposed to be at this party at all, unless he was sweeping up the pieces of another failure.

"Fancy meeting you here, Kitten." I rested a hand on my hip and cocked back my head, so I could look down on him in spite of the height of his perch atop the table.

"Fancy, indeed. I'm impressed you made it past the Bandersnatch." Mau punctuated the taunt with a chuckle, feeling no obvious remorse for the pain he'd put me through, as per usual. He rubbed his claws up and down Alice's arms, who sat entirely too comfortably in his lap. She bit her lip and nestled deeper into Mau's hold, as if that was some sort of safe space. Strange. Almost cute. But genuinely perplexing. "Though I must say, for the White Rabbit, you've gotten awfully slow at the chase, Bunny."

"That's because *you're* not supposed to be the one I'm chasing." I narrowed my eyes and pursed my lips. "But you and Poppet seem to have gotten rather well acquainted." I watched as she turned her flushed face to the side, resting her cheek on his shoulder. She was drenched in blood, I assumed from Arlen, and tea, I assumed from Jacan, and yet still she was so visibly turned on. It was… distracting.

Mau smirked in that way he always did, bearing his fangs as his lips stretched wide. "You noticed?" *As if it was possible not to.* "In all that time you spent doing the devil knows what," *Battling the Bandersnatch and the Jabberwock that YOU sent after me, you mean,* "I've really gotten to know this Alice, and I quite like her. I think I'll keep her, if you don't mind." His hand drifted up to her neck, where he traced its contours with his claws, just lightly enough to trail a red mark behind them without breaking skin. She swallowed into his hold. Nervous, but not scared. Not fighting him. "Isn't that what *you* want, Little Dove?" He purred into her ear at a volume I could barely catch.

She lifted her chin, allowing him more access. Why that made me flinch, I couldn't say. "Yes." She whispered with her eyes closed. She was still visibly on a high from Jacan's tea. But… It wasn't just that…

"Well, if the lady chose you, then you should have her." I taunted, shifting on my feet and giving him a nod. I wanted to see how exactly she'd react. I didn't know quite what to expect of the relationships Alice had formed since I'd seen her last, but I was beginning to gather she'd built up a tolerance to Wonderland. "Go on then. Don't stop on my account." I waved a hand to shoo them along.

"I knew you'd see it my way." Mau hovered breaths just over her skin, as those claws slipped back down to her dress. "How about you see what else *my way* entails." His touch drifted down to her collar bone. Lower. He brushed her breast with careful fingertips, testing and probing. She clenched her thighs together as he slipped his hand beneath the cup of her corset. She let out a soft moan as he ran his tongue along her neck, licking from nape to jaw.

"M-Mau." She gasped as he played with her nipple beneath her clothing. "N-not here. Not…"

"In front of Coello?" He purred against her skin. "No, My Dove, I *specifically* want to do this to you in front of him."

"I…." She stopped herself before she could protest, and instead she squeezed her eyes shut in response. "Then do it." That embarrassment, that discomfort, and that way she was fighting her arousal, while also giving in at the same time—Alice was hard to look away from.

"You found a rather impressive candidate this time around." Jacan, the host I'd nearly forgotten about in my focused irritation, remarked as he glanced back at her and Mau. He hopped down to my level. "The look in her eye when we'd taken every ounce of power from her…" He chuckled, then he moved closer to me. He placed a hand on my cheek and he pulled me to him. He spoke roughly against my lips. "Magnificent. Have you tasted her yet, Coello?"

The Mad Hatter dug his hand into my hair, and he pulled me to him. He nipped at my lip, just enough to take a quick taste, then he pulled back and he laughed. "Her flavor compliments yours oh so nicely, you know. I think you would like it if you gave her a real chance."

I pulled my lower lip into my mouth, just to keep his competing sweet and tart notes on my tongue. Pleased, Jacan took my hand, and he stepped backwards, one slow pace at a time, until he was against the table. "You know you're always invited to my party. Why don't you come and play."

I hesitated to respond, in words or actions, still getting a gauge on the full scope of the situation.

Jacan released his hold, then he hopped back onto the table and returned to her side. While Mau fluttered kisses up her neck, the Hatter took her lips. She was both willing and compliant. Giving me a show didn't seem to bother her so long as both of them had their hands on her. It was almost comical to me that *I* was somehow the only man in Wonderland who she was still afraid of. Begging to get fucked by Cheshire, while terrified of the White Rabbit? I don't know if that's a win for my intimidation tactics or a knock against Poppet's judge of character.

"Will you let him see you, Alice?" Mau asked, low and tantalizing. She nodded briefly and quickly before opening wide to take the Hatter's tongue again.

Mau used a free hand to pull the ribbons on her corset. The bodice loosened. Then she lifted her arms to allow them to remove it.

Jacan dragged the bone corset up, slow and steady. Her soft breasts spilled from the binding as they lifted it over her head, and they bounced into place. Her nipples were pink and hard, complimented by the drips of blood that ran down the contours of her smooth, soft abdomen.

"There, isn't that better." Mau said as much to me as he did to her. She leaned back into him again as he traced light touch down her bare skin, smearing crimson with his touch. Jacan broke their kiss to take her right nipple into his mouth. Mau played with the left, pinching and firming her to assure her nakedness and arousal was so clearly in my view.

When Poppet fidgeted, he pinched down roughly, eliciting a small yelp from her throat. "You're so wet already, Little Dove. It's almost like you enjoy letting him see you like this."

"I-I don't." She shook her head. "I mean, I'm not…" Still so defiant. But her protests and her actions painted two different pictures. My Adam's apple bobbed as I tried to compose myself.

"Really, Dove?" Mau slid his hand down her body, lightly dancing over her navel, then curiously slipping under the band of her skirt. "You're practically drenching my lap." He chuckled as he brought his hand back out. It was slick with her excitement. He slipped his fingers into her mouth. "Suck, Alice." He whispered breathily in her ear. "Why don't you taste that and tell me how disinterested you really are."

She closed her lips around his fingers and sucked her own juices from his skin. She complied with everything he asked, to the point I was nearly jealous. I'd never seen him bond with a woman quite like this. I'd seen him fuck plenty of them, sure, but it was never so… careful.

Mau smirked. He kept his eyes on her, watching her with interest as she cleaned her mess from him. "Now why don't you take off your panties and show *him* how wet you are for me, Dove." He purred. "Won't you let him see who you belong to?"

"Yes." She agreed through heavy breaths. My eyes widened in surprise. The Cheshire Cat's only magic was one of invisibility. He couldn't control or enslave someone. He didn't have any sort of magic charisma or compulsion. Even with an arousing tea, there was no magical enchantment to it that would compel her to do *everything* he asked. This pliable, sexual version of Poppet was completely *her*.

And what a woman she was.

Mau took her mouth, Jacan continued playing with her nipples, while Alice tried to keep enough focus and composure to lift her skirt. She revealed those laced panties, then she slipped a finger under each side. With an excruciating lack of urgency, she nudged the lace over her hips. The material clung to her wetness, until she dragged them down to mid-thigh. While still in Mau's hold, with Jacan pressing her into him, she was only able to get them down as far as her knees, before she fidgeted enough to let gravity take them to her ankles.

She squeezed her legs together, as if trying to hide her bare pussy, despite having just undressed herself of her own free will. She was a curious contradiction of kink and shyness. It was absolutely impossible to look away.

"Almost." Mau licked her ear with the broad side of his tongue.

She nodded, as if understanding his command. Then she slipped her first foot through and used her other foot to toss her lace to me. I caught it. My hand was instantly covered with her arousal. I could smell it without even needing this bit of lace, but having it in my hand was another level.

"That's a good girl." Mau nibbled on her earlobe as he slipped his hand back under her skirt. She was trembling as she spread her legs for him. As she let him slip in the first digit. As she let him finger fuck her right in front of me. "Do you think you can come for me, Dove? Won't you let him see how much better it is in my hands?"

"Y-yes." Her words were breathless. "God, yes." And they were the step too far.

"Enough, Mau." I growled. "You've made your point."

But he didn't stop. He continued to slip his finger in and out, while she covered her mouth, doing her best to muffle her gasps and moans and cries from my ears.

"Hmmm, what do you think? Do you agree, Alice? Do you feel like I've made my point yet?" He slipped in a second finger, this time going all the way to his knuckles. He stayed inside of her, his knuckles visibly flexing as he massaged her inner walls. "Or do you need a little more help to get to the *point*?"

"Not yet." Alice shook her head, urging him to keep going. "I'm not there yet." She used both hands to cover her mouth now as he brought her closer and closer to climax.

Jacan joined his grip. He played with her clit, while Mau played in her pussy, and her breasts heaved under every erratic breath.

"Have it your way." I shot back more harshly now. That only amused him more. I wasn't going to keep standing idly by and watching this. I closed the distance between us swiftly. Alice's eyes shot open as I got in her face. I gripped her thighs and forced them apart, giving me access. Then I started undoing my belt.

Mau met my eyes, and his smile was utterly content. He'd gotten exactly what he wanted. He always did from me. He slipped his fingers out of her, Jacan backed away, and she whined as they both left her on edge.

"I'm so close." She near sobbed into Mau's shoulder.

"Just follow the White Rabbit, and he'll take you there." He spoke against her lips. He gave me a slight nod before he claimed her mouth with his completely. She lifted her hips for me, and I didn't turn down the invitation. I reveled in the way she moaned into Mau's mouth when my cock pushed into that first inch of her pussy. Then the way she practically screamed into him as I shoved myself all the way in.

She was perfectly snug around my cock, wrapping around me with wet heat. Her natural fluids trailed on my pelvis each time I hit into her, until I was dripping in her wetness.

Mau released her lips long enough for her to cry out a desperate "don't stop." Her breasts rippled beautifully under every hard thrust, and the sound of air escaping her lungs on each impact of my hips was music that could rival the most beautiful symphony. We were making a mess of the Mad Hatter's table. Though as she traded over to take Jacan's tongue into her mouth again, I don't think he minded. This was a far more satisfying tea than anything he could brew.

"That's right. Come for him, Dove." Mau commanded her, and she obeyed. I hit her again in that spot that made her moan so deep and guttural, and she wrapped her legs around my waist, pulling my full weight onto her.

Then Alice let go on me while shaking tremors of an orgasmic high over my still firm arousal. She was still riding that wave as I slid out of her. I placed my cock over her clit, and I slid between her folds, rubbing the slickness of precum and her own fluids through her. She was clenching me between her thighs, overwhelmed by the continued sensation when she was already so sensitive. She clawed at the back of both Mau and Jacan's heads for stability. I kept her on that ride until I hit my own limit.

A mess of my orgasm dirtied the tulle of her skirt and mixed with the sweat on her stomach. She was a beautiful disaster, as pretty in come as she was in blood. It was so very worth it to catch her.

Mau braced her by her shoulders as she breathed heavy and undone against his chest. Though his eyes stayed on mine, with a vicious amusement.

"You are so terribly easy to manipulate, Bunny."

Chapter 29

Flushed, hot, and completely unraveled. I *loved* that face on Bunny. Though *this*… I brushed my fingers over Alice's abdomen, spreading semen and sweat and blood up to her naked breasts. I rubbed his essence into her skin as I made it to her neck. This woman in my arms was a masterpiece. I shouldn't have enjoyed watching her come so much on another man's cock, but the way they both got each other off was positively delicious.

It's not like I didn't like to see Coello happy after all. But I think I might like to see this one happy as well.

I nuzzled my face in her hair, enjoying that scent of tea, death, and sex, then I addressed my adorable bunny. "You just couldn't help yourself, could you?" I chuckled. Alice squirmed in my hands, seeming uncertain of how to take the situation. I tightened my hold, and spoke against her skin while still addressing Coello. "Doesn't that mean she failed your test? I thought you were supposed to kill the women you caught."

She tensed ever so slightly in my hold. A touch of fear that I hadn't seen from her in a moment. Was she still afraid of Bunny? Endearing.

"You won't kill me." She said through shaky resolve.

"I won't, Little Dove." I whispered into her ear, then I shoved her over into the White Rabbit's arms. He caught her on instinct alone. "But will he?"

Coello immediately clamped down. He gazed down at the pretty little thing in his hands, then his sights lifted to me again. His expression was neutral, yet not neutral at all if you knew how to read it. His rose gold eyes reflected near imperceptible surprise, then they reflected a flash of understanding. A silent language we both spoke only between each other.

Coello lifted her chin so she had to face him. And he whispered most delicately against her lips. "Tell me now, Alice, how have you been enjoying Wonderland?"

"I…" The conflict on her face was clearly visible. *'Should I be terrified or should I hold my confidence?'* it said. "I've come to enjoy it quite a bit." She settled on confidence. Her eyes narrowed, but not in anger. No, in a satisfied cruelty. A most divine expression. A wicked smirk danced on her lips. "I haven't had this much fun in ages, if you want the truth. But after all that talk, you're only going to fuck me once, Mister White Rabbit? I was expecting my consequences to be much more severe."

A laugh escaped my throat. *Sweet Devil, I adore her.*

Bunny shook his head, but the smile he bore, casted so obviously in her direction, betrayed him completely. "It's not my turn in your pussy anymore, Poppet." He placed his hand around the waistband of her skirt, and he yanked it down roughly. "But I'll be happy to fuck you in another hole."

"I've been a bit spoiled by Wonderland. You're going to have to be more creative than that." Alice gripped his wrist, and she directed it down from her chin to her neck. He obliged her by wrapping his fingers gently around it. "Why don't you show my how dangerous you really are." She taunted him. Shamelessly and fearlessly. If she was bluffing, she was terribly good at it.

I took that as my cue, and I repositioned behind Coello. I gripped him by his shoulders, and I pulled him back against me, freeing Alice from his hold. "You heard the lady." I whispered harshly into his ear. "You don't have to pretend to be so vanilla for her." I drew a line of pressure up his spine before tightening my hold around his airways. "A promise is a promise, Bunny."

Alice took the brief moment of freedom to wriggle out of her skirt. Now completely naked, she mounted Bunny's lap, while she held eye contact with me. "We're playing my game now." She said. "I won yours already."

I reveled in the confidence she'd gained. Surviving one horror after another looked good on her.

She raised her hips and positioned Coello's tip against her still wet pussy. He'd gotten hard again so fast and easy. I couldn't possibly blame him. Then she rested her hands on his shoulders, while Bunny leaned back into me for support.

Coello's face was level with her perfect breasts, yet he managed to look up into her eyes. "You might just be a worthwhile Alice." He added, and she lowered herself slowly onto his lap, until her full weight was pressing into him. Then she stayed there, not moving an inch.

"Obviously." My little dove said with a smirk. "Now let's see if you're a worthwhile White Rabbit." Then oh so mischievously, she nodded to me. "For me and for your friend here."

I couldn't help but chuckle, while Coello's Adam's apple bobbed in my grip under the single pulse she performed on his dick. I was happy to oblige her deviance. "This is for the good of Wonderland, Bunny." I whispered into his ear.

"Then you'd better do your best." He breathed back harshly.

"You know I always do." I nudged his pants down lower, while Alice seemed to delight in teasing him with the slowest possible strokes. "Lay her down, Bunny. I want you to fuck her while I take you."

Little Dove didn't fight him as he did as he was told. She let him press her to the table, shove her knees wide, and position himself on top of her and inside of her. I grabbed a cup of tea and I poured it down on his back. The hot liquid splashed around her as he served as a barrier over her naked body. Then I ran a hand through the liquid and slid down to his ass, where I used that extra lubrication to slip in the first finger.

Alice placed her hands over her head, drawing her breasts upward with the muscles in an attractive stretch, then she craned back her neck to focus on the Mad Hatter, who perhaps had been a touch left out in our usual dynamics.

"I've got room for one more." She said, while tightening her legs around Bunny's waist. "If your touch gives life, I want to know what your come does."

"You are a filthy doll." He chuckled, but he wasn't about to refuse her. *Who could?*

Jacan positioned by her head, freeing himself for her, and she touched her lips softly to the head of his cock. She tapped the tip softly with her tongue, then she widened her tongue broadly and pulled him into her mouth. Her throat moved attractively as she sucked on the tip with soft pulses, and Jacan took the initiative to give her a bit more. He slowly disappeared inside her mouth, and Bunny disappeared inside her pussy as she commanded him with a squeeze of her thighs.

As satisfying as it was to watch, I was straining in my hand to hold myself back. So I worked more of that lubricating tea into Coello, and I decided to join the game. His expression was already slack as he lost himself in her warmth. And it twisted in my most favorite way as I buried myself in his. I entered slowly at first, but my discipline snapped as I watched those eyes close so tight and his teeth dig into his lip. I held his hips firmly as I gave him every inch.

More satisfying still, was the moans that vibrated through Alice's throat, as each time I thrust into him, he pounded that much harder into her. I was fucking her by proxy, and Jacan was bracing himself on Coello's shoulders as he reaped the benefits of those guttural groans on his cock.

The Mad Hatter gave in first. She swallowed all he gave her in a pronounced shift of her neck muscles, then she sucked on him to assure she didn't miss a drop. The way his healing essence rippled through her body had her practically glowing with the strength and power she'd already mastered. She shuddered and tensed, losing herself to orgasm purely through the oral satisfaction of his released power.

I slammed into Coello harder, forcing him to send that pleasure right back upward, and reveling in the way they both trembled as they gave in to release.

I took my time finishing myself, not wanting to give until I'd gotten to watch all of them lost on high, but the sound Alice made as Jacan pulled out of her mouth, when she drew a sharp breath to catch her composure, then the even more satisfying sound she made when Coello halted that breath with a grip of her neck, was enough to drag me off the bridge with them. I shifted my hold to Alice's knees while I slid into Coello one more time, then I pulled out at the last moment, so I could make a mess of them both to stake my claim.

The feeling was everything. I closed my eyes and let myself fall back onto my hands as perfection, heat, and satisfaction crawled through my every nerve.

While I sat back, the last to recover, Bunny helped Little Dove to her feet.

Then, like the queen she would be, she stood atop the table over us all. She placed her hands on her hips, not caring that she was naked and covered in fluids of all kinds. No, this Alice was much too fierce to do anything less.

Fantastic.

Her wary eyes remained fixed on the White Rabbit for several moments. She looked to the Mad Hatter, then she looked to me. A heavy breath drew into her lungs, then she closed her eyes and exhaled through her nose.

"I've survived all of your trials now, no?" She said as she straightened out, unbothered to be so bare in front of us. To be naked before the men who pleasured her was hardly a point of humiliation, after all.

Coello was first to cock his head back and address her. "You passed all our tests." He stated with a confirming finality.

"You smashed all of our tests." I reiterated as I stood up beside Bunny.

"And you were *stunning* as you did so." Jacan smiled widely.

"Excellent." She crouched down and grabbed her bloodied corset. She shook it out, causing the bodice that was still heavily soaked in the March Hare's blood to send spatter across the table in a most delightfully devilish pattern, then she pulled it on and tugged the laces tight. She stepped into her skirt next, then she lifted her chin expectantly.

I took the cue, approaching to better fasten her laces for her. Once it was secure, I straightened and fluffed her skirt, and I stepped back from our Alice.

Alice rolled her shoulders, then she nodded toward her panties that were still on the table. "You can keep those as a souvenir. Now take me to this Queen of Hearts. Let's get this over with."

Yes, she was utterly divine. Whatever it takes, she was going to be our final Alice. I would make sure of it myself if I had to.

Chapter 30

Alice

To describe the Queen of Heart's mighty castle, I could only say it was a fortress of nightmares. Three massive spires shot into the sky, hundreds of feet high, creating a triangular structure that was both sharp and imposing in nature.

One tower was topped with a black club, one a black spade, one a blue diamond, and in the center of the three pillars, crowning the main structure, was a large blue heart that twirled at a slow and steady pace.

The structure itself was a caricature of evil, with its black stones and uninviting, thorn filled ivy snaking along every wall. The outer rim was crowned with blades, and the only windows to be seen, high atop the spires, were small and heavily barred, mimicking a prison more than a home. To top off its commitment to arrogance, no gate or wall had been built to defend it. Only nicely spaced rose bushes stood between us and the entryway. But what more did they need, really? Who would dare be so brazen as to attack such a place? Other than myself and my entourage anyway.

Though it was interesting to think that these men by my side had failed, time and again, to defeat the Queen. Powerful men who could kill without thought or remorse— who could happily and jokingly kill their own allies, no less—were made small and insignificant amidst the darkness of the Queen's Wonderland. How powerful must she be? Coello, Mau, Jacan, even Finn and Tynan… none of them could stand up to her? Was it magic that protected her? Her guards? What was it that made her strong?

More than that, what made those guards loyal to her, when the rest of the land was openly rebelling? I could only assume it was some sort of brain washing. Maybe magical, maybe charismatic, maybe sexual.

But then, why would she not control all of the men of Wonderland? Why even give Coello, Mau, the Hatter, the Hare, the Twins, and the Caterpillar a chance to shape a rebellion?

So little of it made sense to me, but that was nothing new here. I suppose this coming confrontation would hopefully answer some of these questions. Or it would bring even more. It could really go either way at this point.

"So what are the rules?" I turned to my companions. While this place functioned on nonsense, it also so oddly functioned on an unexplainably strict set of parameters. I'm sure this showdown with the Queen would be no different than the so called trials to get here.

Coello ran a hand through his platinum hair, then he caught me in those rose gold eyes. Not too long ago, that look would have terrified me. But now, I had an ally in that deep cruel gaze. He'd become a man who would kill *for* me instead of kill me, and I reveled in that.

"We'll all have a role to play in this final showdown, Alice." He said. I liked it when he said my name. I preferred it to the many nicknames I'd received. "You just have to remember that, no matter what you see or hear or feel, that we are still on your side, and never on hers."

I scrunched my nose. What did that mean?

Mau placed his hand on Coello's shoulder. "Are you saying that for her or for you, Bunny?" He said, before softly whispering something inaudibly in his ear. Then he turned back to me. Their relationship still confused me. Though in a strange way, I liked that these guys all got along. It was strangely satisfying to be able to share these men without hard feelings, but also know they were just as content to share each other. I'll admit that I was proud of being the glue and common denominator that kept them together.

To exist without jealousy… maybe that's what I'd really needed. I'd compared myself and each new partner to my past so many times, because I still held that bitterness in me. But why did I need to? Why settle for one man who never quite made me happy, when I had several who were tripping over themselves to make me feel good, while being completely open about their predilections. Somehow that just felt *right*. We were in this together in every way.

"He's correct though." Mau continued. "We will be your knights, Little Dove, should you need to call on us."

Jacan stepped forward. He glanced between his team mates. "We are your knights, yes. But *you* will have to be the one to take off the Queen's head. Only Alice can kill Alice." A grin of pure madness danced on his pale, painted face. "And no, that is not a play on words or a clever riddle. Her head, you will need."

"And her head, she will have." The White Rabbit gave me a confident nod.

I swallowed. *Wait, were they serious? Was I going to have to literally cut off her head?* Of everything I'd been subjected to thus far, I was yet to kill someone or something myself. I even let the Caterpillar off the hook.

Mau chimed in with his measured, sly, and low voice that sent shivers through me. "You've already braved horrors much worse than that. These trials are meant to scare you, but they're also meant to numb you to violence and turn you into a killer." Mau paced over to me. He swept me against him with a hand around my waist, and he braced me in his body heat. I focused on those violet, flecked eyes and the way his lips twisted. "A woman who can come while bathed in blood, for the men who put it there, no less, is a woman who can't be stopped."

I chewed on my lower lip. I closed my eyes. And when I opened them again, I made sure they were filled with resolve. "A woman who would trust the Cheshire Cat, the Mad Hatter, and the White Rabbit in their own twisted Wonderland is who you *really* need to watch out for."

I smiled for him, and he returned the gesture for me.

Then just like that, with a wisp of the wind, they were gone, and I was alone.

"Hey! What the hell!" I shouted into the void, just in time to get nearly bowled over by a trio of guards. They carried large buckets and were dashing for the bushes.

White roses bloomed on every branch, appearing full and beautiful and uncharacteristically angelic. I watched with confusion as those guards pulled tiny blue Mome Raths from their pails and began chucking them into the bushes. The roses came to life, stretching and slithering over to each tiny animal. They gripped them with their petals, then sucked the animals down into their bud. As each rose feasted, it changed color, settling blue instead of white.

The men, all three decorated with blue diamonds atop their heads and the numbers three, six, and eight on their chests, appeared frantic as they tried to feed each and every rose as quickly and efficiently as possible.

"What are you doing?" I asked, eliciting a pronounced startle from all three of them.

"We're fixing the roses." Number Three said with a shake in his voice. "Eight of Diamonds here stupidly planted white roses, when her majesty wanted blue."

"She won't have to find out if you stop talking and keep feeding." Mister Eight snapped, while dealing out Mome Raths like he was making it rain at a strip club.

"She's going to kill us because of you." Six whined, nasally and pathetic. "You had one job. How could you ever think someone like the Queen would like white? There is nothing good or pure or bright or shining about that woman."

"Hush! Hush! What if she hears you?" Eight shot a dagger filled glare at Six. "You know she has spies everywhere."

"Work faster." Three barked. A command that was overpowered by a sudden parade of large black horses that came bounding past us along the nearby walkway. The walkway where I stood and was directly in their way. They made no indication of slowing, and it was by luck alone that I managed to dodge at the last second. Though not while also keeping my balance. I plunked onto the floor, falling on my ass beside the stone path, while the caravan passed through.

On each horse was a knight, and on each knight was a number on their black armored chest and a card suit on their helmet. The black knights gave way to blue knights on blue horses. I scooted back, still trying to collect myself, when the carriage appeared.

I felt invisible. Not one of the knights even paid me a passing glance. Their eyes were forward with perfect discipline as they marched towards wherever they may have been going. They were probably trained to do that, like the British soldiers who could keep a straight face no matter how much tourists tried to get them to break stance. They were cogs in a well functioning machine that had never before been stopped.

After what felt like an eternity, that carriage rolled in front of me, and without a single word, everything abruptly stopped. I blinked up, stunned and uncertain, at the woman who stood from her plush blue velvet seat. She was a sight to behold.

Long blonde hair wafted down to her waist, shining with the softness of silk–even despite the absence of the sun in the dark, unticking-moon filled sky. Her eyes were a piercing sapphire that was so vibrant they literally glowed, and her body was exquisitely crafted from practical stone, with perfect abs, strong thighs, and large, shapely breasts that perked at their pink nipples—all of which was clearly visible beneath the dress of loose-linked blue chainmail that fell over her chest, and contoured down to a full and puffy skirt, layered with tulle and satin. A long, black and blue blade rested on a leather belt that wrapped tightly around her tiny waist, dark stockings with frilly cobalt garters at the top cascaded down her perfect legs, and baby blue stilettos finish the look, with daggers in place of heels.

But most notable of all was the crown that topped her pretty head, built of sharp upside down hearts.

The original Alice. The Queen of Hearts.

"What nonsense is this?" She said with a voice both stern yet feminine. A sultry, enchanting, seductive voice, yet one that felt severe and threatening at the same time. "Which one of you planted those monstrosities?"

The three guards immediately fell to their knees and bowed their heads deeply. The remaining Mome Raths scrambled from the buckets and started sprinting for the woods in the distance. "We're fixing it. We're fixing it." Six was nearly sobbing. The Queen scowled.

With movements that were more feline than even the Cheshire Cat, she jumped from her carriage and paced over to the men on the floor. She placed the point of one of her knife-like stilettos on Eight's back, then she crammed him into the floor, stabbing straight through his armor like a needle through cotton. Red bloomed from his back as she drove that heel all the way through him. Then she drew her sword.

"If we don't fuck up, we don't have to fix things, now do we?" She said through a deceptively sweet smile. "And if we don't have to fix things, I don't have to take off your *stupid fucking heads*."

Then swiftly, without a moment's hesitation, she swung her blade through each of their necks, sending their loose heads rolling into the walkway. A passing horse kicked one. Another was trampled, smashing the skull in a horrid display of gore and blood. And I just watched on, wide-eyed, as Wonderland found yet another new level of brutality I wasn't quite prepared for.

The blood absorbed into her heels, and her soft blue shoes became a shade deeper and darker. It was as though their death gave her that much more power.

The Queen lifted the blade to her pouty, painted red lips, and she licked the blood from hilt to tip. Her mouth upturned in a wicked smile, then she returned to her carriage and remounted her mobile throne.

Fear. It was fear that she ruled with. Not mind control or magic. That much was clear.

Though as she'd passed me, she didn't even so much as look at me. It was as if I wasn't even here. Perhaps I was too insignificant to even register on her radar. I frowned, then I stood up and dusted myself off, hoping I might get her attention.

"They can't fix things if you murder them." I said boldly.

Finally the Queen's vibrant eyes met mine. That gaze crawled from my toes to my face, then she lifted her chin before she spoke, subtly placing me further beneath her. "And I can't reasonably murder them if they don't make mistakes. They all know the rules when they join my army." She batted her eyes at the carriage driver. A blush could be seen through the sliver of his blue, heart-topped helmet. "The benefits far outweigh the risks."

She spoke so casually to me, I wasn't sure what to make of it. I knew the world reset time and again, but as she was the one who wore the crown, did her memories reset with it? Or did she already know who I was and why I was here? The rest of Wonderland was striving and struggling with desperation, while she was so unbothered, I couldn't help but think she was oblivious to the uprising. Or she saw it as so insignificant, she simply didn't care.

"Do you take pleasure in killing them?" I asked neutrally, probing but not provoking.

"I take pleasure in many things." She said with a shrug. "The death of lesser men ranks high among them." She looked and sounded so young to me. If I were to guess, she'd likely come here and stopped aging somewhere in her late teens or early twenties at the latest. Her body was very much an adult, and magazine-perfect to the point it looked like she'd likely undergone quite a bit of plastic surgery in order to achieve the shapes she flaunted, but I couldn't help but think her soul was that of a traumatized teenager, who was taking revenge against *all* men to get back at one who may have wronged her.

I frowned at the thought. Was I so different? I'd spent so much time wanting to get back at my ex, that it wasn't much of a stretch for me to enjoy the company of true psychopaths. I've even justified it and come to be legitimately fond of them. Would I be any safer or more just beneath that crown?

"Where are you going?" I asked with measured curiosity.

"To play, of course." She pondered for a moment before continuing. "Do you play croquet? Would you like to join me?"

I'd barely even heard of croquet, but something told me not to turn her down. "Of course. I'm not the best, but I would certainly be willing to entertain you." I bluffed, setting expectations as low as they should be, while showing a hint of that submission I was certain she was looking for.

"Excellent. I prefer to win anyway." If not for all the blood and the blatant flaunting of her sexuality, that might have almost come off as sweet. "Come on then." She waved a hand, and I obliged, climbing into the carriage and taking a seat beside her. The precession resumed its march toward the croquet field.

"What's your name?" She asked me with such comfort. I was starting to lean more towards the idea that she truly didn't know why I was here.

I hesitated for a moment, then committed to honesty. I would be killed for lies, I presumed. "Alice. My name's Alice."

"Oh, how delightful. That's my name, too." She said with a please clap of her hands. Cute, sexy, sweet, yet… evil? What a confusing mix this woman was. Despite the earlier display of brutality, I was already starting to kind of like her. "Please call me 'your majesty' in front of others, but should we ever end up alone, I'd love to hear you call me by my name." Her lips curled upwards and she practically winked at me with her words.

Wait, was she flirting with me?

She continued. "Would you like an orgasm or two on the way to the court? I find the rush really helps my game."

I blinked a few times, trying to figure out how that counted as casual conversation. *Definitely flirting.* "Are you… offering?"

She giggled. "Not me, silly. That's what the men are for."

"I think I'm good." My voice was a mess of nerves. I didn't want to upset her, but this just felt strange. She was somehow both the monster I expected and not a monster at all at the same time.

"Suit yourself." She responded with a shrug. The original Alice raised her hands and clapped her fingertips softly against her palm. A guard in black with a spade atop his helm and the picture of the Jack across his chest hopped from his horse and climbed into the carriage. He knelt before his queen, and she responded by placing her ankles on his shoulders. "You may pleasure me now, Jack." She leaned back in her chair, and the guard removed his helmet and followed orders, diving right in.

I simply watched as he buried his face in her powder blue skirt and puffy white tulle, and her expressions danced between dignity and pleasure.

"Higher, Jack." She purred. She had no shame and no modesty. "Slower. *Slower.*" The man was practically sweating bullets as he tried to figure out the right way to use his tongue. She squeezed her thighs around his ears, and she scraped her bladed heels along his black armor. "No. Slower, I said." She snapped at him. Then she locked her heels together behind him. He fumbled his licks, and she sighed in exasperation. Then in a smooth motion, she drew her blade once more, and she sent it careening into his scalp.

I was too stunned to make a sound as the man crumbled, dead, between her legs. His skull had damn near split in half, and a fountain of death erupted from the wound. She drew in her thighs, and squeezed them together, while she subsequently threw her head back and moaned out satisfaction. "Yes, that's better." Her whole body quivered with visible pleasure, while the man fell to the floor of the carriage and resumed bleeding out in a senseless mess. I lifted my legs to avoid getting more blood all over my shoes.

What in the actual fuck.

Any admiration I'd felt immediately deflated. This woman was a monster, somehow even worse than my monsters.

She grinned with a wickedness then raised her hands to clap again. "One more, please."

When we arrived in the croquet court, the carriage was cleaned of its dead guards, and the Queen merrily jumped down while her men prepared the court for her. The way she reveled in death was disconcerting even after all I'd seen. A lot about her was disconcerting, really. She was a strange juxtaposition of erotica and youth in a way that screamed of a lifetime of abuse, and I couldn't help but wonder who the original Alice had been. More than that, was it Wonderland that had corrupted her? Or was it she who had corrupted Wonderland? If the world reflected whoever wore the crown, then I couldn't help but think it was her own viciousness that created this mess.

Still, so long as she hadn't turned on me just yet, I wasn't going to push any buttons or pry too deeply. I wanted to know more about her, but I also knew that the more I did know, the more likely I was to develop some sort of unreasonable, misguided empathy for her, despite or *in spite* of her dysfunction. The way Wonderland functioned, it felt like walking into a well-rehearsed play as a new contestant who was meeting well practiced actors, and I couldn't help but wonder if the real goal here was simply to help heal misunderstood and damaged people who just needed some compassion.

Those were the naïve and pretty things I thought, up until I watched on, in horror, as the Queen removed the heads of three more guards to use them as her croquet balls.

Right, so I think we're somewhere around that point in a serial killer's life, where we have to accept that the time to save them has passed...

"Come, let's play, Alice." She said with a giggle. I stifled a groan, I steeled my stomach, and I took a croquet mallet in hand to begin the game. The mallet had a long handle that I would not be acknowledging was likely made from human bones, and the balls were mostly comprised of painted skulls, that I would also not be acknowledging for what they were.

It would have been nice if my Wonderland men could have given me a bit of a heads up that I'd have to play some ball sports with dismembered corpses, but god forbid anyone ever tell me anything that might make my life easier. Or… *Devil* forbid, I guess? These are definitely Hell's soldiers.

Whatever. They could have at least given me a hint as to what I was supposed to do to get close enough to the Queen to put an end to these cycles. But I suppose if I wanted to live and have any chance of returning to the real world, I'd figure it out, just as I had so many times now.

I could do this.

Chapter 31

Alice

Croquet was a game where, no one should quote me on this because I was, at best, guessing, the players took a long handled mallet and tried to knock balls through little archways in a big field. Or… something like that? I assumed that the game usually had some sort of goal or order, but as one might expect from Wonderland, everyone was just gallivanting about with no rhyme or reason. Sometimes we took turns, and I was mostly doing poorly and losing terribly. Which I only knew because everyone who got ahead of the Queen was beheaded immediately, and I had somehow been spared thus far.

There were perks of not having any athletic gifts after all. My gym coaches in high school who gave me a passing grade only out of sympathy would be so proud to see my failings finally being good for something.

The knight beside me, who usually took his turn after mine, was sweating profusely as he went up to bat. His whole mallet shook as his unsteady hands prepared to swing at the next archway. He swallowed, and he trembled. It should have been easy to intentionally throw the game, but if it was obvious AT ALL that the guards were missing the target on purpose, she'd holler "off with his head" as if issuing a command, only to unceremoniously perform the task herself. How she had any guards left was a wonder. How she managed to keep replacing them, even more so. But it was easy to tell who was legitimately bad at the game and who was faking it for the sake of survival.

I thanked my natural ineptitude at croquet, having literally never played it before, *because who the fuck has.* But still, every time my turn came up, I was sweating just as nervously with the hope that I wouldn't get some sudden burst of beginner's luck. The queen had no patience for anything that she deemed challenging to her, even if she was already winning by a mile.

"You're quite bad at this, Alice." She said with a smile, reinforcing the knowledge that we shared a name. "Have you never played before?"

"The last time I swung at a ball, I was playing soft ball in middle school almost two decades ago." I responded sheepishly, still trying to remain as casual as possible. "Oddly, it's not a skill that has come up in my office job or day to day life."

"Middle school? Office job?" She blinked, as if processing the words. "Are you human, Alice? I've not met another human in Wonderland in…" The Queen looked up and counted on her fingers. "I don't recall. It's been quite some time, and she had to be taken care of rather swiftly, so we didn't chat much. She was also named Alice, now that I think of it. We Alices have a way of ending up in Wonderland, it seems."

My stomach sunk. Though she said everything in a sweet and sing song voice, the implication wasn't lost on me. That settled any remaining confusion as to her knowledge of the cycles and resets. Either she was so unaffected by the efforts of Wonderland that she didn't bother to understand why she was meeting other humans named Alice, or she was playing dumb to trick me.

It was hard to say though, considering the happy murderers I now associated with. I gathered it was pretty rare for one of their precious Alices to actually survive the trials and make it to the castle, so she'd probably not even noticed there was a movement happening. She didn't seem to pay much attention to anyone or anything outside of herself, anyway.

"Yes, I'm human. I lived in Los Angeles, if you know it." I attempted to give nothing away. "I stumbled on this place totally by accident."

"Of course I know it." Her whole face rose with her excitement. "I was born in England, but I visited the United States once when I was a girl. What fun." The Queen knocked her baby blue painted skull through another little arch, then she nodded for me to take my turn. "I also arrived here by accident. I followed a silly rabbit down a silly hole, and my whole life changed."

"I see." I wasn't sure what to make of that. It didn't seem that her life changed for the better, but I'm not sure if mine did either. Actually, no, that wasn't fair to say. I was miserable before. I was just in a constant state of terror now. How I felt about that was a bit of a toss up. I might have developed a fear kink on accident.

I swung at my little pink skull, one that matched my dress, and it bumbled towards the archway. I held my breath as it rolled entirely too closely to her ball. I released the air in my lungs as it narrowly missed giving me a death sentence.

"It looks like I'm going to win again. You should have taken me up on those orgasms." The original Alice giggled, then she continued to take another turn. A guard stepped in to take the next turn, and another guard took the next.

There seemed to be little order to it all. The Queen continued playing, and I took advantage of that chaos just long enough to step aside and take a breather.

I stood behind a bush, and I watched as the disorder unfolded around me. I'd become numb to the death of it. The savagery was so egregious and excessive it was hard to take it seriously. I barely acknowledged that they were real people being killed anymore, or that the constant fountains of red were bodies dying. I was existing in a surrealist painting in my mind, and I couldn't think about the fact that they'd all be permanently dead if I succeeded in defeating the Queen. It was easier to force ignorance than to believe my own eyes.

"So, first impressions?" Mau's voice whispered in my ear. I jumped, but his hands appeared and caught me, holding me still so I didn't visibly flinch to outsiders. Only his mouth and fingers were visible behind me. Everything else existed in another plane.

"She really likes to remove people's heads, I gather." I frowned as she decapitated the Nine of Clubs. It should have been a scene from hell and horror, but at this point I almost wanted to laugh at the ridiculousness of it. I'd become entirely too well accustomed to Wonderland, in my opinion. "I hear you guys get crazier and crazier every time you're revived, but if no one has ever taken down the Queen, then she must just be like this naturally?" It was a statement posed as a question, because it was hard to wrap my head around it.

"I've never been killed either, and I'm perfectly mad too, if it makes you feel any better." Mau purred with amusement.

"I actually never would have guessed that." *But seriously, I NEVER would have guessed that.* "I guess you're a touch less brutal than the others, if I really think about it."

"Am I?" He laughed at that. It seemed involuntary. "I'll take that as a compliment."

"It was."

"You make me want to root for you more and more every day, Little Dove. So please don't get your head chopped off." That sounded unexpectedly sincere. My cheeks warmed.

"No promises." I glanced to the side. "I'm going to do everything I can to stay alive, but I'm not really sure how I'm supposed to take off *her* head, when she has legions of men who will die for her, and a pretty trigger happy swinging arm."

"Powerful as that may seem, you have a legion of men who will *live* for you, Alice." He spoke low in my ear, and the vibration of that deep, sexy purr made my heart race.

I blushed at the implication. Though, pretty as the words may be, I knew I still had to be the one to actually do the murdering, and that idea still made my skin crawl. "Can those men kill for me, too?"

Mau's disembodied lips downturned in a frown. "Sadly, in this singular instance, that's the one limit we can't cross. But I'm confident you have what it takes. I'll cheer for you."

So helpful. I furrowed my brow. "Are you being serious right now?"

"Am I ever not?"

"Are you *ever*?" I rolled my eyes. He chuckled. "I get that I have to be the one to do the actual execution, but aren't you guys supposed to be helping me with this now that I've passed all your trials? Why is this all on me? It's *your* Wonderland, not mine."

"What an interesting thought." He was taken aback by the statement. "*Our* Wonderland. I've never heard such a thing."

"Well, before the Queen's terrifying rule, it must have belonged to all of you, right?"

Mau's fingers tensed in surprise. "I suppose it did." Was that something they'd never considered? Or had they simply all been murdered and terrorized so many times that they'd forgotten there was once a time when they hadn't lived in constant violence.

I bit into my lip as that concept sunk in. To be so deep in neglect and mistreatment that you forget what comfort and peace even look like. Maybe that's what my life had been too. I was so upset when Daniel had broken up with me. I was ragingly mad. I wanted to burn the whole damn world down. And yet… even these psychopaths are kinder, more complimentary, and loving towards me than he ever was. So why had I clung to him so hard?

How did I never see it? Perhaps I was the same as Mau, as Coello, as Finn, as Tynan, as Jacan. I was so deep in my situation that, while I knew it was wrong, I also forgot I still had the power to make it right. I just had to stand up and remember to be on my own side.

And that's why they all brought me here. I was the one person who was supposed to stand up to this Queen. I was *their* chance at being free and finding normalcy again.

Still… cutting off someone's head, despite the display by current company, wasn't exactly something one could just happily and easily do. Not someone like myself anyways.

"Is there a less barbaric method to over throwing the original Alice?" I pursed my lips after I whispered to my companion.

"I suppose you could just *steal* her crown, Alice." He massaged my shoulders gently with those fingertips, while the rest of his hands had vanished. "But what fun is that?"

With that, he disappeared, and I was alone, once more, in a croquet court of nightmares.

Steal her crown? Maybe I could.

Chapter 32

Or maybe I couldn't and that was the dumbest fucking suggestion I'd ever been offered. Because when I went up to the Queen of Hearts and took advantage of the element of surprise to knock it clear off her head with my croquet mallet, hoping to make this as quick and lickety split as possible, I hadn't anticipated that her guards would actually stand to protect her instead of letting someone less murderous take the magic heirloom.

I had an array of heart, spade, diamond, and club shaped weapons pointed at me in an instant, and the Queen's face turned a shade of red that would make the blood soaked courtyard jealous.

And now here I was, running, running, *RUNNING*. Again I was running. I thought I was done with that when Coello switched to being sweet and friendly-ish, but clearly that's just the kind of place this was. I could stop, technically, but I wasn't over the whole 'having a head' thing, so thus is life.

I dashed into a nearby hedge maze, the only out from this hell scape of a ball court, and I found myself having to make one hair trigger decision after the next as I delved deeper and deeper into the maze. My gut instincts seemed to be serving me well. So long as I didn't pick wrong and hit a dead end, I'd likely survive. Though the chances of that grew infinitesimally smaller with every fork.

I could hear the guards clamoring behind me, some becoming more distant as they chose the wrong path in each split in the maze, and others sounding eerily closer as they chose right.

By a numbers game alone, I had no chance of escaping. Even if I guessed every direction correctly, there would be at least one other who did the same. It was utterly hopeless, regardless of my survival instincts that kept me sprinting toward the slim chance of victory.

I'd come too far to die here. *Please don't let me die here.*

"Find her and take her head NOW." The shrill Queen's voice bounced through the hedges. This was not working out how I imagined at all.

Not that I ever imagined having to behead a magical fantasy Queen in a land of nonsense, but I thought if I could just get that crown on my head, I wouldn't need to. I frowned, and I kept running.

I rounded one bend, and immediately it was a dead end. I turned back and narrowly dodged the swinging blade of one of my pursuers, using the advantage of my smaller size to get past them and dart in a better direction.

Shit shit shit.

Well, now they knew exactly where I was, and now they were all following me without making any wrong guesses. I pumped my arms, I practically skidded around a turn, and I swore I saw a hint of the light at the other end of the maze in my periphery. If I could get into open air than someone like Mau or Coello or Jacan could help me. I just had to get out into the open.

Another fork came up quick. Left or right, left or right, *left!* I dashed left and I ducked under another swing as one of the guards with a diamond on his helm nearly caught me. He stumbled under the weight of his sword, and the blade caught in the branches of the hedge. His bumbling acted as a lucky barrier that slowed the whole group.

Yes! Fucking idiots.

I smirked despite the fact that they were pretty damn likely to be successful in killing me regardless of this negligible misstep, then I darted for a three pronged fork in the maze.

Straight. Straight is fastest. I decided based on nothing but hope and instinct and a belief in rainbows and unicorns.

I propelled myself further, launching off that springy grass like a goddamn gazelle. As graceful as one too, probably. I rounded another bend, then another and another and another and *there!* The light of the exit shone beautifully, and I put everything I had into that final sprint towards freedom.

And I came skidding to a halt, to the point I toppled backwards and fell on my ass when I came face to face with the Queen of Hearts, standing at the exit, holding her sword drawn and pointed perfectly in line with my neck.

I scrambled backwards, while she closed in on me with slow, steady, catlike steps. She forced me back into the maze, where her men easily caught up to me. And I was surrounded.

With a heavy swallow, I met her gaze.

"There's no reason to kill me." I attempted, though even I knew that wasn't true. She would be dumb to *not* kill me after that transgression. And it's not like murder was a difficult thing for her even when people were actively on her side.

"No reason except the fact that you tried to steal my crown? I've killed men for *much* less." She snarled in a way that distorted her otherwise pouty face. *I've noticed.* Though I wasn't going to mock her out loud, even if I wanted to. "What made that seem like a good idea, *Alice*?" She used the broad side of the blade to lift my chin, better connecting our eyes. "I've done everything I can to give these creatures a thrilling Wonderland to play in, and time and again they send women like *you* to steal my crown. And time and again, you make the foolish mistake of doing as they say. What is it about them that compels you ignorant wretches to be their sacrificial lambs?"

I opened my mouth, but I failed to answer. So she continued with none of the sweetness she'd feigned before. No, I was seeing the real Queen of Hearts now. "I've been toyed with, used, and jerked around by this horrid half of our species since I was too young to understand how wrong it was, and this…" She lifted her arms with dramatic flair, giving me brief respite from the knife at my neck. "This is my escape. From drugs, from chains, from humiliation— I've been a toy. I've been a slave. I've been everything I never wanted to be, and Wonderland was my bid for revenge. It is the one place where I get to be in control of everyone and everything. Yet you stupid, stupid girls always stand with these brutal, vicious animals." Her words came out in a snarl.

"Yet you kill the girls and leave the animals." I said, now no longer holding back from challenging her. If I was going to die here, I could at least say my peace. "If you hate the men of Wonderland so much, then why don't you join forces with these other women? Why not stand together with me instead of living in such senseless violence?"

"Because I've already beaten the frivolous creatures of Wonderland." She laughed. Cackled even. "The other

Alices have never helped me, so they can die too for all I care. This is *my* Wonderland, and I will watch it crumble for my amusement." She pointed the blade back at me. "The fact that you thought you could ever wear this crown is laughable. Utterly *laughable*."

"It was that or cutting off your head, and I thought you might prefer the former." I stated with a casual shrug of my shoulders. The more she talked the less she scared me. I'd seen far worse and far more malicious already. By comparison, simply swinging a sword around like a maniac was tame and boring.

"My head?" She fluttered her eyelashes at the madness of such a statement. "Why my body is far too beautiful to not have a head. But yours? Yours is far too plain to deserve to keep one."

Okay, now I *wanted* to take off her head.

I inched back, and she stepped forward. When my back was against the hedge, she allowed me to stand, following my neck with the point of her blade at all times to assure I felt adequately cornered.

"You say you want Wonderland to crumble, but you don't have to be here. Why not go back to the Commonland." I attempted, though I didn't have much hope it would get through to her.

"Because the Commonland is worse. So much worse." She had a point. I'd clearly always been a masochist, if my relationship history was to be analyzed. And looking at Wonderland, the kink of it all was a little addicting. Still, admitting that wasn't going to help calm her down. "Why don't *you* go back to the Commonland and leave my kingdom be?" Her eyes narrowed.

And she had another point. "Is that an option?" I swallowed, feeling that sharp tip on my skin. But I couldn't help but notice she seemed to be hesitating. She'd severed the necks of her guards with reckless abandon as if they grew out of the woodwork—maybe they did, actually. Wonderland is weird like that—but with me, she was taking the time to talk. To intimidate.

"Not anymore it isn't." The Queen's mouth twisted in a growl. It didn't suit her face. "But truth be told, you're not even worthy of my blade, *Alice*." Every time she said my name, it was like a mockery of the whole situation. Though it was her own, she'd taken on the identity of the Queen of Hearts through and through. There was nothing human left in her.

I calculated my chances of dodging, or running, or somehow slipping through both her and her guards, but it was all starting to look pretty bleak for me. I couldn't fathom that this could be my end. I couldn't accept that something so ordinary would kill me here anymore.

And apparently neither could she, as she stood up straight and she snapped her fingers.

Mau appeared at her side. His arms were crossed over that burgundy suit, and his violet eyes were beaming with satisfied cruelty. He took off his hat, ran a hand through his dark locks, then he knelt before Her Majesty. "You rang, Your Highness?" He said with words that stabbed straight through my heart. I stared, wide-eyed, at the man who I'd come to trust humbling himself before her.

The original Alice looked down at him, then she shifted her blade over to his chin, where she leveraged his head upward to face her. "My sweet kitty cat, we have another of these wretched women here to kill me. What do you think of that?" Her tone had shifted to full on baby talk. I fought the urge to cringe outwardly.

"I think that is deplorable, my beautiful Queen." It was impossible to tell if he meant it. Either he was a good actor, or I was still every bit as much a sucker as I'd always been. Perhaps all of Wonderland had fallen for his act. Or perhaps… perhaps only the Queen had been fooled.

No matter what you see or hear or feel, we are still on your side, and never on hers.

Coello's words played in my head, and I tried my best to believe him, no matter how convincing the display. These men may kill without a moment's hesitation, but… I believed the hints of compassion that leaked through their facades. I had to.

The logic didn't stop the clenching pain that radiated through my chest, however. "Mau…" I said his name absently. He didn't flinch or acknowledge it in the slightest.

"What do we do to women who try to hurt me, Kitty Cat?" She grinned widely.

"We feed them to the Jabberwock." He responded with finality, like it was a well-rehearsed skit between the two of them.

The Jabberwock. I remembered it. I'd escaped it once before. But could I do it again? I tried not to let the fear show on my face, but I could feel it so viscerally through my entire being.

The Queen rested the blade on his cheek. She slid it across his skin until she drew blood, then she licked it clean in a display of dominance. Mau held his position firmly. "Won't you call him for me? I miss my dearest pet, and I do so enjoy watching him feed."

"Of course, Your Highness." Mau stood. He placed his fingers on his lips, and he whistled loudly. "I'll call upon your Bandersnatch as well if it pleases you."

"It pleases me." She idly twirled her blade in her hand. It didn't matter that it was no longer pointed at me with all of her guards at my flank, but I was recalculating my chances of escape despite.

The Cheshire Cat followed up his whistle with a twirl of his hands, sending a beacon of light into the sky. The call for the Bandersnatch, I assumed. Though I'd not met that monster myself.

Birds scattered from the hedges, like they were fleeing a coming disaster, and everyone stilled as they waited for the beasts to appear.

And they did. Oh, the beasts were certainly happy to oblige their Alice. *And by beasts, I mean...*

"That's enough, Your Majesty." Coello appeared beside the Queen with a swiftness that was nearly invisible to the human eye. He caught her wrist, and he gripped it hard enough to crush the bone of a normal person. The blade fell from her palm and bounced on the springing grass. The Queen of Heart's eyes widened in sheer befuddlement.

The guards began to rise into action, when a flash of darkness brought Tynan to one side of me. He held them all back with a blade of black. A blinding surge of light brought Finn on my flank. He swung a blade of white at the horde of card warriors.

"You'll be good for me, won't you?" Finn said with a gleam in his eye.

"I won't be mad if you're bad." Tynan added with a wicked jeer.

"You're late." I addressed Coello. My heart beat slowed, and I let a complacent smile settle on my face.

"For a very important date." Mau finished the thought as he glanced between us with a mischievous and mocking rise of his finger.

"What's going on here?" The original Alice growled.

Mau stood back and stroked his chin with feigned confusion. "Why, it seems your Jabberwock and your Bandersnatch have been murdered in cold blood, my Queen." He shrugged his shoulders. That only made her more angry.

"How?" She was reaching a point of hysterics. "Who is strong enough to kill my pets?"

Mau bore his fangs as the corners of his lips turned upward. "The only person who could possibly kill a Jabberwock is the only other person in Wonderland who you've never been able to kill, perhaps."

"And it turns out uniting our powers made the Bandersnatch a breeze." Finn struck down a guard without mercy.

"We just had to find something we enjoyed more than hating each other." Tynan struck horizontally, taking out four men in a single swing. "And that unity was fucking invigorating."

The Queen's eyes darted between the four men. The sweat on her brow was growing increasingly visible, her eyes squinted, and her nose scrunched, as the White Rabbit crushed her wrist. Her stubbornness was no longer enough to mask her pain. "You…" She was absolutely seething. "Since when do you all work together?" She jerked in Coello's hold, and when she couldn't get free, she made a last ditch effort for a backup weapon: a small dagger, hidden in the lace of her garter belt.

She gripped the hilt swiftly, then she swung as hard as she could at Coello.

One gloved hand covered her mouth and her nose, the other wrapped so tightly around her neck, she was remaining conscious by strength of will alone. Her hand stilled and her expression immediately began to placate as the paralyzing scent of the Mad Hatter's tea began to infiltrate her system.

"Calm now, Queenie." The Mad Hatter whispered in her ear. "No need to make such a fuss." She struggled only for a moment, but the magic hit her hard and fast. Her eyes drooped slightly. The dagger fell from her hand.

With the Queen fully restrained, Mau stepped forward. He gave the Queen a bow, then he took hold of her blade on the floor. With one last nod, he turned back to me.

"The time has come, my Little Dove, to see what's in your heart." He paced over to me, steps so smooth and feline, and he placed that blade on my shoulder. He let the sharp edge graze my neck. I kept my eyes locked in his, unflinching, as he slid the cutting metal along my skin, just enough to send dribbles of blood down to my collar bone. My essence gathered on the gemstones of my necklace.

A few more steps, and he grabbed me by the waist. He pulled my body against his, and he removed the blade from my neck to twirl it around and present it to me by the hilt. "Can you take off her head, Alice? Or will you let the Queen have her way with you."

I stayed in his arms for several moments. I stared into his eyes. I let him hold me in that violet galaxy of his spirit.

I built my resolve, then I gripped the hilt, one finger at a time, until a firm fist held her weapon. Mau kissed me softly, like a wish for good luck, then he stepped to the side and cleared a path between myself and the original Alice of Wonderland.

All I had to do was take off her head, and it would all be over.

… All I had to do was murder a woman with an overgrown knife, while intimately looking into her eyes as I severed flesh and bone and painted myself in her blood.

My heart caught in my throat. A cold sweat started to bloom on my blood covered skin. I'd seen so many atrocities now. I'd survived near death countless times. I'd even gotten off while doing it.

And yet, this moment of truth, where I was expected to kill someone in cold blood all by myself…

It was impossible. Even knowing she'd do the same to me, how could I? She was damaged and broken, but was it truly impossible to save her?

Even if it was, I wasn't a killer. I was a normal girl. I was a people pleaser, a doormat, a girl who got used and rejected. I wasn't strong, I wasn't tough, and I wasn't someone who stood up for myself when others were stepping on me and blatantly rubbing their heels in. I was unworthy and undeserving. I wasn't going to win. I wasn't ever going to be anyone's end game. I was never a girl who was special or strong or worth marrying.

And standing in the face of someone who would have so happily killed me but moments ago, I was still going to drop this blade and let her live.

Because murder was wrong. Hurting others was wrong. I would rather take that burden on myself, be the one who got hurt, and be the one who took everyone else's pain. I was going to choose her over me, even though she didn't deserve life more than I did. I was going to let myself get kicked while I was down, because my suffering was okay, while standing up for myself and returning equal treatment, was not.

That's who I was. That's who I would always be.

Unless…

My internal battle was interrupted by the low purr of Mau's voice in my ear. "There's nothing unspectacular about you, Little Dove." He said as if he'd been reading my thoughts. Maybe he had been somehow. Or maybe he'd just come to understand me better than I understood myself.

"Your drive to survive despite it all is something you should be proud of, My Dear." Finn turned to face me as the last guard on his side fell.

"Not to mention you're fucking smoking hot when you get off, Princess." Tynan drew his blade back into his personal darkness as he finished off the last knights on his side as well.

"And you are fierce and unfaltering, even when you're cornered, Doll." Jacan met my eyes as he tightened his hold on the Queen. He dropped his grip to her chin, where he lifted her head to better expose her vulnerable neck. Her breathing was steady, but they'd left her helpless.

"And you are an Alice worthy of all of our loyalty, Poppet." Coello released the Queen, and he approached me next. He held me in the gaze of rebellious pink, as he moved in close enough to hold me. Then, he drew his thumb along the cut on my neck, collecting the still fresh blood.

And he used that same thumb to draw a line under each of my eyes. War paint. Just like he'd given me back when he'd saved me from the Mouse. But he didn't stop there.

Still using my own blood, he colored his lips, one at a time, then he leaned in close and pressed them to mine. He painted me with a kiss, then he took a step back, clearing a path between myself and the original Alice.

"So tell me, Little Dove, can you fight for yourself for once? Or will you forever be but a toy to those who don't deserve you?" Mau cocked his head back. A mocking question.

The perfect question.

He extended an arm towards the temporarily disabled queen, as though he was presenting a fine dish, and he took a bow. "Show us the Alice who we've all fallen in love with. And we will show you what it truly means to be prized by this magic and vicious world."

I laughed at that. I should have been appalled, but I wasn't in the slightest. Because they were right. They were all right. And they were counting on me. They believed in me. They were… they were who I wanted to protect.

No.

I was who I wanted to protect, and all of them felt I deserved that.

I smiled broadly, and with eyes wide open, I walked forward. Jacan stepped back, while still holding her in place with firm grips on each of her biceps.

Face to face with the Queen of Hearts, whose rage blazed in every inch of her expression, I pulled the necklace from my shoulders and I placed it around her neck.

The necklace of total control. One that only worked for the person who owned it. And as it had been covered in my blood, time and again, that person was now myself.

"On your knees." I said to her, testing that power. Jacan released her completely, and despite her visible frustration, she obeyed.

I couldn't help the warm sense of delight that filled me. To delight in such humiliation was wrong but, well…

We're all mad here.

I lifted the Queen's blade like it was a baseball bat, and I swung with every ounce of shame, self-loathing, depression, fear, and anger left in my body. My sword connected with her neck, and the sharp edge tore through muscle, bone, and tendon: smooth, swift, and sudden.

I watched through a detached gaze as her head tumbled to the ground. Her body remained upright for an extended second, then it crumpled down with the rest of her. I stood strong while I was bathed in her blood, and I didn't look away as the light faded from her once glowing blue eyes.

First I collected my necklace. I replaced it where it belonged. Then I tossed the blade aside and listened to the sound of it bouncing in the grass.

When all was calm and quiet, I crouched to the ground beside her lifeless skull, and I lifted the crown from her pretty blonde hair.

Then, like the queen *I* was, I placed that Crown of Hearts atop my head, and I drew one full, deep breath through my still living lungs. A warmth radiated downward, comforting and secure. It filled me with light, power, and magic.

First, the few remaining guards kneeled.

Tynan and Finn followed, bowing deep and low. Jacan tipped his hat and placed it over his heart. Mau did the same.

And it was Coello who slowly lowered himself to the ground before me, extended his hand to take mine, and pressed a soft kiss upon the back of my hand.

"Beautifully done, Alice." He said. "I have never, in my immortal life, seen anything so breathtaking."

My heart fluttered despite myself.

It was this White Rabbit who brought me here. Under the pretense of a violent game, he thought he was going to torture me. And now, he was on the ground, worshipping my feet.

But that wasn't what I wanted.

"Stand up." I said, firm and resolute, so all of them would hear. "From here on out, you are not my subjects. You're not my play things. You're not my scared and trembling minions who will be forced to do my bidding." I placed a hand on my hip, and I shifted proudly on my feet. "This Wonderland is yours as much as it's mine—no, *more* than it's mine. And I have no intention of taking it from you."

"Yes, Your Majesty." The guards shouted in unison. A trained response. I shook my head.

"Alice. My name is Alice, and that's what you will call me. I'm not your queen or your ruler or your tyrant. I'm just a woman who wants a better Wonderland."

As those words left my lips, the moon began to tick again. It ticked and it ticked and the arms rapidly wound forward, as though it was at last allowed to release the tension holding it back. As hour after hour spun away, the moon melted into the sun once more, and a burst of light returned to this great castle of Wonderland.

The ivy on the brutal stone walls receded. The flowers bowed towards the sun. And the outgrabe of Mome Raths danced in the air like a beautiful birdsong.

Welcome to Wonderland.

Chapter 33

Alice

After everything in Wonderland settled down, I set everyone free, and the people started to rebuild something hopefully more wholesome and pleasant—whatever that meant to… any of us at this point. Then, content that order and peace had returned, I asked Coello if I could return to the Commonland, as they so accurately called it. Dejected as he was by the request, he obliged.

I didn't know if I wanted to live in Wonderland forever. I was happy to have helped them, but I was sure my little sister was wondering what happened to me. And whether or not I ever returned, I wanted to grab some clothing that didn't consist of suffocating whale bone corsets and tutus.

I hadn't been in Wonderland that long, but returning gave me the sensation of being an alien visiting a foreign planet. The grass didn't spring when I walked through the park near my old apartment. The trees were statically grown in place, no longer accordianing into view as I approached. The birds flew right-side-up, and the flowers never ate the bees. It was all very ordinary and common and predictable in what now seemed so incredibly… boring.

But what did I expect from Commonland? … Err, *Earth, I mean*: My *real* home on the *logical* side of the looking glass. This world was easy, simple, and made sense. It was everything I knew, and everything I was used to. Well, mostly. Little had *I* known, it had been the mirror in my *own* bathroom that served as the portal Coello used to tunnel me to his dungeon. Perhaps magic existed here too, right under all of our stubborn, mature, and skeptical human noses.

Once I'd gotten used to it all again, I stopped in to a small café in the suburbs, where Dinah met me for a quick brunch. It had apparently only been a single day since I'd left this realm, so naturally, she'd not been terribly worried. She pried me for information about who I'd left with, I did my best to hold in a laugh as I tried to explain I'd been won over by a guy who called himself the White Rabbit, and that turned into a whole group of deviants with different kinks. Maybe one day I'd tell her about Wonderland in earnest. Maybe I would even show it to her. But for now, I'd leave her begging for more details about the five gorgeous men I'd played with.

After we parted ways, I returned to my apartment, and I glanced at my phone. Missed call after missed call cascaded down my notifications.

Daniel.

Daniel.

Daniel.

Daniel.

Daniel.

Holy fuck, how many times did he call me?

I deleted a barrage of voice mails unheard, then by the devil, my phone started to ring in my hand. His cursed name flashed in my caller ID.

But being I was choosing violence lately, I decided to just go ahead and answer.

"Alice!" He sounded incredibly surprised and relieved that I'd at long last answered. "I thought you'd never pick up. I need to talk to you."

"Go on." I said shortly.

"I want to apologize. Clara was a mistake." I remained silent. He kept going. "I've called off the wedding. I was such a fool. She had been playing me the whole time, and I don't know how I could have been so blind to how good I had it. How good *we* had it." He blabbered on and on about the most absurd nonsense I'd heard to date.

"What? You mean someone who would cheat with you would also cheat on you? That's wild." I had no emotion in my voice as I said it. Even burning him didn't excite me anymore. "Sorry about your bad luck." Flat and disinterested.

"Why don't you meet up with me for dinner, Ally-gator? Just you and me. Let's talk about it." That stupid nickname that I used to think was so cute, paired with that slightly higher pitch he used when he was trying to win someone over, made my stomach churn. How had I fallen for that for so long? Daniel's '*Ally-gator*' felt like an entirely different person from who I was now. "You don't have to forgive me right away, but please just give me a chance to try and make it up to you. Hear me out."

I pondered that for a few moments. "Why?" I asked, still incapable of conjuring anything that resembled caring. I had no such thing left for him. "Why would you even want to work it out with me?"

"Because Alice, I miss you, baby." He said, his voice sounding genuinely sorry. *Genuinely* desperate to see me.

And a couple days ago, I might have even entertained him.

But a couple days ago, I was pathetic. Today, I just laughed. "Yeah, I would miss me, too. Go fuck yourself, Daniel." I hung up and blocked his number before I tossed my phone back into my purse.

Then I grabbed a bag of my favorite clothing, slung it over my shoulder, and I returned to my bathroom mirror. There, Coello was sitting on the counter, waiting to take me back through if I so chose.

Today, I chose.

"Got everything you need?" He asked before extending his hand. His rose gold eyes sparkled under that shaggy, sexy platinum hair.

"Absolutely everything." My entire soul seemed to smile as I said it. Then I took his hand, and we interlaced our fingers. His grip was warm, firm, comforting, and strong.

"Let's go home, Poppet." He said.

"Lead the way, my White Rabbit."

The End (For Now!)

AFTERTALK

And that's a wrap! Thanks so much for coming along for the ride! I've always been fascinated by the original Alice in Wonderland, and I also always found it to be pretty dark for a kid's book, so I thought this would be a fun way to twist the tale myself. This is my first ever Reverse Harem/Why Choose story (though not exactly my first Dark Romance, but I typically write MM under a different pen name (Anni Lee, for anyone who's curious and likes Dark and queer!)). As a long time fan of Japanese Horror in particular, who grew up obsessed with stories that I probably shouldn't have been watching OR reading, I'll admit that I really enjoyed blending erotica, fantasy, and splashes of horror into one vicious little package.

I tried to be mindful of going TOO dark, not wanting to cross that fine line of sexy psychopath into violent creep, so I hope I succeeded. In between the senseless and frivolous sex and violence, it was still important to me to keep a thread of deeper emotional value throughout, so I hope it still resonated. Something about Wonderland just felt like a free pass to write the story I wanted and not have to censor myself too much, so I hope I didn't scare anyone away!

On that note, my next story in the Vicious Wonders series will be a RH retelling of The Wizard of Oz, so if you enjoyed this, I hope you'll stick around for that! (I'm also planning Willy Wonka, and a few other, perhaps less popular, fairytales!) If you have any particular stories you'd love to see, I'm always excited to hear from readers!

All that said, if you enjoyed this story, it helps me a TON to leave a review! I always appreciate feedback, and I'm always looking to improve my craft.

Also for updates and teasers for upcoming projects, feel free to follow me on social media! I'm most active on TikTok, but I hop in everywhere regularly!

Goodreads: https://www.goodreads.com/author/show/19238551.Leann_Belle

Instagram: https://www.instagram.com/leannbelleauthor/

TikTok: https://www.tiktok.com/@leannbelle

Facebook: https://www.facebook.com/LeannBelleAuthor

Amazon: https://www.amazon.com/Leann-Belle/e/B07SRHFP2Z

Thanks again for reading! Until next time, go fast and take chances!

OTHER WORKS BY LEANN BELLE:

We're All Mad Here

A Dark and Twisted and very high heat Alice in Wonderland Reverse Harem

There's No Place Like Oz

A Dark and Twisted, High Heat Wizard of Oz Reverse Harem

Stalking Cinderella

A Dark and Twisted Cinderella Reverse Harem, with a bully step brother, a stalker prince, and a manipulative, gender-swapped fairy god mother

What Happens In Vegas

A Billionaire Office Romance Comedy (Also available in audio!)

Sing With Me

A lightly dark, erotic Battle of the Bands, Reality Show Rockstar RomCom

Rise With Me

A lightly dark, erotic Music Industry Romance with Secret Relationships and Mafia

www.ingramcontent.com/pod-product-compliance
Lightning Source LLC
Chambersburg PA
CBHW070426120726
47910CB00003B/669